THE

Passion, Murder and a Quest for a Sporting Grail

Karl Spracklen

The Parrs Wood Press
MANCHESTER

First Published 2001

THE PARRS WOOD PRESS
St Wilfrid's Enterprise Centre
Royce Road, Manchester, M15 5BJ
www.parrswoodpress.com

© Karl Spracklen 2001

ISBN: 1 903158 20 6

This book was produced by Andy Searle and Helen Faulkner of The Parrs Wood Press and Printed in Great Britain by:

MFP Design and Print
Longford Trading Estate
Thomas Street
Stretford
Manchester M32 0JT

CONTENTS

About the author

Karl Spracklen has been writing for as long as he can remember. He attended school in Bramley, Leeds and an FE College in the centre of Leeds. From there he went in 1990 to Pembroke College, Cambridge, where, after three years, he graduated with a First in Natural Sciences. From Cambridge he moved back to Leeds, where he did research for a thesis on rugby, masculine identity and community at Leeds Metropolitan University, culminating in the award of Doctor of Philosophy in 1996. Karl was a co-author of the CRE and RFL-funded report into racism in rugby league, published in 1995. Karl has worked in the past as a brewer's assistant, a reporter for a number of rugby league periodicals, a researcher for a leisure consultancy, a lecturer in research methods and leisure studies and a political researcher for Bradford Council. He now works as a national development officer for Sporting Equals, an organisation devoted to equal opportunities in the sporting world. Karl has been involved with the Word Hoard, a Huddersfield writers' co-operative, since 1996, and in 1999 won a place on the Arts Council funded course 'The Opening Line' for Yorkshire's most talented up-and-coming writers. He combines this with an editorial role for 'The Greatest Game', the magazine of the Rugby League Supporters' Association, to which he is a regular contributor. Karl Spracklen's first book, Green-Flavoured Gobstoppers and Aliens, was published by Spout Publications in 1997. He now lives in Bradford.

This book could not have been written without the enormous amount of research Tom Mather has done into the Chorley club of the 1870s and their captain, Humphrey Whittle. Tom's work laid the foundations for this story, and gave a real-life context to the older, darker themes within. If there are any historical inaccuracies or errors in this book, they are mine alone.

Karl Spracklen, Shipley, June 2001

For Beverley

PREFACE

IN THE FIRST HALF OF THE THIRTEENTH CENTURY, the Arthurian Romances were the equivalent of today's sports pages. Then, as now, the struggle to prove one's strength of character - in particular, the socially-acceptable manliness of men - was played out by other people for our entertainment. There are many parallels between the Sir Gawain of the later Romances and the flawed, sporting folk-heroes that England's tabloids nurture. Like Gawain, the tabloid folk-heroes are brash, brave and - at their prime - unstoppable. But like Gawain, when the sun turns, they are shown to be moody, petulant, wife-beaters, alcoholics.

At the heart of the Arthurian tale is the Quest for the Grail. Set aside from the slaughter and colour of the tournaments, and the masculine tales of infidelity, the Grail is a simple tale of morality. Sir Lancelot, the champion of the Arthurian world, the Ellery Hanley of his day, ultimately fails to win the Grail because he is, like the rest of us, an imperfect soul. Only someone true of heart can ask the right question and win through to the Grail. The Quest for the Grail is mirrored by the rise and fall of the Arthurian kingdom, which is torn apart at its peak by events arising from the infidelities of Lancelot and Guinevere, Arthur's wife.

In the second half of the 19th Century, the kingdom of Arthur was reborn as the British Empire. Then, as now, new industries and processes arose that challenged established orders. Villages became towns, towns became cities, and large parts of the countryside were turned over in the search for the raw material that, like the Grail, seemed to provide the vitality of the Empire itself: coal. Towns, like Chorley in Lancashire, were transformed by the development of new industries, which in turn were fed by coal. Chorley was connected to the outside world by the railways. Machines improved production in Chorley's mills, improving profits and demanding more casual labour to handle those machines. Mines spread in the countryside around Chorley, and a new class of wealthy individuals and families emerged, replacing the old order. The rapid development of steam-powered industries demanded the mining of coal to heat the water that turned to steam that turned the wheels that sent goods, people and ideas from one corner of the Empire to another. Pit-heads became a common-sight in many places in the Empire, as mines became factories for the production of coal. And with the pit-heads came the mine-owners - wealthy capitalists who had made successful speculations or who had had the luxury of owning land under which ran deep coal-seams - and the miners themselves. The money made by the mine-owners funded a growing sense of municipal pride in the provinces where coal was mined, but no public improvements and ornate town-halls could disguise the harsh conditions the miners worked in, and the mean lives they were forced to live.

As the century neared its end, the legend of Arthur had been resurrected by the ruling-class to justify their status and hide, like reflections in a series of mirrors, the scarred hills and the crowded terraced-houses of the landscape. The knights of King Arthur were seen as perfect Christians: loyal, strong, active, white Englishmen. The cult of muscular Christianity, of equating the health of the soul with the health of the body, encouraged the creation of myths of racial excellence. The English nation, as typified by Arthur, was the best nation because it was the strongest, and the strongest were that way because they were God's chosen people. This belief led to a political will to improve people's lives through the great public health works of the day. But it also led to a cult of manliness that, in turn, led to the rapid proliferation of organised sport.

People in the English countryside had always played football. But in the 19th Century the traditional games had fallen out of favour as people moved from the countryside to the towns and cities. Football may have disappeared in much the same way as bear-baiting, if the missionaries of muscular Christianity in the Empire's public schools hadn't taken it up. By the middle of the century, England's major public-schools, factories for the production of the Empire's new Knights of the Round Table, had all adopted football and codified it for the purpose of inculcating strength and discipline in their pupils.

Eventually, the boys who had played football at school became teachers themselves at less-exclusive schools, and spread their enthusiasm for the game to the middle-classes. Others then formed teams to continue playing as adults, whether they were living in Chorley or Canterbury. The fashion soon spread, with the help of its evangelists, to the working-class men of the country's towns, where it was deemed to be an improving influence.

One version of football was adopted by Cambridge University and then, with the creation of the Football Association, and the later acceptance of professional players from the working-classes, became the standard game known throughout the world. But another, based on the rules of Rugby School and including a permission to handle and run with the ball in one's hands, was arguably as popular in the years between 1863 and 1895. In particular, this football code spread across industrial Wales, the Midlands and the north of England, adopted by miners, factorymen and mill-workers as an expression of their way of life.

Rugby football, originally a game of the ruling classes, mirrored the growth of association football by becoming in the north of England a spectator sport for the working-classes, played by the strongest, fittest men the new clubs could find. Rugby was the number one sport for working-class men in the mining villages, towns and cities of Lancashire, Cheshire, Yorkshire and Cumberland. But in this sudden expansion of the game, the middle-class men who had brought Rugby to the northern counties in the first place were, in many areas, pushed out of the game. The clubs in Yorkshire and Lancashire looked to the professional association football clubs for their inspiration, not to the amateur rugby clubs of London and the Home Counties. Inevitably, this led to the charges of professionalism in the last two decades of the century, which culminated in the establishment of a breakaway 'Northern Union' in 1895. The Northern Union was a move by the big clubs of Yorkshire and Lancashire to compete with association football, and led, through a chequered history, to the code of Rugby League that rivals Rugby Union in many parts of the world today.

But the 'Split' of the northern rugby football clubs from the London-based and amateur-obsessed Rugby Football Union came to late to stop association football from establishing itself in the Northern Union's own heartlands. The rugby-playing cities of Liverpool and Manchester had largely given up on rugby in preference of association football before the Split of 1895. And the same was true of other towns in Yorkshire and Lancashire - including Chorley, where the memories of the hugely successful rugby team of the 1870s had almost, but not quite, faded by the time the Century ended.

In the 1870s, Chorley was a boom-town, a small part of the machine that turned the wheels of the Empire. And its rugby club, perched between the amateur ideal of its founders, the entrepreneurial drive of its backers and the demands of the paying public, was renowned throughout Lancashire. So much so that it seems natural for a man looking to promote the first-ever rugby football Challenge Cup at Blackpool, at a time when the resort was becoming the working-class Mecca of the North of England, to approach the Chorley club to take part. Chorley's rugby footballers were the best, but they were also from a town that prided itself on its industry. Chorley was a town on the cusp of greater things. Its civic leaders were building a new Jerusalem. Chorley's coal was the Grail that gave life to the Empire. The very idea of a cup competition - in which the aim of the game would be to be the best in the North of England - would not be shocking to the men of Chorley, as it would be to men who still believed that playing the sport was all that mattered.

The Cup was, for the football players of Chorley, their particular Grail. For a moment, it was all that mattered to the supporters. For the players and their captain, Humphrey Whittle, it was a moment in which the kingdom of Arthur was about to be reborn. But as the Arthurian romances tell us, the Grail can only be won by those with a pure heart. And once won, it will only remain before our eyes so long as we stay pure.

1.

The Council Meeting

HUMPHREY NORRIS WHITTLE KNEW that the revolution was bound to happen soon. It was already 1894 and clear from the newspapers that the socialists were about to take over. They would come in their thousands and seize everything he owned. They would eat from his silver plate, using their fingers instead of forks. They would take down the pictures on his walls and burn them, laughing as his portrait went up in flames. They would open the banks and steal his money, sharing it out just as she had shared it out with Shellard. Then the winding gear would come to rest and the men would forget the coal that kept the world in motion. Not even the army who had shot and killed three miners in Featherstone would be able to stop them.

Whittle could see the workers now, standing outside the main entrance to the town hall, ready to destroy all that he held dear. They would wave their ragged red flags and spit on the stone steps. Women would laugh at the tall windows as young boys threw lumps of coal. Glass would litter the street. And they would come for him, as they would come for all the Council, every single man who had devoted his life to the town of Chorley. They wouldn't care about the work the party had done to make life better for them. They wouldn't understand that he and his colleagues were benefactors of the people, job providers and school builders, modernisers intent on making their miserable lives better. They would neither know or care about the natural order. They would barge their way into the Council chamber, tipping over the urns at the sides of the doors, smashing the mahogany panels on the backs of the benches, and they would allow their women to feed their babies in the Mayor's oak chair.

He thought about the rugby club. He had been right to vote against the decision to play the professional's game of association football. Working men had always had their place in the club before then but it had been understood that the game was there to make those men into gentlemen. And it had worked, and for that brief moment the workers in the club had understood they could elevate themselves from their fated position into the pantheon of the gods. But at the same time they had been playing to his rules, the rules of the modern gentleman, of the Game of Life.

Now, of course, it had changed. The club played association football and the chaps who had founded the club were all gone. It was barely twenty years since the club had been formed, back in the summer of 1874. The spirit that had existed then, conjured up by their collective understanding, had gone. In its place were material things, the grubby ambitions of the artisan, the hand that was always extended asking for more. The idea that the game was played as a means of improving the soul was mocked by the working men, who ran the club for their own ends. It had left a bitter taste in his mouth.

The town had changed, changing like its neighbours Preston and Wigan were changing, like every other town in Lancashire. The socialists were spreading dissent in the mills and down the mines, inciting the normally placid workers into making unreasonable demands without realising the economy was depressed. They did not know the responsibilities he had. If he allowed all their demands he would be bankrupt. The business would close, and they would all be without a job. Now they had organised themselves into a party and were talking about winning all the council seats even though barely half of them could read, let alone fathom the complexities of government. They were talking about putting up a candidate against him, a man from one of his mines who shirked hard work and who had tried to form a union as an excuse to earn more for working less. The man reminded him of Shellard.

He thought about his wife. They had taken his club, changed the rules of the game and forgotten why they were supposed to play sport in the first place. It had been fifteen years since they'd put northern Lancashire on the map, made people all over the country scratch their heads and look at the small town of Chorley as if it was the centre of the world. Fifteen years since he'd shown there was more to the town than coal and cotton. Now they were taking over his mines, taking over his town. And in six years time it would be a new century, their century.

They had taken everything from him: they had even taken his wife.

The Council Meeting, held on the first day of June 1894 in Chorley's soot-stained town hall, was for a special purpose. Councillor Humphrey Whittle walked up the steps into the town hall, ignoring the small group of unemployed men standing in the street. They shouted at him about jobs and pay, watched by the policeman who was on guard at the top of the steps. They were dressed in shabby brown suits, cut from the shoddy cloth cast off from the end of the lines at mills up and down Lancashire. It was stolen, of course, but Whittle knew it was mean hearted to take these poor people to the Courts for such a small transgression. It was an act of charity not to set the police onto them.

As he passed the policeman with a polite nod of his head he heard a carriage draw up on the street. The driver bellowed at his team and their hooves clacked against the cobbles. The unemployed men laughed as the driver cursed one of his horses for not standing still. Whittle turned to look at the men and the carriage. His large frame, unbowed and untouched by the passing years, filled the porch of the town hall. Next to him the policeman was a shadow in the corner. Only Whittle's grey eyes betrayed his age and the sadness of his life.

Getting out of the carriage was a grey-haired man in a grey suit, carrying a black top hat and a black coat. This man was small, as small as the driver of the carriage, but his large belly more than compensated for his lack of inches. He took from his breast pocket a clip of paper money and proffered a large denomination to the carriage driver. This seemed to satisfy the man with the reins, whose face burst into a satisfied smile when the pot-bellied old man waved away the offer of change.

The unemployed men were watching this exchange with wry smiles. Whittle watched them in turn. He clenched his spade-like hands, the leather of his gloves creaking under the pressure of his fists. A few nightshift workers were passing on the street with their knapsacks over their shoulders, and a respectable looking couple were taking a walk along the other side of the street in the direction of the train station. The evening sky was overcast, and the air was still. Although the summer was still young the smog from the factory chimneys had already descended on the town, where it would stay until the cold winds of autumn blew the heat and smoke away.

The unemployed men were standing between two gas lamps, so that their faces were riven by dark shadows like those of demons.

'Harry, old man, let me help you up the steps,' shouted Whittle, so that the unemployed men knew he was watching them watch the old man. He went back down the steps, unbuttoning his coat so that it flew behind him as he jumped onto the street. The driver whipped his horses and the carriage rolled away as Whittle came up to the old man.

'Harry Hibbert! How good to see you!'

They shook hands. The unemployed men did not move or say anything.

The old man grinned, his hairy jowls moving as he spoke.

'Humphrey Whittle, what a pleasant surprise to find you here before me. How's the business?'

'Excellent, Harry, just excellent,' replied Whittle. He had become so accustomed to lying it no longer felt like a sin every time he opened his mouth. He glanced across at the unemployed men. 'I've just made some rationalisations and there's good hope about the end of tariffs, thanks to your sterling work.'

Harry Hibbert shook his head and then put on his top hat. Whittle offered him a cigarette, which he took graciously, then they slowly climbed the steps to the town hall. They walked in silence. The old man coughed and wheezed as they reached the top, then sucked on the cigarette until his lungs settled. Whittle lit one for himself.

'How are things at the House?' he asked.

'Horrible,' replied Harry. 'The Tories are as dogmatic as ever, and London remains a den of iniquity. I fear for the moral fibre of our nation. Believe me, Humphrey, it is not Germany we should fear but England's own people. It is a matter of fashion now to mock the idea of God.'

Harry stopped speaking as one of the unemployed men below shouted something in their direction. Whittle listened as the rough voice shouted again:

'Get art o' Chorley, 'ibbert, we don't want thee as MP no more!'

Harry's hands moved. He ground his teeth and started to turn around to shout something back. But Whittle held on to his shoulder and gently pulled him into the quiet reception of the town hall. Here a number of council serving men were stood to attention, waiting to take their hats and coats and usher them into the Mayor's Rooms.

Above them, hanging from the boss at the centre of the domed ceiling, was a fan operated by an electric generator somewhere in the bowels of the town hall. It reminded Whittle of another innovation, that glorious failure of Harry's when the club had tried to play a match of rugby football under electrically powered floodlights. It brought a smile to his face – the memories of the club were the only things he had left - and he turned to Harry, who had been divested of his coat and hat and was fuming on a red carpet emblazoned with the town's coat-of-arms.

'Remember when we tried to play Swinton, Harry?' asked Whittle, handing his own coat to one of the blue-uniformed men.

Harry frowned.

'Did you hear what they said? Layabouts! The people of Chorley voted for me, the socialists conveniently forget that fact when they rant and rave!'

'Ignore them, Harry,' said Whittle.

'We all want to be wealthy and well, but they don't understand that it is ours to seek our fortune, not to steal it from those who have it,' said Harry. He pointed at the walls of the staircase up to the next floor, at the paintings of Chorley's elders. They looked to be drained of all colour in the light of the gas lamps. 'We built this town and now they want to take it away from us.'

Just as they took the club, just as they took my wife, thought Whittle. He tried again to think about the good times, but the phantom of the floodlit match had disappeared. They had taken his wife. Now he was giving them the Cup, so they could have everything of his.

Harry looked back at Whittle, who was staring at the cigarette in his hands.

'I say, old man, cheer up, they haven't got us yet, eh?' he said. He saw the ghosts in Whittle's eyes, and grinned nervously. 'Well, the chaps are waiting for us. I hope you've put together a good speech, Whittle, I don't want to fall asleep until after the port's passed around.'

They were led by one of the servants up the staircase, past the portraits of the dead men who had made the town prosperous. Whittle's own father stared back at him. His face was stiff, disapproving. The portrait was telling Humphrey that his sister had to be sent away for the good of the family, and that he would have no hesitation in sending Humphrey away too if he showed any signs of the same illness. Whittle remembered the eyes in the painting glaring out from behind a belt as he was punished for not being a gentleman. He remembered his sister, with whom he wasn't allowed to play after she had done something wrong which no one had explained to him.

He thought about his wife, but not for long. He dismissed that demon and brushed the dandruff from the shoulders of his suit. He was giving the Cup away.

It had been his idea, but he had told Harry in such a way that Harry believed it was his idea. Harry thought it was a nice gesture towards the town, a reminder of the good old days and a good way of getting some photographers from the local press along to see Henry Hibbert MP being charitable. Harry had enthused about the flash of cameras on the polished sides of the trophy, wondering how best to hold it so that readers of a newspaper could see both its size and his face. If Harry had thought about it more he could have demanded that it was he and not Whittle who was to hand over the trophy. But the promise of a photo was all he was bothered about, and if the council wanted their man Whittle then he had no complaints.

'Now then, man, 'ow's the cook this evening? Are we to get good portions or 'as 'e gone all Parisian on us?' asked Harry of one of the servants once they had reached the top of the steps. During the climb he had lost his statesman's voice and found the one he'd been born with. Whittle's left eye twitched at the old man's flat vowels. His father had made sure they spoke with no trace of the Lancashire accent. A man had to control his vowels like he controlled his family.

'Best sirloin steaks tonight, sir, straight from t'butcher, with taters to match,' answered the servant.

'Steak, eh? Fit for a football player, eh, Whittle?' grinned Harry. He dipped his cigarette into a plant pot next to the oak doors to the Mayor's Rooms. These doors were flanked by two Grecian statues, one of Heracles bound by the snake-like Hydra and the other of Odysseus with a bow in his hand. The hero myths of the town, the inspirations behind the football club. Whittle had fancied in idle moments whether he would join them in legend, the conquering hero of the town, the wise and benevolent ruler. But that was long ago, before he had lost his wife, when the moment of victory had been his and his alone. Now the dream of a statue was just a dream.

Another flunkey stood at the doors and opened them with a deferential bow. In the town hall, at least, Whittle was still a man to be respected. Inside was a large reception room with windows overlooking the town, on which were glazed the names and arms of famous families from the district. Whittle knew his family was somewhere up there, but he had never been able to find it when he looked. Curtains of red velvet hung from brass rails on either side of the windows, matching the dark red plasterwork of the walls. Electric lamps had been installed against the advice of many of the councillors, who had business interests in gas. But the Mayor had insisted on the novelty as a way of showing other towns like Wigan and Preston that Chorley was ready to face the 20th century. They gave the room a dirty look, shining on all the dust and showing the retouching done on the mock-Georgian filigree on the ceiling. Whittle considered it an unnecessary extravagance.

At the far end of the reception room was a painting of the town hall at night, its stonework blackened by soot. Underneath this painting was a small table on which were a number of sherry glasses and three unopened bottles. A handful of men in black suits stood around the table smoking and drinking. Another, larger group of men were standing near the windows. These looked around when Harry and Whittle entered the room.

'Harry! How good to see you, old chap!' a man with a huge beard shouted.

'And yourself, Charles, I see you're running the town admirably,' replied Harry.

Whittle chased one of the servants and found a large glass of sherry. That the Mayor had chosen to speak to Harry was not unexpected. He was the Member of Parliament, and Whittle was just a councillor. But Whittle knew there was more to it than that. His old friends, men who had played for the club, men who had stood at his side as he recited the rites of passage in the Hall, knew what had happened. They knew why he was giving the Cup away.

The men under the painting were the opposition. They were good people and some were members of the same clubs, and as long as they didn't discuss the matter of trade they were a friendly bunch. But things were changing. If the socialists got their men elected, then the reasoned debates in the chamber would be replaced by angry rhetoric and simple-minded

7

ideology.

Whittle drank his sherry then took another from the servant carrying the bottle around on a silver tray. He took a deep breath, then followed Harry to join his own party's councillors.

He stood at Harry's shoulder, listening to him telling anecdotes about the House to the Mayor. The Mayor laughed politely, raising his glass to toast the punchlines. He was older than Harry, and had served the town for more years than anyone could remember. In the past he had been Whittle's father's most trusted companion. His hair had gone from the top of his head, but what he had at the back he grew long like his white beard. He wore round spectacles and dressed in fashions long out of date. He carried a handkerchief in his shirt sleeve, and used this to dab his sweating forehead at frequent intervals. Around his neck he wore a chain of gold links bought by a list of subscribers that had included both Harry and Whittle's father. When Harry had finished speaking, the Mayor turned to Whittle.

'Whittle, the town's grateful for this, you know, an important part of our history this trophy,' he said, playing with the glass in his hands. 'Your lads did well to win it.'

Whittle nodded, remembering what he and Fish had worked out between themselves. Not even his brother Leo knew the truth.

'Well, now that it's all soccer there's no point in keeping hold of it,' said Whittle. 'No call for it being in my possession now.'

The Mayor stroked his beard. He frowned at Whittle.

'Aye, Humphrey, we'll take good care of it now. No need for you to worry. They do a grand job at polishing things up in this place.'

'It were a good win, that was, put this town on the map,' said Harry. 'All thanks to me of course.'

'Don't you go spinning a yarn with us, Harry Hibbert, you'll be telling us you fixed the matches next!' laughed the Mayor.

Whittle smiled.

'I might have done, and this lad 'ere 'll be none the wiser,' said Harry, slapping Whittle on the back and winking at the Mayor.

'Do you hear that, Whittle, he's saying your game were nowt but a fix,' said the Mayor, looking at Whittle.

Whittle thought about the game. It had been all so simple then. So pure. Yet even then, those halcyon days had been tainted by his deal with Fish, the entrepreneur who'd organised the Cup in the first place. His memories betrayed him, betrayed his faith. He shook his head.

'Excuse me, I must get another drink,' he said.

Harry watched Whittle walk away, his shoulders tensed to knock people out of his path. He knew what had happened to Whittle, everyone did to some extent. He sighed. There was no point worrying about one man. He turned to the Mayor and grinned.

'So, tell me, old chap, how's the business these days? Anything I can do to smooth things through?'

The Cup had been placed in front of the Mayor's chair, on the mahogany desk overlooking the rest of the Council chamber. In the dim room it shone as if there was an internal light deep inside the silver, giving it an aura extending out across the desk and into the brass knobs and rails at the desk's edge. Its bowl was tall and wide, a hero's cauldron which suggested some mythical cup of plenty, although the inside was empty and smooth sided. Embossed around the lip of the Cup, and draped down its sides, were garlands of silver flowers, blossoming in the light and frozen forever in a metallic skin. In a space between the flowers in the centre of the Cup was an engraving of an open field, bordered by tiny flags, with a large stand behind which seemed to stretch out of the side of the Cup, as if the thing was a real stand shrunk to the size of the Cup and seen through a magic lantern. The engraving and the lips were lined with gold, which touched the edges of the flowers where shadows should have been.

On the other side to the engraving was the coat of arms of the Chorley family, surrounded by heraldic flourishes and mythical animals, above the inscription:

'North of England Football Contest, Raikes Hall Park, Blackpool, Challenge Cup won by Chorley 1878'. The inscription was a reminder of better days, but also a reminder for Whittle of his own deceit, his own compromise. They had won the Cup a year after they had agreed upon the inscription.

Whittle sat at the Mayor's side in the Council chamber. It was the first time he had been elevated to the dais above the benches, and he could look down on balding heads glistening with sweat and small clouds of tobacco smoke. The air in the chamber, as in most places in Chorley in June, was humid and still. Although the boilers in the cellar were cold a smell of coal still lingered in the chamber's dark corners, mixed with beeswax and soap. The windows in the chamber were situated high up near the roof, stained glass examples of trade and industry – a man hewing at the coal face, a mill with its old-fashioned wheel dipping into churning water, an engineer instructing the construction of a new building, an official standing in front of a train, the inside of a factory and, finally, a gathering of the builders of the town in a miniature council chamber, with a tiny stained glass window in the background repeating the image.

The chamber was designed to seat seventy prosperous men, so there were gaps and empty benches even when every councillor attended a meeting. Whittle's party, who had led the town for as long as the town hall had existed, sat on the wooden benches to Whittle's left, busy discussing business amongst themselves. The smaller party – the party of the past, of the parson and the squire, the anachronism in the age of capital wealth – sat across the empty space in the middle of the horse-shoe shaped benches to the right. They discussed their own business, ignoring the jokes cast their way by the younger members of Whittle's party.

No one sat in front of Whittle, where the two curving sides met at the middle of the arc. But that was where the socialists would sit if they were elected, mocking the free debate and the assembly of learned men before them. Whittle could see them already, lounging on the benches, still wearing their caps, talking loudly during other men's speeches.

He grimaced as a pain shot through his left shoulder. He gripped himself and gritted his teeth, waiting for the agony to go away. It never lasted, but he knew he would always suffer.

'I say, Councillor Whittle, feeling all right?' asked Ramsbottom the Town Clerk, who was sitting on the other side of the Mayor's chair. He was a small man with a long nose, down which his spectacles slipped whenever he spoke. He had fought in the Zulu campaign as a young man when Whittle was playing rugby football for Chorley – but he had never won a Cup.

'I'll be fine, Ramsbottom, just an old injury,' replied Whittle as the pain slowly dissipated, dissolving like an effervescent pill in water.

'Must be with seeing the Cup, eh? Bringing back memories, that sort of thing,' smiled Ramsbottom.

'Perhaps,' nodded Whittle.

Up in the visitors' gallery, a small balcony running around the walls above the benches, people were gathering. Whittle recognised most of their faces, ex-players from the club, other men from the Hall. There were the Mockett brothers, looking as formidable as they'd been on the pitch, still indistinguishable from one another in their black coats and bowler hats. He could see Dr Marsh at the far end, sitting quietly by himself as he smoked a pipe. They had had heated arguments about politics, sometimes while they were playing, but he was glad at least that he'd bothered to come to see the Cup presented to the town. His brother Leo was at the back, where he had played in the team. He hadn't spoken to Whittle since the day of the Inquiry. Now he was talking to Harry Hibbert, laughing loudly at the MP's stories, charming the old man with his politeness and interest. There was no sign of Fish, or Scheidler. But then no one except Whittle would have expected them to be there.

There was movement behind him, and a man in a blue uniform walked in carrying a gold plated mace with a marble handle. He stood at the doorway leading into the robing chamber and said at the top of his voice:

'Honoured gentlemen of the Council, guests of honour, the Mayor of Chorley!'

The chamber went silent as everyone stood. Whittle knew the socialists wouldn't stand if they were in the chamber – and they would mock the ceremony that bound the assembly to its Mayor and the town the assembly represented. He screwed up his eyes in anger, and his moustache trembled.

The Mayor entered behind his footman, dressed in a black evening suit and a long red velvet robe trimmed with ermine and stitched with gold thread. On the left breast was stitched a badge representing the office of town mayor in arcane heraldic symbols, a lion rampant over a stylised town on a black and white checkered background – the black for coal, the white for cotton. It had been the fancy of the Mayor to have the badge designed, to give his office an air of antiquity and mystery. His chain had been polished so that it rivalled the Cup for brilliance, although it slipped under the ill-fitting robe as he walked. He sat down in his chair, belching softly so that only Whittle and Ramsbottom could hear it and smell the whisky. He smoothed down his beard, waited until the footman had found his seat at their feet in front of the desk, then rapped his knuckles on the arm of his chair. This was not a tradition he'd inherited.

'Be seated,' said the Mayor. The councillors and the public in the gallery sat down. Whittle glanced up and noticed that Leo was whispering something to Harry.

'Urrah for Chorley!' shouted someone from the gallery. Whittle recognised the voice – it was Garstang, one of the players who had never been much of a gentleman, but who had at least respected the way of things. The chamber pealed with laughter, which echoed off its high ceiling as if the chamber itself was laughing. The last to stop laughing was Leo. His laugh was a deep boom, an opera singer's laugh, full of confidence and comradeship. Whittle watched his brother's face slowly settle like an engine's piston coming to rest as he finished laughing. Leo wiped his eyes, then his mouth, then looked down at the chamber with a grin still on his face, as if all along he had been waiting for them to continue. He waved a hand.

'Item One on the agenda, prayers,' said the Mayor, reading from the piece of paper Ramsbottom had placed in front of him.

He bowed his head, and the rest of the men in the chamber followed suit. Whittle shut his eyes and thought about God and forgiveness. He had tried to lead a good Christian life but he knew that the Devil had his soul. He pleaded with the Lord to forgive him his sins and allow him a reprieve from the fires he had seen so vividly when he'd been a child. He had seen the demons take over his sister, spirits that possessed her and who would not leave despite the administrations of the Reverend Smith. He had seen them invade other members of his family too, until they came to the gates of his own soul and demanded to be let in. He hoped that the Lord would see that it was the work of those demons that had made Whittle sin, and that his soul was pure. It was a foolish hope, he knew: for he could not hide from the final judgement, even if he evaded its earthly forms.

'Amen,' said the Mayor, breaking everyone out of their silent confessions. Whittle noticed that Ramsbottom's face had gone pale and clammy, cold with secret guilt. He touched his own face to see whether he betrayed himself. It felt as it always did – like a hard stone façade.

Ramsbottom pointed at something on the Mayor's paper. The Mayor nodded and looked up at the council chamber. Whittle could tell that the Mayor had had too much to drink. 'Before I go on, I'd just like to say what an honour it is to have with us our town's Member of Parliament, the 'onourable Henry Hibbert, whose idea this is.'

The councillor's from Whittle's party cheered and clapped. One of the men on the back benches, a young chap who owned an undertaking business, shouted 'bravo!', and this call was taken up by his companions. The opposition clapped politely. Up in the gallery, Harry stood up and waved down at his friends and political rivals, enjoying the adulation. Whittle watched with envy. Someone called for a speech but Harry shook his head with a wry grin and sat back down to yet more applause. The opposition did not clap this small act.

'Item Two on the agenda, apologies for absence,' said the Mayor once the applause had died. Whittle gave Ramsbottom a sideways look. They were there so that he could present the Cup to the town and get rid of the thing. How long would it take? Ramsbottom shrugged his shoulders and mouthed the word 'tradition'. Whittle sighed and fidgeted in his chair. It was too small for him. He looked at the clock ticking away on the wall above the main entrance to the chamber. Ramsbottom scratched away with his pen as the opposition Whip read out three names – Forshaw, Lockett and Grubb. Then Whittle's own Whip stood up.

'Mayor, I give apologies for Councillor Lever,' said the Whip. He looked at Whittle, who bowed his head. He had not seen Lever in the chamber or at the drinks beforehand. He knew why the team's stand-off half wasn't there. Lever had been a good friend of Whittle's wife's father: indeed Lever had introduced Whittle to her.

Ramsbottom nodded at the Whip then whispered something to the Mayor. The Mayor nodded and picked up his piece of paper. To Whittle's horror, he could see that the drunken fool was about to make a speech.

'I turn now to Item Three on the agenda,' said the Mayor. He stumbled to his feet, still gripping the paper, and put his free hand on the lip of the cup. He smudged the sides, leaving greasy fingerprints where he caressed it. He smiled at Whittle, giving him a conspiratorial wink from under his bushy eyebrows, then addressed the chamber. 'Gentleman, we 'ave crossed swords in this chamber for so many years I think we were 'ere as children.'

He paused, expecting laughter at his joke. When it wasn't forthcoming, his hand holding the paper started to shake, but he ploughed onwards. Whittle sighed and looked at the Cup as the Mayor talked about unique events that could bring men together. They had won the Cup after some delay in staging the final, and as such the excitement of the competition, the novelty of the event, had been overshadowed by the wrangling over when actually to play the match. Like Harry's experiment with electric lights, the victory had been Pyrrhic. The club had failed to survive as a rugby football club, as a club for gentlemen. The game had deserted the town, had left Whittle with only the memory of his mistakes and sins. The Cup had brought him prosperity and contacts, but these were only material things; he had lost his soul when his wife had been killed.

The old injury in his shoulder throbbed at the memory.

'If I may say, my friends,' continued the Mayor, looking at the Cup and smiling at the sound of his own voice, 'what we had, indeed what the town will have from here on, is, my friends, a chalice most fitting the ah the...'

He paused, and turned his piece of paper over.

'...the example of the knightly quest. And indeed this is no poisoned chalice. This is a Grail, won by Chorley's finest men, many of whom I see before me, but none so fine, if I may be allowed to indulge in a little flattery, than my good friend, earnest businessman and charitable councillor, Mister Humphrey Norris Whittle.'

'Bravo, Whittle!' shouted a few of the people in the gallery. Neither Dr Marsh, nor Whittle's brother Leo, joined in this exclamation.

'Speech!' shouted one of the Mockett brothers.

'Gentleman, please,' requested Ramsbottom, his lips pursed close together.

'It's all right, Albert, I'm Mayor 'ere,' muttered the Mayor. He looked back to his paper to find his place. 'Many of you will remember the Hercule... Herclee... big tasks the Chorley football club overcame to win this exquisite Grail I see before me, 'ere. But for those who don't pray let me indulge you, and suffer my voice but for a few moments longer. You will remember as in those days there were many folk involved in rugby football who thought that Chorley football club were too ambitious. But our lads, and the club's dynamo of a secretary, who shall remain nameless, showed them that Chorley is a town that has no limits to its ambitions. Just as we can build the finest town hall in Lancashire, just as our miners produce more coal for every 'our of their shift than any other, our football players were the finest of their generation.'

There was more applause at this, from both sides of the chamber and

14

the gallery. Whittle looked at the Cup and dreaded what the Mayor was about to say. He felt the sweat dripping off his back as he heaved in the scrimmage, pushing the Rossendale forwards back across the grass. He heard the excited shouts of the crowd, and Lever's shouts for the ball. He saw the ball hacked towards him in the middle of the scrimmage, before he in turn kicked it clear in the direction of his half-backs. He remembered Leo slapping him on the back once the game had been won, and Fish leering at him as he presented the Cup.

He thought about Shellard, watching that match with his betting slip in his hands, then later, slipping into his bed – Whittle's bed – to make love to his wife. Then the pain in his shoulder tormented him.

'Friends, citizens of Chorley, this great town of ours, today is a day in which we remember our heroes and celebrate their victory on the field of battle, remember their deeds on the rugby pitch, and celebrate that magnificent brace of wins which won them this fine trophy,' smiled the Mayor, delicately stroking the sides of the Cup. 'The Chorley club swept all before them like a tidal wave, a mighty 'ammer smiting football teams from across the land. Their deeds will not be forgotten, no, not while men are alive to say I was there that day at Blackpool, I saw Whittle's lads come out on top.'

Whittle groaned, but the chamber erupted with cheers. The Mayor started to clap in Whittle's direction, and was soon joined by every man in the room. The pain in his shoulder pulsed with the rhythm of their applause. He slowly got to his feet, looking at the Cup. He rubbed his eyes, then took the Cup in both hands. The chamber went silent.

He lifted up the Cup. He looked up at his brother and Harry. They stared back impassively. He looked along the gallery, searching for some sign of understanding. And there, at the back of the gallery, sitting by herself behind the Mockett brothers, was the girl, Prudence. His wife's maid. She was dressed in black. She frowned as she saw Whittle looking at her, and all his strength left him. His shoulder seized up, and he dropped the trophy back onto the desk, where it made an awkward clanging noise.

'Humphrey!' whispered Ramsbottom.

Whittle shook his head, and motioned for the Mayor to take up the Cup. He smiled at the men in the council chamber, then he looked back at the Mayor. His voice, croaky with weakness, barely reached the ears of the council as he said:

'He should have great pleasure in filling the Cup with wine, and to pass it round as a loving cup'.

The Mayor picked up the trophy, hesitant claps echoed around the chamber, and Whittle sat back down. It was over.

2.

Chorley Football Club

LEO WAS THE FIRST OF THE WHITTLE BOYS to be caught by the new football craze. Their father made sure that both Humphrey and his younger brother Leo were thoroughly drilled at school and at home, and from an early age they had been put through a rigorous programme of exercise using the latest scientific ideas about the relationship between the body and the mind. They were familiar with the need to develop one's soul through physical exertion, and were put through their drills at the Chorley grammar school by a missionary who had taken the Good News to the heathens of New Guinea before settling in Lancashire to do the same. They were also trained in the sports of gentlemen, so that they could mingle in society: at school they learned cricket, at home they were taught the fine arts of hunting, fishing and riding.

Humphrey had left school by the time a new master arrived fresh from Oxford anxious to show the boys the new game of football, based on a game played since the turn of the century at some of the best schools of England. In this he had the approval of the missionary teacher, who had become through the grace of God the grammar school's headmaster. Mister Whittle, their father, was at first dismissive of the fad, considering football as a relic of the dark ages used by rustics as an excuse to miss work, drink too much and fight. It was a diversion, and he thrashed his children to warn them off such diversions. But the school quickly reassured him that football was a gentleman's game, now played by all men of society, and taught to their sons. It was a game perfectly suited to the modern world of capital and colonies, a testing ground for the men who would govern. The master from Oxford saw Whittle senior in his office in town, and explained that football was played according to a number of rigid codes set out in the late 1850s and 1860s by men of great standing – learned scholars, wealthy sons of lords and businessmen. He showed Whittle senior cuttings from southern newspapers that carried reports of matches between respectable teams.

The master explained the game's glorious history. Football owed its origins to the codification of rough-and-tumble games in public schools in the first half of the century. Any idea that the game had anything to do with the working-class was, said the master, a deceit spread by radicals, Chartists and other assorted Jacobins. At that time, there was only the one game played by decent boys: that of football. This game, which had been popularised in a number of public schools by masters looking to make spiritual and colonial conquests, was played to differing rules depending on which school one attended. Matches between schools, and later between clubs organised by gentlemen, happened only when a set of rules for the particular match were agreed by both sides. Although it was generally agreed that the round ball was only to be controlled by the feet, some schools - famously Rugby - allowed players to catch the ball with their hands, or even pass it with their hands.

By the 1860s it was clear that football was becoming fashionable among middle-class men, as well as those who had been to the best public schools. Its relationship with the fashionable muscular Christianity - a belief that physical might and athletic prowess protected one's soul and purified the mind of sinful thoughts - had allowed football to grow beyond its limited public school roots. Clubs, claimed the master, were appearing in various parts of the country where there were enough gentlemen to play the game. At the same time, this expansion had led to some rationalisation and consolidation of the loose rules governing the game. This had culminated in the establishment of a Football Association in 1863, formed by a number of clubs who agreed to play to a code established by Cambridge University. Those clubs who preferred the Rugby School rules, which allowed for limited handling, rejected the invitation to join.

The rules used in a football match therefore differed, being dependent on the code that the competing teams followed. They also differed in that the rules of football were neither fixed nor absolute. The Rugby code was a match of a man's honour in the unregulated chaos of the scrum. It was in the long scrimmage that gentlemen learned how to impose order, to exert discipline, to support each other in the pursuit of an elusive goal. And even in failure, there was the honour of knowing that one had done one's best in that engine of manliness. Football was a game for making gentlemen out of boys: Whittle senior decided he would have no objections to Leo playing the game.

The master taught the boys football played by the Rugby rules after Whittle senior learned of the formation of the Rugby Football Union from the newspaper. His attempts to tell the old man that the Football Association had been in existence for some years failed. Whittle senior had decided, and even the headmaster knew it was better if they let him have his way.

Football played by the Rugby rules differed from the Association's game. Leo learned how to pick up the ball, how to make a clean catch and how to pass it to his team-mates using both his feet and hands. Association rules barred players from using their hands. The Oxford master was constantly reminding the boys of the differences between the two games to such an extent that he discouraged dribbling of the ball and preferred to see a static scrimmage where the strongest boys won. But although the Rugby rules demanded that the ball pass over the cross bar instead of under it, the aim was the same - to use the leather-covered bladder, twice the size of a boy's head, to score goals.

Leo wasn't a strong boy. He had taken after his mother and was small and compact; unlike Humphrey, who was as big and tall as their father. But he could catch a ball, and his flair for bringing a boy down by tackling his legs made him a natural choice as one of the full-backs guarding the goals. In the school games this would suit Leo well. He could stay at the back with his hands in his trouser pockets and watch the forwards scrambling over each other in the middle of the field. If the ball came out to his half-backs he would run up the field to try to get the ball from the backs for a run. If their opponents had the ball he would jog across the pitch watching their attack, mirroring their every movement, sidling up to their runner before diving for his legs to send him crashing to the ground. Or he would watch the ball spinning in the air as it came off someone's boot, watching it tumbling towards the ground, and he would dash across the grass to be the first boy under it. As he caught the ball he'd bring it close to his chest, smelling the mud and wet leather, enjoying the feel of its rough skin against his shirt. It was a prize he cherished – when he caught the ball he understood what the missionary had told them about sport and the soul. When he followed his forwards up the field to congratulate a fellow for kicking a goal from the middle of a seething mass of muddy shirts, or when he stopped a rival from crossing the line and setting the enemy up for a try at goal, he knew what it meant to be alive. He enjoyed the praise of his team, the applause from the young boys and masters around the field. His father never came to watch the matches: Leo was old enough to understand that his father was a distant man, but he would listen when Leo retold his exploits in the evenings.

Humphrey listened to Leo's tales and watched their father nodding with approval. Not once had Humphrey seen the old man so full of interest in his family's affairs. Not once had the old man approved of Humphrey's work in the pit office. He had confronted rebellious foremen, dismissed idle drunkards and dealt with buyers from across the country. All this he had done and not once had his father approved, not even when he had won the school medal for wrestling, beating John in the process. He knew his father still remembered what had happened in the orchard, though he tried to forget it with every stroke of his stick.

They were sitting in their father's study, letting their evening meal settle. Humphrey was smoking a long, thin cigar and lounging in his seat by the fire. His father was in the chair opposite him, which was built up with cushions. He was smoking tobacco from a small white ivory pipe and staring disapprovingly into the distance. Leo, being still a child, had to make do with the carpet between them.

Their father wasn't a studious man. The only books in the room were account ledgers in an old bookcase with a glass door. These were behind the old man's desk, from where he conducted the affairs of his seven coal mines. Humphrey had told him it was time the business progressed, that there was money to be made in speculating on new factory machines and land for housing. He argued that their profits had to be channelled into other enterprises, as a means of protecting them from the fluctuations of a single industry. His father, however, saw no need for changing their ways. Coal had made them rich, made Chorley rich, and he would live or die by coal. His father didn't listen to him: he said Humphrey, being only twenty-two, had no experience of the real world; he said Humphrey's arguments were too fashionable, which Humphrey thought was rich coming from a man who encouraged his son to play football.

Leo's stories made Humphrey jealous. When he'd been at school, in the shadow of his brother John, there hadn't been a football team for him to join. They had proven themselves in a different way. He remembered the time they had dared him to climb the spire of the new town hall. He wanted to please his father, to be on top of the town. He'd scrambled up in the middle of the afternoon, past the windows and gargoyles and onto the roof. Then he'd shinned up the timbered sides of the spire, watched by his friends down in the street, climbing higher than his father would ever go, above the council chamber until there was nowhere else for him to climb. Gripping onto the spars he reached out for the weathercock and placed his school cap on the rooster for the whole world to see. From the top of the spire he could see across the entire town, across the entire world. He felt that if he stretched out his fingers he would be able to touch the clouds and feel the moisture on his skin. The cheers of his friends made him look down and for a moment he went giddy with excitement. They were so small, so insignificant. An urge came upon him and he considered jumping, to see how far he would reach before gravity took him back to the ground. He resisted it, and climbed back down. The other boys had carried him on their shoulders through the streets as if he was a new Alexander. That evening he'd foolishly told his father about his achievement and received a sound thrashing with the belt.

'It sounds like a fascinating game to play, for schoolboys,' said Humphrey, ignoring the fact that he was barely out of childhood himself.

'It's not just for boys, Humphrey, old men like yourself can have a go for nothing,' replied Leo confidently. 'I hear there are clubs being formed all over the county, from Barrow to Oldham. Why, we're thinking of forming a club when we've left school, to carry on the sport. Keep ourselves active.'

'Well if you do I'm sure Humphrey will want to join, won't you, Humphrey?' said their father.

'The girls all love a football player, better than a hussar,' said Leo.

Humphrey nodded. He didn't particularly like women, yet he needed their company. He felt uncomfortable when talking to them, especially the working-class ones who made all kinds of sordid suggestions whenever they thought he wasn't listening. They were a nuisance. They shamed him whenever he was near one – his guilty secrets made his face go red, made him feel sick inside, sick at his own weakness.

The idea of football, of using it as a millrace to divert the flood of energy and convert it into something more noble, appealed to Humphrey after that conversation. He was converted to the cause of rugby football, and started to read reports of other matches in newspapers, matches between newly formed teams such as Liverpool and Manchester, Leigh and Broughton, Bradford and Halifax. Leo fed his prejudices, explaining that the rugby football code was the superior version, and often took him out to the school field with some of the younger men from the Oddfellows Hall. When Leo left school that summer, he showed Humphrey an advertisement placed by Harry Hibbert in the local paper. It was well timed, and Leo didn't have to work hard to persuade Humphrey to forget about the office for the afternoon and go with him to the park where Chorley Football Club was about to be born on a summer's day only four years before the North of England Challenge Cup matches.

At the gates of the town park, Harry Hibbert stood by himself, looking impatiently at his pocket watch. He knew through his contacts that a number of young gentleman had taken to playing football. He had watched the boys at the school, and observed the Oddfellows being put through a rigorous training session by young Leo Whittle. It was clear that football had a big potential in the town, especially since most of his contacts were wondering how they could make some money out of it. Men who already had large amounts of money from their mills and pits were talking after dinner about setting up a club for the purpose of taking part in competitive matches against Chorley's neighbours in the county. Some were even talking about the club taking on the cream of the London clubs, so that they could expand their businesses in the south of the country.

No one was as sharp as Harry in placing a newspaper advertisement for sporting gentleman. If there was to be a Chorley Football Club, he would run it. The advert had been quite specific about his motives, and about the character of the players he was hoping to attract. It had told all interested gentlemen to attend a football gathering to be held in the town's central municipal park that afternoon, with the intention of establishing a rugby football club. All he had to do was wait for them to turn up.

Humphrey waited impatiently for his older brother to finish talking to the pit-head manager. Leo had gone home to fetch their hobnailed boots and a clean set of clothes to wear, leaving him to convince his older brother John that he deserved a free afternoon. John was more affable than their father – although he was only five years older than Humphrey, and not even out of his twenties, he behaved and looked like a corpulent, port-soaked alderman. Humphrey considered him a dullard with no more wit than one of the workers. The men in the mines liked John Whittle because they knew he was quite simple and could be easily fooled. It was, thought Humphrey, the natural way of the worker – they were sluggards.

Through the smoked glass of the office door, Humphrey could see the slump-shouldered silhouette of Mister Garstang the pit-head manager. He had been in the pay of the family for ten years, and his loyalty had earned him a measure of white-collar respectability that belied his time at the coal face. He was a favourite of both John and their father. Humphrey didn't trust him. He may have been a manager, but he still went to the pub at the end of the shift with the black-faced men he sent into the ground. He suspected Mister Garstang of being a suitable conduit for the desires of the more troublesome workers, those who made unfeasible demands over pay.

He looked at the grandfather clock in the office atrium. The pendulum swung back and forth, like a scythe slicing through the harvest. He was running out of time, and all because of his dullard brother. He couldn't wait any longer. The clerk at the small desk in the atrium had told him to wait for 'Mister Whittle' to finish his meeting. But didn't he run the business as well? Who was the clerk to decide whether or not one Whittle could talk to another?

He knocked on the door. The clerk looked up from his copy-book. He was a young man a few years older than Leo, who was wearing a waistcoat cut thin about the shoulders and embroidered in an Oriental manner in pale gold. Humphrey thought it was an ugly fashion, but one which the middle-classes had taken to with great relish over the summer.

'Excuse me, sir, but Mister Whittle said he and Mister Garstang were not to be disturbed. He were quite persistent in that, sir.'

'Listen, boy, I am in a hurry,' replied Humphrey, 'I have a football club to join this very afternoon, and I am sure that you would not object, as a gentleman yourself, to my determination to get to the football meeting on time.'

He opened the door, leaving the clerk open-mouthed, unsure of whether Humphrey had insulted or complimented him.

John was sitting behind his desk, fiddling with a pen caught between his stubby fingers. His blue suit was too small for him, or rather, he was too large for his suit, and when he moved the seams stretched ominously. Humphrey found him disgusting – of course, the missionary had arrived too late to save John through the application of muscular Christianity. Behind John was a painting of a Welsh mine in the style of Constable. Rain lashed the winding gear and black mountains of slag loomed up in the background, merging into the storm clouds so that the break between air and earth was not distinguishable. Men emerged from the shaft as dark shadows, smudges of ochre paint against the greys and browns of the ground. In the foreground a tree's green leaves contrasted sharply with the bleakness of the mines. It had been one of their father's more extravagant buys. Humphrey suspected it was bought thanks to the influence of their mother, who knew the artist's sister.

Standing in front of the desk was Mister Garstang, a man in his early fifties. His hair was still thick and healthy except for patches of grey about his temples and down his large sideburns. He was always clean-shaven, and immaculately dressed in a sombre black suit. He nodded at Humphrey, deferring to his superior. John stirred behind the desk. His chair creaked.

'Humphrey, what can I do for you that's so important you have to interrupt my meeting with Mister Garstang?' he asked, looking at Humphrey then at Mister Garstang.

'John, I have to leave this afternoon. Will that be all right?' asked Humphrey, grinning at his older brother.

'What on earth for, Humphrey? You have the stock-taking to see to,' replied John.

'It is only for the afternoon,' said Humphrey. He looked at Mister Garstang for support. The manager smiled.

'It is for a football meeting Mister Hibbert has organised. Leo says it is for the formation of a football club, a football club for the town. But Mister Hibbert needs players… you know how I like this game, John, it is not a fickle amusement, it is about improving one's body and mind.'

Humphrey wondered whether that argument would work with John.

'It could be very profitable for the business if Leo and I are players at the club. Football is attracting the interest of the best businessmen across Lancashire – and only the best gentlemen play it. Just think of the people I would meet after the matches. And consider this: Mister Hibbert is a very influential man in town. They say he could be an MP you know, and he knows just about everyone. He's a good friend of father's too – you wouldn't want this scheme to fail, would you?'

John frowned and looked at Mister Garstang.

'What do you think, Herbert?'

Mister Garstang shrugged.

'Well, Mister Whittle, m'young un's got 'is 'ead full of this football, it's right popular nowadays. If the likes of them in Yorkshire can play it then ah can't see why we can't play it in Chorley. Mister 'umphrey 'ud make a fine footballer too... if there's a club in Chorley then my lad'll be keen on it.'

'You see, John? Even the men are dead keen. If there's to be a club then it needs to have a Whittle involved. What do you say? Leo's too young to have an influence on these things, and he hasn't the right character for business. I need to go, John, for the sake of the family,' said Humphrey.

John nodded.

'Very well, Humphrey, off you go.'

Harry Hibbert was grey before his time. His silver hair, glistening under a thick coat of oil, went well with his grey, worry-lined face. The world was moving fast for Harry. It was no longer enough to run a small family company; that type of business had no place in the future of huge factories, fast trains and free trade. Harry's world ran on the tracks of railways, down the wire of the telegraph. For those who knew how to make the most of it, there was money and glory to be had better than any prize a knight errant in a fairy tale could find. God had given Harry the opportunity to build a better life in anticipation of the world to come, and he wasn't about to let God down.

The park was full of young men in shirts and trousers, all sweltering in the heat of the afternoon sun. He had gathered them in the middle of the lawn, in between two parallel sets of blue and yellow flower beds. The only shade was provided further up the park, under the sycamores, or in the municipal bandstand near the pond. Luckily for Harry, he had brought with him a large umbrella, which he used as a sunshade. The men, who were more than Harry could count, stood or sat on the grass. They talked amongst themselves, or smiled at the old maids and young nannies walking along the gravel path.

One of the young men, who was in the process of growing a moustache, walked over to Harry. He was lean, and carried himself like a dandy. He had large blue eyes and soft, feminine skin. But his voice, when he spoke, was hard and blunt.

'I say, Mister Hibbert, I have been here twenty minutes. Are we to have a football game or not? I can always go and play for another club in Preston, you know. They want me to play for them.'

Harry smiled at the lad. He knew his father – Councillor John Lever, of the soap-making family. He had not inherited his father's looks, though he had the voice.

'I said three o'clock in the newspaper, and at three o'clock we'll start, Mister Lever.' He pointed at the nearby town hall, at the clock on its side. 'That says it's still five minutes to. Football's a popular game, Mister Lever, we 'ave to give everyone the opportunity.'

'I don't want to play with everyone, I don't want to play with people who don't know the rules,' said Lever. He looked at Harry. 'Do you know the rules, Mister Hibbert?'

Harry laughed.

'Course I do, young fellow!' he replied, trying to remember what the rules were exactly. He had a vague idea that the rugby code of football allowed the use of hands because he'd watched the Whittle brothers at play, and he knew the objective was to get more goals than the other side. It was on account of that and the school that he'd put rugby football in the advertisement, but he was flexible enough to allow whatever rules the chaps wanted, just as long as they had a club.

'Then if you know the rules, why haven't you brought a ball?' asked Lever cockily. 'Surely you know we do play football with a ball. I imagine even the savages in the South Pacific are aware of that.'

'A ball?' frowned Harry. A ball! No plan was perfect. He hadn't got to be the most influential man in Chorley without being able to improvise. He laughed at Lever's suggestion. 'My lad, this is just to see whether you lot 'ave the commitment to make something of thiselves… when we 'ave a club then you'll have thi ball.'

Lever looked beyond Harry.

'Never mind that, Mister Hibbert, I see someone has had the sense to bring a ball along.'

Harry turned around.

Humphrey strode across the grass, holding Leo's ball under his arm. He was wearing a white shirt and black trousers with grass stains over both knees. He smiled at Harry, glorying in the attention from the older man, then looked at the others. He imagined himself to be Alexander, inspecting his troops after the rout of Darius. They were all staring at him in wonder, looking at the ball he carried. He recognised many of them as his lesser companions from the Oddfellows Hall, men who looked up to him and respected him for his daring. He glanced up at the town hall spire, remembering the past.

He kicked the ball into the midst of the other men, who scrambled for it like boys.

'There you are, Mister Lever, I knew Humphrey would bring a ball,' said Harry. He left Lever and walked over to shake Humphrey by the hand. 'Humphrey, dear boy, I am so glad to see you... and young Leo as well. Tell me, how is your father's business?'

'He won't diversify, Mister Hibbert,' said Humphrey, 'I worry that he is going to get old and John will make a mess of the whole thing. Quite awful.'

'A shame. I was rather hoping that you Whittles would be dipping your hands into your wallets to make Chorley Football Club the envy of the north of England,' said Harry.

'I'm sure we can convince father it's a good thing, he encouraged me at school,' said Leo, who found himself standing behind Humphrey's back.

'Well I'm glad you two came, if there's going to be a football club in Chorley then I need to make sure the best gentlemen in town are members,' said Harry.

'For their financial support?' asked Humphrey cynically.

Harry grinned at him.

'By lad, you'll do well, you will.'

Humphrey nodded.

The other chaps had arranged themselves in an ad-hoc fashion into two uneven teams. Lever had gathered about him seven of the likeliest lads, all strongly built, and was urging them on in a rough scrimmage against a dozen of the others. He was shouting at the top of his voice and slapping them forward. They pushed, and the legs of those in the row immediately in front of them buckled under the overwhelming force. Losing this forward wall, the rest of the scrimmage moved unexpectedly forward. Like skittles the other men stumbled and lost their balance, losing sight of the ball as they were thrown to the ground by the momentum of the scrimmage.

One of Lever's men found the ball and hacked it back to another man behind him. Then the scrimmage moved slowly forward, pushing the men on the floor out of the way. They tried to regroup, but they were like hopeless navvies trying to stop a railway engine at full steam. Lever's men moved their legs like pistons, pounding the grass into the mud and stamping over the handful of men too slow to get out of their way. Lever joined the scrimmage at the side, pushing away those who tried to get around the men forward and thus break their stride.

Harry nudged Humphrey.

'I say, young feller, these lads have spirit, don't they? That fellow Lever looks like he knows a few tricks.'

Humphrey looked at Lever. He didn't like the look of him, nor the way in which he was basking in the glory of the men who were doing the hard work for him.

'Come on, Leo, let's show Mister Hibbert how Whittles play!' shouted Humphrey.

Not caring to pause to see whether Leo followed him, Humphrey ran onto the park's pristine grass. Grabbing the arm of someone spiralling away from the scrimmage he shouted at the men about him to dig their heels into the ground. He threw the man he had grabbed into the wall of defenders, then put his shoulder into their backs. The force of the scrimmage knocked him back a yard or two, but he gritted his teeth and pushed forward with all his might. Someone cried out in the middle of the scrimmage for air but Whittle ignored them. He bent his knees and strained as the pile of men threatened to roll over him.

'Push, damn you, push!' he shouted.

The men nearest him, finding their feet for the first time since the initial attack, howled and screamed with rage as they pushed back. It was the turn of Lever's men to find themselves wrong-footed. One of the men at the sides crumpled and Whittle pushed some of his men into the breach. The scrimmage twisted around and both front rows collapsed in a pile of laughing bodies.

Whittle continued to push, seeing the ball loose near the back of the scrum. He scrambled over two men and reached out for it, but too many legs were in the way. He cursed and fell to the floor, trying to squeeze his hands through the mass of limbs.

Lever broke away from the side of the scrimmage and saw Whittle straining forward by his fingernails. He followed Whittle's eyes and saw the ball.

Whittle glanced up and saw Lever looking at the ball. 'No!' he cried.

Lever smirked. He ducked down, pushing one of his own men on top of Whittle, then scooped the large leather ball up in his hands. Whittle tried to pull himself out of the scrimmage but there were too many men who had given up the game and were laughing at their predicament. Lever saluted Whittle, then started to run away.

He got five yards before Leo crashed into him on his blind side, sending the ball one way and Lever the other. Leo let go as Lever fell to the floor then jogged over to where the ball had come to rest. He looked across at Mister Hibbert, who was clapping his hands, then at Humphrey. His brother had got to his feet, and was dripping with sweat. His face was red but his anger had gone.

Humphrey found his handkerchief still in his pocket, and wiped the sweat from his face and moustache. Someone slapped him on the back. Lever stood up and shook Leo's hand, then grinned at Humphrey.

'You're like a bloody stampeding elephant,' he said.

Humphrey smiled back at Lever. 'And you managed to get those fellows whipped up like devils!'

'We're all devils,' replied Lever. He extended his hand. 'Lever.'

'Whittle,' said Humphrey, stepping out of what was left of the scrimmage to shake Lever's hand. 'Humphrey Whittle. This is my brother, Leo.'

Lever nodded and looked at Leo, who was still holding the ball.

'Well, I think we three make rather a splendid team, don't you?'

Harry Hibbert smiled to himself. Even he could see most of the men who had turned up to have a go were appalling. They would have to make do with a second team, or play for someone else. But Lever was right.

There was promise in a few of them – the sight of Humphrey's shoulders holding back the scrimmage had made even Harry's heart jump with excitement. He had looked around and noticed that the young women in the park had also been interested in Humphrey's feat of strength. All he had to do was to persuade enough people to give him the money, and he would build a mighty club around Humphrey Whittle, one where the entire town would watch in amazement. He was sure he could find more men like Humphrey before the start of the season, and he knew when they played it would be like an earthquake in Lancashire - Chorley Football Club would play to win.

3.

The Apple

THINGS HAD BEEN SO DIFFERENT when Humphrey had been a boy. It had been a better world, one of sunlight and trees and adventures at the end of the garden. There had been long-tailed newts dappled brown and black kept in jars of slimy water, and swirling clouds caught in marble tors. There were long days searching for highwaymen's treasure in the hedgerows leading out into the endless countryside. There were nights spent in haunted houses, sitting beside old black kitchen ranges covered in dust as tales were told of ghosts and goblins.

They had played football, even though they didn't know its name, nor any of the rules. They would find a meadow and roll about on the grass, then afterwards they would listen to John telling them about Merlin and magic as the sun went down.

As the eldest child at Primrose Cottage John would always be in charge, a situation about which Humphrey was never happy. When their tutor, Mister Mytholmroyd, the ancient head of the school, read to them the tale of Caesar's death at the hands of his friend Brutus, Humphrey sympathised with the man who betrayed his leader. His anger at John stemmed from the day they took Frederick away. Humphrey was ten at the time, and Frederick was only just eight. They had gone down to the bottom of the orchard to play in the stream, even though their mother had forbidden it. Frederick was a simple child. Humphrey remembered the fuss after Frederick was born, and how for nearly four years their father refused to acknowledge the pathetic creature's existence in case he died from any one of the many ailments from which he suffered.

But Frederick lived, even though he struggled to say a proper sentence and had trouble walking in a straight line. Humphrey sensed that something was wrong with him: he knew that Frederick was stricken by some wasting of the brain, and that their father would have left the infant to die if it had not been for their mother and the nursemaid, who conspired with the doctors to keep Frederick alive. This he found out later. At the time young Humphrey had to make do with the whispers and the warnings, and the wild guesses he made with his older sister Jane. John, of course, accepted the fact that their brother was not allowed out of the sight of the nursemaid, even though he was old enough to feed and clothe himself.

Jane loved Frederick. She was older than Humphrey by three years, and in his eyes she was like a strange and frightening grown-up who smiled when no one had told a joke. She reminded him of his place as a mere child in the grand scheme of things, but at the same time she joined in their games like another boy. When he'd been five, Humphrey had watched her pull off the legs of a frog in the pond at the back of the house. John had found the frog, and had carried it in his chubby little fingers nervously, trying to stop the water trickling down his shirt sleeves. He said it was going to be his pet, and he was going to keep it in a small wooden castle he had made under his bed. Jane had asked him whether she could feel it, and he had stupidly passed the creature to her with a cheery smile. Once she had it her hands she declared it was hers, not his, and she was going to call it Puddledum and crown it Prince of all the Frogs. He was going to live in a real palace, not a wooden castle with walls that always fell down. They started to argue, and Humphrey, who was sitting between them pulling at his blue shoes, had naturally thought the frog could be his if only he could grab at it. So he'd pulled at Jane's dress and held out his hand impatiently. She had laughed, and said that if she wasn't to have Prince Puddledum then he was to die a hero's death.

Then she had pulled at the legs until the frog split in two, oozing out silver-grey guts and a black liver and heart. These insides fell over Humphrey, and he screamed for their nanny. Jane threw the remains of the frog at John and then ran away into the orchard to climb the tallest apple tree. She'd stayed in the tree for the rest of the day, until their father had found her and dragged her home, ignoring her pleas for forgiveness. He had beaten her soundly that night, and the next day John had found his favourite lead soldier hanging from a rafter with a splint for a cane glued to his hand. She told them she would never obey their father again, and warned them to keep that secret on their souls or suffer in Hell forever.

Jane said Frederick was backward, but she didn't let that stop her looking after him like her favourite doll. She helped the nursemaid dress and wash Frederick every morning, and was constantly combing his yellow curls with a bone comb she had made for the purpose. Frederick would sit there chewing his nails with a grin on his face as she pulled at the knots and tried to straighten his naturally bouncy locks. Their mother never interfered, and stayed well away.

The day Humphrey took Frederick down to the stream their mother had gone with Jane into town to collect some material for a new dress. They had left in their father's carriage with Jane still complaining about not being able to take Frederick with her. But their father had insisted that Frederick was never to be taken into town, so he was left with John and Humphrey.

It was easy enough for Humphrey to trick the nursemaid. He had pushed Frederick over into a patch of nettles in the orchard, and his terrifying moans of agony were enough to send the nursemaid away to look for dock leaves. Of course she didn't know there was a patch under the beech tree, where he took Freddy to soothe the rashes and stop the tears. It was a little harder to convince John that they should take Frederick out of sight of Primrose Cottage and down to the stream at the bottom of the orchard. John knew it wasn't allowed and agonised over the different threats to his well-being – the real threat of being called a coward by his younger brother, and the potential threat of being found out and beaten by their father. Once, when he'd followed his father into the orchard, Humphrey had seen him place a card on an apple, warning that it mustn't be plucked. Humphrey hadn't cared about this. He couldn't read his father's crab-like script, and only knew afterwards, with the taste of apple in his mouth and the sting of the rod on his backside, the meaning of those words. But the beating was nothing compared to the sweetness of the fruit.

Since that day they had been banned from the orchard. Humphrey wanted his older brother's approval before they went, so in desperation he offered him a share of his sherbet if he let them go. He agreed, taking the sherbet with eager hands. They would go.

Primrose Cottage was a quaint name for the family house, one which the elder Whittle had chosen to remind himself of the agrarian roots from which he supposed his ancestors came. In later years Humphrey detested this act of middle-class affection, and refused to call his home by anything other than the Old House. This was at least a more accurate name than the one his father had provided in a fit of whimsy one summer's day. Primrose Cottage was a huge, sprawling manor house on the western edge of Chorley, built over and around an ancient hall by one of Lancashire's first merchant kings in the previous century. His taste had been eclectic – the architects had been given a free rein to include all the trappings of a transient fashion which appealed to the elder Whittle when he purchased the house. It had a sweeping frontage with two windows to every room. Although half of these had been bricked up to reduce the tax bill by the sensible heir of the builder, the elder Whittle had put the glass back in, so that every room was lit by the natural light of the sun. The porch was colonnaded and decorated with griffins in the niche between the house and the roof of the porch. Inside, the hallway was spacious, with tall alcoves and mahogany panels between the openings that led to both wings of the house. The rooms inside had a perfect symmetry, balanced on all three floors of the house, except for the kitchens which were a later extension at the back.

To Humphrey, the Cottage was a castle. Its big gardens and ponds were the bailey to the house's keep. The orchard was the 'King's Forest', protected by a tall brick wall which met and joined the smaller wall that marked the boundaries of the Whittle land. And at the bottom of the orchard, beyond the apple trees, was the stream: the castle's moat. The stream was the boundary between the Whittle land and a farmer's field, which in turn had a small hedge around it. Beyond that were hills, the sea, dragons.

They walked through the orchard, seeing who was best at whistling like a bird. It was a cold spring day and they had a number of birds to choose from. Humphrey favoured the rowdy chatter of the sparrow, and whistled as loudly as he could at the young birds in the lower branches of the apple trees. John tried to copy whichever bird sang the loudest, but struggled to purse his lips narrow enough to make sufficient noise. In the end he produced a passable imitation of a wood-pigeon, which made Frederick laugh and fall over. Humphrey picked him up and gave him a piggy-back. Although John was bigger, Humphrey was the stronger of the two and they both knew it, even though John's pride would not allow him to accept this. Humphrey carried Frederick along, pretending to be a horse, dodging the trunks of the trees at the very last minute so that Frederick threw off

Humphrey's cap and grasped his hair in excitement.

'Steady on, Humphrey!' shouted John, who was trying in vain to keep up with them. He picked up Humphrey's cap and leaned against a tree, puffing and wheezing. Ahead of him Humphrey had turned round, and was scraping the ground with his foot.

'I'm a charger, and this is Sir Frederick of Whittle, a Knight of the Round Table. He will defeat any Saracen cur in a joust. Dare you accept the challenge of my master?' asked Humphrey. Frederick shouted something in his strange, indecipherable manner, and kicked his feet in the air between Humphrey's arms.

John grinned and looked up at the tree. He found a straight-looking branch within reach and pulled at it, watching the bark peel away from the trunk until it was narrow enough to give with a twist of his wrist. He snapped off the twigs and the leaves, then held it out in front of him with both hands gripping the thickest end.

'And I am Lord John, no, I am King John, of Primrose Cottage, and I am master of this entire forest,' answered John, glancing around at the orchard. The sunlight made patterns in the grass, moving as the wind moved through the trees. Humphrey and John looked around and saw huge oak trees covered in moss and mistletoe, their eaves dark and damp, the shadows hiding bears and unicorns and giant stags with antlers twice the size of scrubbing boards.

King John's burgundy velvet suit became silver armour, shining inside itself, and his sword was as long as he was tall, and red with the blood of his vanquished enemies. Sir Frederick's face was hidden behind a black helmet which matched his black armour. Humphrey realised that the others had been transformed into knights whilst he was only a horse. It was not how he wanted to play the game.

'You're not a knight, I've already said, you have to be a Saracen cur,' said Humphrey, shifting Frederick about on his back. 'You can't be the King because Frederick is sworn to serve the King. A good knight wouldn't betray his lord and master by challenging him to a fight, would he? A good knight obeys his King.'

'But I don't want to be a Saracen cur,' complained John. 'Why can't Frederick be the Saracen and I can be King then.'

'It was my idea, Frederick challenged you, so we decide who plays the baddy, so there, be a sport,' argued Humphrey.

'But you challenged me, not Frederick,' said John, using his sword to make a hole in the ground.

'Frederick challenged you, I just spoke for him, don't be such a weasel, or I'll wrestle you into the stream like Robin Hood,' said Humphrey, raising his hands and clenching his fists. Frederick did likewise and lost his grip. The weight on Humphrey's arms was too much and he let go of Freddy's legs, letting him fall silently into the grass.

'If you're Robin Hood then I'll be Little John. And Little John pushed Robin Hood into the stream, if you remember,' sneered John.

'All right, let's see if you dare, then,' said Humphrey. Frederick brushed the grass from the seat of his shorts and pulled on Humphrey's leg to try and get back up. Humphrey ignored him: he stared at John, trying to twist his angelic face into a manly grimace. He had never dared to keep one of their arguments going before, and the thrill of doing so made his blood rush. It pounded in his temples, between his clenched fingers. He could feel himself growing taller. 'First one in the water loses.'

John looked at Humphrey and smiled nervously.

'No weapons, just hands.'

'Very well,' nodded Humphrey. John dropped his stick.

The stream was only a few seconds away. It cut a ditch through the ground between the wild grasses of the orchard and the swaying hedgerow. Beyond the hedgerow the first shoots of barley were breaking the ground. At the height of summer, when the wheat was a sea of gold crashing against the green hedgerow they would cross the stream to hide under the ripening ears. As it was only spring, they knew there would be nothing of interest beyond the stream.

On the orchard side the banks of the ditch were shallow, opening out into tiny beaches where the flood of winter had taken part of the soil away. Small pools out of the fast-flowing centre harboured fishes and other creatures, and were deep enough for the boys to swim in during the summer months. In the middle of the stream rocks and pebbles formed small islands and shallow banks for paper boats to run aground on. At one point the boys had arranged the trunk of a small tree as a makeshift bridge across to the field. It was a couple of feet above the water where the width of the stream narrowed between two outcrops of rock. The water there was shallow but raced through over a multitude of lesser rocks, from where the stream widened into a pool carved out by the water's force. The bridge was strong enough for them both to sit on it and shin across to the other side, or drop pebbles into the water.

Both boys knew without saying that this was to be the place they would fight over. Between them they pulled Frederick along in a series of jumps, then left him on the bank by a growth of sweet-smelling soapwort. John took off his jacket but kept on his shirt and shorts. Humphrey copied him, then John shinned across the trunk to reach the middle. He came to where a branch had been torn away and used the bump sticking out of the trunk to steady himself turning back round to face the orchard. His legs dangled limply over either side of the trunk.

'Come on then, Robin Hood,' challenged John.

Humphrey frowned.

'You're wrong, John, I'm sure it was Robin who pushed Little John into the stream.'

'We'll see, my little brother,' replied John.

Humphrey scrambled onto the trunk until he was face to face with John. He didn't want to be reminded of the fact that he was younger than John, and that John would be the Lord of the Manor instead of him. That wasn't fair. He knew he was better than John. Whoever had invented the rule that the eldest son inherited everything and the others had to go rot was stupid. He would show them.

'First one in the water loses,' said Humphrey.

John nodded, then lunged at Humphrey with his hands. Humphrey ducked and brought his own hands up to punch John in the belly. John's hands grabbed Humphrey's hair and he tugged, dragging Humphrey's head upwards. Humphrey yelled, lashing up with his arms and John lost his grip. Humphrey continued to lash out and caught John's shoulder.

'That's not fair!' cried Humphrey, his eyes full of tears. The roots of his hair felt like they had been shrivelled by a hot poker. John had slipped slightly and was struggling to find his balance using one of his hands. Humphrey brought his clenched fist down on the hand, and John shrank away howling in pain.

Humphrey moved forward, but in doing so he was forced to sit up like a jockey in the saddle. John saw this and threw all his weight forward into

Humphrey. They fell backwards. Humphrey's legs twisted awkwardly and John's body crushed him into the smooth bark of the trunk. John tried to shove Humphrey into the water but his own body trapped Humphrey. He lost his balance and they both slipped over the side of the trunk, still gripping each other by the arm. Humphrey brought his legs around the trunk and clung on upside down, the top of his head inches above the water. John held onto Humphrey, knowing that if he let go he would fall in.

'Let go!' shouted Humphrey.

'Give in!' pleaded John.

There was a splash. Something fell in the stream. Humphrey knew straight away who had gone in the water. They had left him by the large pool.

'Frederick! Let me go!' ordered Humphrey, trying to twist around so he could see what had happened.

'I can't, I'll fall in…' moaned John.

'Frederick! Frederick!' shouted Humphrey desperately. He tried to pull himself up using John, but his legs were caught under John's body. 'Help! Help!'

John suddenly realised what was happening.

'Help! Help!' he screamed.

'Let go, John, hurry!' begged Humphrey.

'Help! Help!' repeated John.

'Help! Help!' they cried in unison.

Humphrey pulled at John, ripping the cloth around his collar. John tried to push Humphrey away but only succeeded in loosening his grip. He slipped and clung onto Humphrey's belt as his body flipped over. Humphrey, released for the moment from John's weight, moved his legs. Then John's momentum dragged him off the trunk.

They fell on the rocks, cutting themselves and ripping their clothes. Water splashed about, drenching them and making the blood smear over their faces where they both suffered deep gashes. John sat in the water and started to cry – Humphrey looked at him with disgust. His older brother, crying! He wanted to hit John to make him cry even more, but he remembered Frederick and scrambled out of the stream.

He raced along the bank, looking for Frederick. In the direction of the house he could hear someone – one of the gardeners – shouting in their direction. He shouted back, shouting as loud as he could that they needed help. In the pool beyond the trunk Frederick's tiny, awkward body, as still as a leaf, was floating face down on the water.

'Frederick! Freddy!' cried Humphrey. He looked around and saw the gardener walking towards him through the orchard. He was a young man, one of the collection of young men who worked for the gardening company their father had contracted to look after Primrose Cottage. The man looked nervous, as if he was expecting some kind of trick. He removed his cap and scratched his uncombed hair. Humphrey looked back at Frederick. The current had moved him out into the middle of the pool, where he was slowly turning round with his limbs outstretched. John was still crying further upstream and screaming out for their mother. Humphrey realised that he was crying too – the drops of water in his mouth were salty, mixed with the iron taste of his blood. He looked back at the gardener.

'Quick! Frederick's bin drownded!'

The gardener ran the last few yards, saw Frederick's body in the water, and without a moment's hesitation jumped in the stream. He waded through the pool, dragged Frederick out, then laid him face down on the grass. Humphrey watched with horror as the man slapped Frederick's bent back.

'Go get Missis Shaw, Master Whittle, tell 'er to call fer doctor,' said the gardener to Humphrey. He bent down to listen to Frederick's heartbeat. He heard John's cries of despair.

'Is yer brother all right, young Master?'

'Don't care... care about Freddy... is he alive?' asked Humphrey.

'I don't know,' shrugged the gardener. He gently shoved Humphrey away. 'Go get Missis Shaw to get the doctor, lad, and be quick!'

Humphrey looked at the gardener in horror. He had never before heard any of the servants except their nanny talk to them in such a brusque manner. He wiped his nose, then his eyes, to make sure there were no more tears, then ran up to the house shouting for Mrs Shaw the housekeeper.

He was glad to get away from the stream, away from John. He couldn't listen to John's cries a second longer. It was a relief for him when he reached the gardens, where those cries were hidden by the sounds of the birds and the housemaids singing. When he was in the house, and the servants were rushing around giving orders to each other, he found a hiding place in the pantry. He stayed there until they found him two hours later and told him that Frederick was alive.

They left Frederick on a reclining chair wrapped in blankets and waited for his mother to return from town. She cried for her son, and would have beaten both John and Humphrey if the gardener hadn't spoken out in their defence. He said both Humphrey and John had alerted him to the danger, and acted like true gentlemen in the moment of crisis. When Mrs Whittle brought both boys to stand in front of her they went red and had to be told to look at her. She asked them whether the gardener had told the truth, and Humphrey was about to say yes and that they could look after Frederick, but John burst into tears again. He ran out of the room, and the gardener was forced to confess he had lied to her. Only the fact he had saved Frederick's life saved him from instant dismissal.

Jane was distraught at hearing her beloved Frederick had almost drowned. She hit Humphrey across the face and called him all kinds of names, ones which shocked the housekeeper and their nanny. Mrs Whittle sent Jane to her room, but she refused to go, and it took the intervention of two of the men who carried her scratching and biting out of the front study where they'd placed Frederick. When she had gone and her howls stopped echoing down the stairwell Mrs Whittle forced Humphrey to tell her everything.

He felt completely humiliated. Surrounded by adults, fearing for his own life, Humphrey tried to defend himself as best as he could. But no matter how he explained the events at the stream, he and John sounded guilty. As he stood there burning with shame, unable to stop himself from crying, he vowed that he'd make sure John was never their leader again. It was his fault they had had to fight in the first place. It was his fault they had started the fight without making sure Frederick was all right. It was his fault they hadn't been able to fish him out of the water before the gardener arrived. He concluded that John had failed – they could have got to Frederick before he passed out, and if they had, then they would have been able to save him as if nothing had happened at all.

When Whittle senior returned he refused to listen to Humphrey's story. He gave both him and John a severe thrashing with his belt, then left them to cry to themselves behind the locked door of their bedroom. That evening he decided that Primrose Cottage was too dangerous for Frederick.

There was water on his brain, they said. He was never going to be anything more than a cripple. For the boy's own good they had to make sure something like the incident at the stream never happened again. Through the night Humphrey stayed awake, listening to the raised voice of his father and the desperate sobs of his mother. Elsewhere, he could hear Jane crying for Frederick. In their room, he could hear John snoring.

The next morning Frederick had gone.

4.

To Snuff Out The Moon

HUMPHREY'S FATHER REFUSED TO WATCH the floodlit match, and saw it as the beginning of the end for the coal industry and the Whittle empire. He had hoped the idea would please his father, show him how he was worth something, how he and the club were taking Chorley into the 20th century. Electricity was the future, Harry Hibbert had said. With electricity came more power, more light, so that workers could work shifts in the middle of the night. It was progress, the mighty dynamo engine of the Empire, making Britain the ruler of a fifth of the globe. And there was still room for coal, but instead of fuelling steam engines and producing gas the mines would be sources of electrical energy for huge power stations, each one serving a thousand homes and a thousand factories every second of the day. Electricity would snuff out the moon, as if Phaeton had taken up again the reins of his father's fiery chariot, warming poor houses in the middle of winter. Electricity would power huge steel ships, so that they cut through the water without a sound to sink an unsuspecting enemy fleet, and armoured waggons, which would race across the battlefield firing projectiles from magnetic-repellent cannons. Electricity was the future. It was a practical means of improving society, of securing the country, of making a fortune.

He suspected there was more to his father's refusal to watch the floodlit match - something to do with the apple, and the beating he'd received when his father had found the core hanging from the tree. He wanted to show his father he was capable of something, that he was the captain and the star player adored by the simple people of the town, not Leo and certainly not John, who had no sport in him whatsoever. The floodlit match had been Harry Hibbert's idea but he'd consulted Whittle first – he'd asked Humphrey for his opinion, and had listened when Humphrey had said it would be a success. But his father had refused to listen, pretending that Humphrey was like Frederick, a simple man with no mind of his own who wasn't mentioned in polite circles.

Leo was more forgiving than Humphrey, and tried to explain to him that their father was old-fashioned, a man who had seen Chorley grow from a small town into a black mass of stone and smoke, who had made his money and was determined to keep it. Humphrey didn't answer Leo, but he raged silently at the sanctimonious attitude of his brother. Leo had taken on the manners of the Oxford master, copying them exactly but applying them to everyday situations instead of converting insolent boys. Leo was a good football player – but Humphrey determined to show that he was better.

'1878 is going to be our year, Humphrey, my boy, we'll sweep all before us and be the cocks of all Lancashire,' prophesied Harry Hibbert.

Humphrey grinned, feeling his muscles growing under his freshly pressed shirt. He was twenty-six, and felt as if the whole world was his. He sipped at his pint of porter, glad of the drink after the evening's jerks on the field.

'Soon everyone will know our names, Harry.'

'Aye, well they'll know your name, lad, and there's nothing wrong wi' that for an ambitious man like thisself,' replied Harry, raising his own glass. 'Your good 'ealth, Humphrey, you've done me proud, you 'ave.'

'I've done the club proud,' said Humphrey, winking at the older man.

'We've done the town proud,' smiled Harry, 'and it's not 'armed us any, either, if you know what I mean, young Mister Whittle.'

Harry and Humphrey were sitting in the snug bar of the *Rose and Crown*, the public house favoured so much by the club when it was in its first season that it soon became their official headquarters. The backroom of the pub was set aside for the use of the players and officials by 'Flash' Jack the landlord, though this was only used when entertaining visiting clubs. On weekdays the club's members, supporters and players mingled in the public bar, drinking away the worries and pains of the day and forgetting about work and wars in foreign lands. Flash Jack was the club's first sponsor, and supplied the players with their whisky and steak expenses after the officials from the Union had gone home. He was too old and too fond of his own stock to be a good player, but he felt he was almost out on the pitch whenever he had the young men around him.

The front end of the pub was thick with smoke from men's pipes, which stuck to the walls like a translucent sepia paint. In the dingy shadows, where the gas lamps failed to reach, working-class men in their best suits and caps guzzled their beer, gambled on the next game and argued the merits of types of play with each other. Closer to the bar, in the small snug, by the fire and under the window, more respectable men mingled with the players, talking about business and chasing compliments. It was a place Humphrey knew his father would hate, as Leo hated it, preferring to go home after training to read books. But Humphrey was happy there. He enjoyed the attention he received whenever he moved to the bar or the door. The other players – his good friend Lever, the working men like Garstang – respected Humphrey because he was able to show his manhood on the pitch, proving himself every week like a gladiator in the Circus Maximus in front of a hard-to-please Roman emperor.

The snug bar was a comfortable table partitioned from the rest of the room by a wood and smoked glass panel on which the name of the pub was etched. As Harry was the club secretary and the most important board member, he had taken the snug as his own. When he wasn't there, Flash Jack was paid to put a small 'reserved' card on the table. It was, Harry said, his club office, where he met potential sponsors looking to make an investment, businessmen who were keen to make a deal through the club and the game, and players who had had enough of their own clubs and were looking to associate themselves with success. Humphrey suspected that there was more to it than that, but he knew not to question Harry's methods or motives. Harry did his job, business was going well, and the team was successful.

They continued drinking, and Harry explained to Humphrey about the logistics of electric floodlighting, and what he had seen a few days earlier at Broughton, where a game against Swinton had been played even though it was a dark, stormy night. Humphrey made a show of listening but the technicalities bored him, rather like the engineering of mines and mills. It was the sort of clever stuff men like his brother John loved, but all Humphrey wanted to know was whether it worked. On this, Harry was adamant that soon every football club in the country would have its own electricity generator and floodlights to turn the winter nights into summer days. The Broughton match had been three days ago, the first under lights.

It had made Humphrey jealous and annoyed at losing out the glory to them. He was determined that Chorley would at least make the best night of it.

As Harry was retelling his encounter with the Swinton club secretary and the bet they had on the side about the size of the gate, Humphrey's thoughts turned to the Swinton team. They were a good side, though he suspected their quality was more to do with the salaried jobs their board members could find in their works for the best working-class players west of Manchester. There was nothing in the Union rules that forbade club officials finding work for men who happened to play in their team, but everyone knew those men weren't employed strictly for their particular skills. There were some gentlemen in the Swinton team but on the whole they were a rough set of players who played to win, like Yorkshiremen. Even though their game with Swinton under the floodlights was to be an experiment, he knew he'd have to play his best to match them.

The door of the front bar was slung open and three young men walked in, staggering with stomachs full of cheap beer. They were mill workers, dressed in their shoddy brown work clothes and poor men's clogs. It was clear from their dishevelled appearance they had gone straight from their shift into the hostelries of the town, spending the last of their wages even though there were still two days to the end of the week. One of the men was much more inebriated than his two companions, and he was being carried along between them while singing a bawdy music-hall song.

'When I saw your face my pretty Annie, I had to take you up the alley....' He crooned, laughing to himself and staggering into his two supporters, who were having trouble keeping upright themselves.

Humphrey looked at Harry, then out of the snug at the three drunkards. The conversation in the bar stopped as every man looked at these new arrivals. They staggered over to prop themselves up against the bar, and one of them ordered three bottles of pale ale in a loud, slurring voice.

Next to them, Garstang stirred and looked to Humphrey for guidance. He was a huge lad, the biggest player in the team, built like a giant. When he'd first joined the club Humphrey had been suspicious of the fellow – he didn't like it that Garstang's father was one of the family's employees and the voice of the men down the pit, and wondered for a moment whether his presence was part of a cruel trick by John. But unlike his father, Garstang was stupid and loyal, and as strong and brave as a Viking warrior.

His face was bent and scarred because of his recklessness, but he didn't care – the blemishes were Garstang's badges of honour, every one a memory of a great deed on the field. In the scrum Garstang would be in the vanguard, and Chorley would use him as a battering ram to push their rivals off the ball.

Humphrey shook his head, then excused himself from Harry. He stood up, smiling at Garstang, and nodded at Flash Jack, who served the three drunkards. They cheered and the man in the middle sagged, his head falling to one side. His friends shook him to wake him up, and he called out for more beer. The bottles arrived and they drank straight from the top, ignoring the glasses Flash Jack placed on the bar.

Humphrey stepped up to them, swerving through the silent crowd of players and supporters. He tapped the man who had ordered the drinks on the shoulder, and the man spun around angrily.

'Gerroff me, sir, that's my shoulder that is,' said the man, sneering at Humphrey.

Humphrey smiled. He wanted to punch the fellow for his ill manners but he didn't want Flash Jack's pub and the club to get a bad reputation, not the night before their floodlit match against Swinton.

'I was just wondering, my man, whether it might be better for you and your friend to take your companion home. I see he is rather ill.'

'When I saw your face my pretty Polly, I had to see your frilly folly...' muttered the man in the middle, who had put down his bottle and was clinging onto his friends as if he was about to pack down for a scrum.

'I know who you are, Mister Whittle, ahv seen yer playing fer Chorley, yer think yer the Tsar of Russia yer do,' said the first man.

'Less of that, lad, or ahl ahv to throw yer out,' said Flash Jack, glaring at the man. Garstang moved so that he was standing behind them, ready to act on Humphrey's word.

'We've come to join yer team, we fancy the women love a football player,' said the third man, smiling at Humphrey. He was the smallest of the three, and his eyes, although glazed with the beer, were a dark blue, like the bottom of the ocean. Humphrey looked away from him, trying to avoid the man's stare.

'You men could never play football, and if you want to carry on as you are we shall soon prove it, Garstang and I,' warned Humphrey.

The first man, who was the most sober of the three, suddenly realised both Humphrey and Garstang overshadowed them by a clear distance. He put down his bottle, and pulled at his companions. The man in the middle slipped but the first man dragged him towards the door. The third man stayed to glare at Humphrey, but the first man returned to pull him away, leaving the second man in the hallway. The players and supporters of the club watched as the third man struggled with his friend.

They reached the door and the third man spun around. He spat on the floor, then the first man pulled him out.

'Come on, Shellard!' he cried, tugging at the third man's arm, before they left the pub with their inebriated friend.

Humphrey looked at the spittle on the wooden floorboards. The noise in the pub returned to normal, and Harry sidled over to Humphrey, grinning.

'Well. Humphrey,' he said, 'it's a shame they're not playing for Swinton tomorrow night.'

There was no need that night to remember Shellard's name.

The game of rugby football had evolved far quicker than any of the creatures Darwin had examined, proving to those who played it that Huxley's rule, the survival of the fittest, was a true rule of human society. It was, thought Humphrey, a perfect test of the hypotheses of improvement and position he had been taught at school. The game had spread so fast that Harry had to turn down offers of fixtures, for the card was already full with teams from every part of Lancashire and as far afield as Kendal, Chester and Huddersfield.

The gentlemen amateurs who ran the game, the ordained ministers and the university scholars, allowed the men who played to shape the game as they saw fit, allowing for the creativity and invention that the other code and its proletarian supporters lacked. In this they were following the traditions of sport and sportsmen through the ages, believing that the only essential rule was to play the game, and play the game well.

At first, this casual approach to how the game was played, which set of rules should apply and the number of players each side could field, actually worked surprisingly well because of the instinctive knowledge players had of the informal regulations applied at school or college. One could have up to a maximum of twenty players in a team; one could interpret the fixed rules of passing behind, of making a clean catch, of kicking out of play and throwing the ball back in very loosely if both umpires had gone to the same school. As for the scrimmage, although hacking at shins - the catalyst for the split between the association and rugby football clubs - had been struck off the rugby list of gentlemanly behaviour, there was still little the umpires could do to regulate what went on when the forwards were pushed up against each other in the scramble for the ball. And since the umpires were chosen by the teams who were playing, and were usually the club secretaries or some other luminary, there was little incentive to regulate the seething, sweating scrums that dominated the game. So the honesty and integrity of the players themselves were the lubricants that led to the smooth operation of the game's central mechanisms.

Consequently, and very quickly, by a process no one could quite chart, the number of players on each team was fixed, definitively, at fifteen. Humphrey and the other players at Chorley accepted this number as sacred, something in which was found both perfection and balance. It was the right number because it was the right number. The ruling had been declared only after practice and convention had reduced the number of men in the scrum to a more manageable level for the umpires, a safer level for the players, and a more enjoyable level for football's growing band of spectators who cared only for the value of their gate fee. Chorley had not invented this process, and had for a few matches tried both the twenty-a-side and the fifteen-a-side games, before settling on the accepted Lancashire method of fifteen, with nine men in the crucial scrum, men who served to push back the other side.

At first, the aim of the game, like the association code, was to score more goals than the other side, but rugby football developed a number of crucial variations on this theme. First, a goal was scored by kicking the ball over a crossbar between the two posts, so there was no reason to have a man keeping the goal area. To score a goal one could drop the ball and kick it in play, kick from the ground for a penalty, or have an undisturbed try for goal if a player managed to put the ball behind the other team's goal-line. The try, as it soon came to be called, was worth something in itself if the number of goals was drawn – though a goal was always given precedence. However, the danger of the try necessitated the strategy of having two defenders fully at the back, to try to stop any rogue who happened to escape the scrum and the maul to run free at the line. If there was a tie on both the goals and the tries, then the winner was decided by the side which had touched the ball down fewer times behind their own line, who had almost scored by hitting the post, or who had touched down least in the goal area, with some debate in parts of the country about which took precedence. It was a complicated business – though fortunately for the supporters the winner was usually clear without having to resort to a report in the next day's paper. The game was a testing ground for a man's strength, a crucible in which men were made in the long, unrestrained struggle for the ball.

Both Humphrey and Harry were wary of any new ideas on the way the game was played. Humphrey wanted to win, and Harry wanted to make a tidy profit out of the team winning. But Leo, who proved to be the keenest student of the game's strategies and tactics, convinced both of them of the need to introduce new ideas as often as possible. With Lever's support, he told Humphrey about any new style, any new pass or position reported in the press, that had led to a team winning. Humphrey could understand this, the advantage of progress; in the scales of reason it outweighed the frustration he felt at the way other people were changing his game's meaning, turning the struggle for supremacy into a mere circus. It was, as Leo explained, the natural way of things that the lesser was inevitably replaced by the greater: the horse by the train, the sword by the rifle, the shoving game by the hacking game. As for Harry, his fear was that innovation would lead to the game changing so much that it became unpopular. He didn't mind so much the team trying out new things, as long as the mob around the side of the field showed their approval by cheering.

In its short life, Chorley Football Club had attracted such a large following in the town that it was necessary to find a field where the crowd would not spill onto the playing area and, in their enthusiasm, get in the way of the game. In their first season this had happened on more than one occasion, with eager young lads from the grammar school stealing the ball and running away until Leo tackled them back into the crowd. After the first couple of seasons it wasn't just the grammar school boys - the novelty of watching men compete in scrums and mauls attracted first of all men who wanted to be seen to be better than they were, then workers who saw in the struggle on the pitch a reflection of their own struggle, then folk from all sections of the town who followed any fashion like sheep looking for clover in a field. Harry had visited the big Yorkshire clubs in Leeds and Halifax and knew that they were missing a way of using their fame to make a decent amount of money. What Chorley needed, he realised, was a field enclosed by a fence, to stop the spectators getting in the way, and for this to be in turn enclosed by a sturdy wall. That way they could make people pay a small fee for the right of watching the players, which in Harry's eyes was a fair tax that allowed the club and its beneficiaries to prosper. Football was no different from the music-hall – it was something people queued up to watch, a new spectacle like nothing before it, and the basic laws of supply and demand dictated that the club would be foolish not to take money. Capital was the coal for the engine of commerce, and commerce was what made Britain the ruler of the world. If people didn't want to pay, as Harry had told the *Chorley Standard*, then they didn't have to watch the football.

Thanks to the club's friends on the Council it had been a simple task to find an unused strip of land on Dole Lane close to the centre of the town, which was used only by gypsies to graze their horses. The legal technicalities of covenant and deed were dealt with by Mister Ditchfield, the Town Clerk, who happened to be on the club's membership committee. The only difficulty proved to be the rights of access to the land claimed by the landlord of a row of terraced houses whose gardens formed one of the borders. A compromise was reached whereby the club left that side of their ground open, on condition that the tenants of the houses, who were all respectable people, ensured that people did not pass through their gardens to watch the matches for free.

The fence was the first thing to go up, after the players had helped the town's bailiffs remove the horses and their irate owners. Then, while the pitch was laid out and the goals were collected from their former home down the road, Harry engaged those supporters who were skilled bricklayers in building a solid wall on three sides of the ground with a solid iron gate at the side of the road. In a matter of days Chorley Football Club was in a position to advertise entry to its matches in the forthcoming season on condition of a small gate fee, with a sliding scale to be decided at the Annual General Meeting.

On the sunny side of the ground the Club built a fine wooden pavilion, painted in the most brilliant white Lever's factory could provide, so that visiting teams were often caught unawares and dazzled, like men stumbling across the Lost City of El Dorado. The pavilion afforded a fine view of the football action, being placed near enough to the centre of the pitch, and there were seats there for the ladies, who would cheer on the players as if they were princesses watching Sir Lancelot take on Sir Gawain over the honour of Guinevere. Whilst the Club's directors had the chance to meet rich friends from other teams and discuss business, Harry invited politicians and assorted philanthropists, reminding them that his own ambitions and those of the town at large were so much the same as to make no difference in the greater scheme of things.

Harry wasn't so much bothered about the price they fixed for gate entry, allowing it to fluctuate by a ha'penny to tuppence depending on the affairs of the stock market and the importance of the match. What concerned him was that Mister Ditchfield, who had volunteered to be in charge of the gate, would have to be watched to ensure he didn't pocket a fraction of the profits that should have gone to the cash float kept in the possession of the Club secretary, whether it be Harry Hibbert or not. Harry knew that the Council paid Mister Ditchfield a pittance of a wage, a respectable salary for a working man but small change for a professional clerk - and he knew that Mister Ditchfield, through his status in the Oddfellows Hall, was a man determined to live beyond his means. Mister Ditchfield took the money, being familiar with the method of accounting for income and expenditure, but Harry always made sure he counted the crowd and checked to see whether his figures matched Ditchfield's at the end of the day.

The back of the pavilion was no place for the teams to change, so they made do, as they'd always done, with the rooms provided for them at the *Rose and Crown*. Flash Jack had given over two rooms for the players to change into their kit and bathe in once the game was over, and made sure everything they asked for was given without question by the boys he appointed to keep the water warm and the men supplied with clean towels and soap.

Normally this arrangement suited everyone. On a Saturday dinnertime the morning shifts were finishing, and the mills were closing down for the weekend. The pub would be packed tight with men quenching their thirst after being in hot spinning rooms or down dusty pits hefting rock from the coalface. When word spread that the visiting team was present upstairs the pub would rock with songs and jokes about how Chorley would be the 'Pride of Lancashire', that they were the undisputed Kings of the Football Pitch, that the visiting team resembled the French army facing the might of the Prussians at Sedan and their captain was the double of Napoleon the Third.

The night of the floodlit match was different.

At the window of their changing room, Leo Whittle looked out at the rain lashing the glass, obscuring the gas lamp that stood outside on the street. Its flame flickered doubtfully, casting erratic reflections through the streams of water running down the window between the lead borders and the yellow-stained roses. Leo sighed and wished he could have a smoke of a cigar – Harry Hibbert had banned smoking before a match since he'd heard some quack say it was bad for a sportsman's lungs. Some of the players had objected to that, including their new half-back Marsh, the medical student who turned out for a number of clubs and who had, it was said, an 'arrangement' with Harry. Marsh would sneak out to the back of the pub's yard and always have a cigarette before they went round to Dole Lane. But Leo respected Harry's orders, as he'd been told to do about all orders from his betters by their teachers.

'For goodness sake, Leo, come away from the window, people outside will be put off coming into the pub for a drink, and then Flash Jack will have us all out by the ear,' joked Lever, who was sitting at the table finishing off his steak and tucking into what was left of the buttered mashed potato. Those of the team who were still eating laughed, and Lever raised his glass of beer gratefully.

Humphrey stood at the mirror, inspecting his new moustache. He had allowed it to grow, and had trimmed the bristles around it and his chin so that the hair was bushy and manly. It was the latest fashion, although barely half of the Chorley players were sharp enough or connected enough to realise it.

He knew he was the best, that was clear enough from the comments made by the reporters and the supporters and the women who sent him suggestive letters about his status as a bachelor. The other players, especially those like him who put their shoulders into the scrimmage, respected his ability. Men like Garstang and the Mockett brothers, simple but respectable sorts striving to be gentlemen, didn't doubt his status. Even

Lever, a cocky chap who didn't believe in being polite to the opposition, accepted that Humphrey was a footballing Heracles, Chorley's hero who had led the club to victory over the north-west's finest teams, such as Liverpool, Manchester and Leigh.

Only his father was suspicious of the adulation afforded to his second son. Leo said that it was just his way of being fair to his two footballing sons, to honour them both without raising one to the hero's podium. But Humphrey didn't believe that: their father showed little interest in the actual football, and barely spoke of the hard work and ingenuity that went into their play. Humphrey would convince his father of his worth. It was a challenge as stiff as any Heracles faced, but one which Humphrey knew he was capable of achieving.

Humphrey tried to focus his anger. He saw the face of Smith, the Swinton forward he knew he'd have to face on the flanks of the scrum, and tried to turn the man's pockmarked and hairy cheeks into the flabby jaw and grey sideburns of his father. He thought about poor Jane dying after the water treatment at the asylum down in London, saw her shivering as ice-cold water was blasted over her tiny frame by a hosepipe. Their father believed in unscientific remedies suited more to the age of alchemy and bloodletting than the modern world of progress and invention. Jane had died of pneumonia in that cold place, denied proper treatment because of an untested German fashion. Humphrey thought of little Frederick, and what their father had done to him.

He exhaled loudly, blowing away his nerves about the match and forcing the anger and rage to concentrate in his throbbing temples.

'I say, Humphrey, do come away from that mirror, anyone would think you were Narcissus himself,' said Lever, in between swigs of beer. 'Do I have to tell all the Whittles to sit down and finish their meals? Were you taught good manners the pair of you?'

'There'll be no beer left soon, Mister Whittle,' said one of the Mockett brothers.

Leo, who was still standing by the window, laughed and sat down at the table. Garstang passed him a bottle of beer and a glass. Leo looked up at his brother, who had moved from the mirror and was sitting next to the fire unfastening his silk cravat. He hoped for his brother's sake that Swinton would arrive in time for the match.

At the Chorley ground at Dole Lane Harry was standing behind Mister Ditchfield as he organised his gatemen. The rain was pouring down and it was dark even though it was only just six o'clock. A few spectators had already arrived straight from work, and were standing around getting soaked, huddling inside their sodden coats and pulling their caps down around their ears. It was cold for October, and the gatemen were complaining about not having their fingerless gloves to sort out the loose change they would keep in the leather purses one of the club directors had given them. Harry had had the sense to bring his umbrella and a warm black raincoat with matching black leather gloves, and he looked at the gatemen with a mixture of pity and scorn. It was a miserable evening to be a volunteer on the gate, but they'd had plenty of warning from the rainstorms which had drenched them earlier in the day.

'Mister Ditchfield, 'ow's things this side of the show?' shouted Harry, as he struggled to make his voice heard above the north wind.

Mister Ditchfield was a man who from an early age had appeared to be at least sixty years old. He suffered from a reddening of the face in the most clement of weather, and the wind and rain coupled with his baldness made his head look like a purple cherry, with a thin moustache painted under his black eyes and tiny nose. The position of Town Clerk had given him access to the most powerful men in Chorley but for the most part they despised him for his servitude and obsequiance. Harry knew the man came from a modest background, and that his greatest fear was to return there, or worse, be cast adrift in the debtors' prison where unlucky gamblers finished their lives.

'It'll be a big crowd tonight, sir, look at these young fellers queueing up outside, even in this weather!' replied Mister Ditchfield. 'If we're not careful some of 'em 'll be using their bonces and sneaking ovver wall.'

'Well, we can't 'ave that, the cheek of it! Trying to watch my boys without paying a fair price!' gasped Harry, clutching at his heart in a theatrical gesture, touching his wallet only by happenstance. 'There's nowt wrong with enterprise, Mister Ditchfield, but every man's got to make his way in this life the best 'e can. If they try to take my money then ah'll defend it best ah can. There's some gas tar left from doing the roof of the pavilion, find some likely lads and get the top of them walls covered in it.'

'Right y'are, sir, all over you say?' asked Mister Ditchfield.

'If any cheeky monkey's after climbing in for nowt then 'e'll 'ave the price of a new suit to pay for - let them know about it!' warned Harry. He looked out at the spectators who were already outside. They were all working-class men, the sort of chap who was the average football spectator, too lazy and weak to play but keen to watch his betters like peasants at a medieval joust. Sixpence, the cost of entry into the match, was a high price for these men to pay to get their pleasure, especially when they probably had children to feed and bills to pay. But Harry knew there wasn't room for sentimentality in business. He was upset by starving children just like any other right-thinking gentleman – his party considered itself the protector of the poor, unlike the deluded men of the past on the opposite benches – but it was not up to businesses to say who could and could not spend their money. The markets had to be free, and if that meant Harry earned money at another's expense then that was just the way the market went. The poor always had the Council to give them some relief from their wretched lives.

He turned away from them just as one of the oil-covered men from the electrical company, Messers Parker and Bury of Manchester, stepped out of the darkness that had swallowed the playing field. He was a stocky built Scottish engineer, a man who twenty years younger could have graced the football pitch as a player, if it wasn't for his obvious rough manners and uncouth upbringing.

'Mister Hibbert? Ah need to crave a moment of yer time, if yer'll gi' it ter me,' the Scotsman said, putting on what he evidently considered to be his politest voice, which amused Harry greatly.

'Och aye, I will that, Jock lad,' mocked Harry. The engineer smiled at Harry, showing he was man enough to take the joke, especially since he was being paid time-and-a-half, as well as supposedly getting to see a floodlit football match for free.

Supposedly.

He took off his cap, which was oozing black, greasy water. He wrung it between his fingers and more of the stuff splashed down onto the gravel the club had put down around the entrance.

'Mister Hibbert, sir, we're having a wee bit of trouble wi' the lamps.'

Harry frowned.

'What do you mean, a bit of trouble?' he asked.

'Ah mean wi' the water everywhere we dinnae know where the problem is, yer see the lamps will no' light, whitever we try and dae,' said the engineer, stepping back from Harry.

Harry kicked out with his muddy shoes, missing the engineer's shins.

'Blast it, Jock! Do you know how many people the papers say are going to be here tonight? They're saying there'll be a crowd of over three thousand! Three thousand people, and the Mayor of Chorley, and the town's MP, and a hundred guests, all here to see a match of football played under lights! Your electricity was supposed to snuff out the moon, now what am I going to say to everyone?'

'Am jus' sayin', Mister Hibbert, sir, that you'd maybe be best to tell the Mayor and your guests and the fellers standing ootside that there may not be any floodlights tonight,' said the engineer nervously.

Harry shook his head.

'Never. Where's Mister Bury? I want to see your boss, Jock, and I want to see those lights working. I saw them working at Broughton, now I want to see them working in Chorley. We have an arrangement.'

The engineer nodded and asked Harry to follow him onto the dark, muddy field. Harry did so, careful not to slip or get too much muddy water over his shoes. Behind the nearest goalposts was a huge black machine, its motors silent, with a tall pole holding aloft an array of electrical lights. Three men were at the back of the machine, tinkering with the motor under a makeshift tarpaulin shelter. At the opposite end of the pitch Harry knew there was another generator and another set of lights, but he couldn't see it. The faint glow of gas lamps from the houses at the near end made the far end of the pitch harder to see.

Harry passed under the goalposts, trying to imagine what it was like to try for a goal. He couldn't see the sense in it, though he was glad his team were the best. The electricity generator was some kind of dinosaur monster, rearing up out of the grass with cold, lifeless eyes at the end of its long neck. Its body was dark and surrounded by a black frame, covering its metallic innards and intestines of wrapped cable. Harry had heard Mister Bury explaining about standard candle power, charge and current, but technical words were as foreign to Harry as the language of the Zulus. All he remembered was the claim that the cost of each light in carbon was estimated at two and a half pence per hour, which meant nothing until he was told that eventually electricity would be free, and it was a cheap source of energy. When he had boasted that the cost was only two and a half pence per hour to the club's committee they were suitably impressed, and just as eager to pretend they knew what he was talking about.

The engineer shouted for Mister Bury, and a tall, thin gentleman clad in a black raincoat appeared from under the tarpaulin. He didn't appear to be covered in oil, unlike his assistants, though he was carrying in his hands two sets of insulated wires. He didn't have a hat, and his foppish yellow hair hung to his ears, soaked by the rain. Mister Bury was, as Harry knew, a young man of great intellect, who had left Oxford halfway through his degree to turn his scientific ideas into a practical business. Harry suspected that Bury wasn't his real name, that he had chosen a northern sounding name when he had settled in Manchester to appeal to the local market. It was a trick Harry would have pulled himself in the same situation, for Lancashire was a hard place for outsiders to make a living.

'Ah, Mister Bury, what's all this Jock tells me about you not bin able to turn these lights of yours on? I thought we 'ad an arrangement, Mister Bury,' said Harry indignantly.

'I'm afraid there seems to be some unwanted conductor in the system acting as a bridge to pass current to the earth, so that the circuit is inevitably shorted,' answered Mister Bury, holding up the wires in his hand.

'Eh, sir? I don't understand a word of what you're saying,' frowned Harry.

'Water, Mister Hibbert. This rain is quite severe, and it is shorting out the electrical current before it has a chance to flow through the elements in the lamps.'

'What? What do you mean? What's this blasted element in the lamp doing?'

Mister Bury sighed. 'We are doing our best to replace the affected cabling.'

'Will it work? That's all I want to know, Mister Bury.'

'At the moment, perhaps it would be wise to delay the match.'

'Delay the match? I can't do that, the Mayor of Chorley's coming, man!' shouted Harry. He looked beyond Mister Bury at the machine. 'Get them currents fixed.'

'I will do my best, Mister Hibbert,' said Mister Bury nervously.

'You will do it, or you won't do it, you won't just do your best, you'll get nowhere in life with that attitude. What's it to be, Mister Bury? Do I have my floodlit match? Do I let the crowd in and take their money?' asked Harry.

'I… I'm not sure,' Mister Bury muttered, stepping back from Harry.

'I will have my floodlit match, Mister Bury,' said Harry sternly.

Mister Bury thought about the generators. It was all too much to explain to people like Harry. Electricity wasn't just something that they could hack out of the ground or weave together in a mill. The electromagnetic dynamo could generate enough electricity to light the filaments in the lamps arrayed at either end of the ground, but to do that there had to be an unbroken circuit between the dynamo's magnets all the way up the poles to the lamps. And all that was no good if the motor's steam-powered piston failed to turn the dynamo's crank and create the electricity in the first place. The problem could be anywhere.

He nodded, smiling weakly at Harry.

'You will have your floodlit match, Mister Hibbert.'

At the *Rose and Crown* the Swinton team arrived in matching blazers straight from the railway station. Humphrey greeted each in the back room, saying a few friendly jokes to those he knew and testing the grip of those he didn't know. He deliberately slapped his counterpart Smith hard on the shoulder, just to let him know that although the evening was unique it would be the same joust in the scrum. Smith asked Humphrey about Marsh, who had played for Swinton in the past, and asked how his studies were going. Humphrey ignored that particular barb: at least Marsh was a gentleman, even if his interest in the game was more to do with its pecuniary benefits rather than the spiritual ones.

When Smith – along with the rest of the Swinton team - had passed up the stairs to change, John Whittle arrived. He still had his umbrella up, which Humphrey considered to be most impolite. He wasn't a superstitious man, but he knew the working-class men in the team were ill-educated and prone to believing anything they heard said by old women.

'John, for pity's sake fasten that thing up before the rest of the players come down, you wouldn't let a woman down the mine, would you?' complained Humphrey.

John, who had grown in size at the same rate as the club, snorted but did as Humphrey ordered. Then he unfastened his raincoat and went over to warm his backside against the fire. He looked at Humphrey through the mirror above the mantelpiece.

'The lights aren't working yet, Humphrey, and there's a huge crowd there now. Harry's arguing the figure with Mister Ditchfield, but there must be at least three thousand in the ground, and loads more waiting to get in.'

'Three thousand,' gasped Humphrey. He thought about the number... three thousand people, mainly working-class men, all in the same place. What would happen if they happened to get out of control? He shivered – what John had said finally made sense.

'John! What's this about the lights?'

'They're not working, Mister Bury has said he thinks he can get them going if the rain stops, there's some discussion about how long we wait,' said John.

Humphrey glanced at the grandfather clock next to the door. It was five minutes to seven. They were already late.

'Three thousand men, John, three thousand men who will get very angry when they realise they've paid sixpence for nothing,' Humphrey shouted. The door opened and Leo, Lever and Marsh entered the room. Like Humphrey they were wearing white shirts, especially tailored for the evening match, with black trousers and leather boots.

'Is everything all right, old boy?' asked Lever.

'There's some problem with the lights... I'm sure it's nothing, really,' said John.

'There's three thousand men, at least three thousand, who will be getting very angry when the lights don't go on in five minutes,' said Humphrey.

'So what do we do? Swinton are just getting changed...' said Leo, leaning against the side of the door. Marsh grinned and stayed with one foot in the corridor.

'Mister Hibbert wants you down at the ground. As soon as the lights go on we'll get started, and if not... if not, he wants you to help disperse the crowd,' said John.

'Disperse the crowd? I'm not doing that,' complained Marsh.

Humphrey sat down in a chair. Harry had said electricity was the future. It was supposed to be a great moment for Chorley, a measure of their worth. He put his head in his hands, and concentrated on trying to turn

Mister Bury into an image of Smith, an image of a tree to kick, a horse to whip. Then he thought of the crowd, the mob. If the match was abandoned, he thought, at least there was something to take away the anger.

At Dole Lane Harry stood under the shelter of the pavilion and watched the crowd heaving against the fence and pushed back against the wall. Some of the drunks were beginning to boo and complain, especially those who were stood at the back where the tar had poured down on them from the top of the wall. After some argument they had shut the gate after five thousand had paid, and Mister Ditchfield was standing next to him with the takings in a large briefcase. The guests in the shelter of the pavilion were complaining, but only about the weather.

At the far end of the field, Mister Bury was arguing with his Scottish engineer, and kicking the machine in desperation.

At the front of the pavilion, standing in the freezing rain and thoroughly miserable, the combined Chorley and Swinton teams were watching the crowd for any sign of trouble. Humphrey looked back up at Harry, who was too busy looking at the crowd to acknowledge him. Humphrey realised the other players were breathing hard and heavy, readying themselves to stop the mob attacking the pavilion. He realised this, then noticed that he could hear himself breathing. The rain, which had worsened, was stifling speech, stopping people from shouting.

From out of the darkness of the field came Mister Bury. He looked as if he had thrown himself into the canal. He pushed his way through to the pavilion. Humphrey watched him speaking to Harry.

'Mister Whittle, look at what's 'appened to m'son!' someone cried in the crowd. Humphrey looked around and saw a rough-looking man holding up a young boy smeared in thick, black tar. The boy seemed to be happy with this situation, but the father was livid. Around him some of the more active members of the crowd started to mutter 'shame'.

Humphrey looked back up at the pavilion for support. Harry, Mister Ditchfield and Mister Bury had disappeared, along with the Mayor of Chorley and a few of the other guests. The man with the boy tried to push his way through but Garstang and Crumblehulme held him back. More people took up the cry of 'shame', and the man pointed at Humphrey. 'You're 'is 'ero, do something abaht it!'

Some of the players were looking at Humphrey, waiting for the word.

Leo was remonstrating with a woman in the pavilion. Lever had moved surreptitiously around the back of the man in the crowd, separating him from the others who were supporting him. The Swinton players had moved backwards, guarding their club's directors in the middle of the pavilion.

Humphrey could smell the sweat of the crowd.

They had failed. He looked up at the pavilion, at the old men sitting where his father should have sat. They nodded, and got up to leave. It was over. They had to take their chance.

'It's cancelled!' cried Humphrey. 'The match is off!'

The crowd roared and swarmed onto the pitch, surrounding the generators. The engineers from Parker and Bury slipped away, those at the near end climbing into the back gardens of the adjoining houses. The people in the pavilion joined the dash for the gates, and squeezed their way through with a large part of the crowd eager to escape the rain.

Humphrey started to follow the Swinton players out of the ground.

'Humphrey!' cried Leo. 'Shouldn't we protect the generators and clear these people off the pitch?'

Humphrey looked at the men on the field. They were angry, but they seemed more angry with the machines than with the club. It wasn't as if they were Luddites – this time the machines had failed.

He shook his head.

'Let them take out their anger here, before we do the same,' said Humphrey. 'Let's go and make sure the gate-takings are safe.'

'Where are they?' asked Leo.

Humphrey smiled, but inside he felt humiliated, violated. The lights had failed. They had become a joke.

'They'll be where Harry Hibbert is, where else would they be?'

5.

Prudence

PRUDENCE SAT IN THE HEART of the town hall after the presentation of the Cup, ignored by the ghost-like men who wandered in and out of the doors, waiting for Whittle. She thought of George Shellard, and the coroner's decision that had condemned his soul to wander the earth until - as the scientists said - the universe's cogs wound down and everything died a death of cold. She had never liked Shellard, never trusted the feel of his hand on her arm and the glance of his eye when he thought she wasn't looking. It wasn't her place to ask Nellie why George Shellard was chosen, why him and not any one of dozens of charming, young craftsmen and delivery boys who flirted with the maids at Derwent Lodge. But her mistress had told her things in the middle of the night, when they'd huddled close for comfort, that went some way to explaining her motives - about the cold in Whittle's touch, his hatred of her for being a woman, a reminder of his own weaknesses, and about the vitality that existed in Shellard's smile, his jokes, his mocking differences. She spoke of her despair at her marriage, the dark clouds that had covered the sun ever since she'd had his unloved children Dorothy and little Kathleen, reminders of the moments they had shared away from the world, moments which now shamed Humphrey. And Prudence knew part of it was because George Shellard was not Humphrey Whittle.

Humphrey was in the banquet hall, after he'd given away the Cup. His shoulder no longer hurt. He had become invisible, lost in the noise and movement of hungry men, hidden by wine glasses and silver plates piled high with roasted potatoes and turnips. The councillors and ex-players merged into one drunken beast before him, their faces blurred by the alcohol they'd supped, their voices sounding the same platitudes about old times and new ideas, the new century ahead, of electric entertainment and professional sport, and the long years that had passed since the Cup final. They were blind to the revolution that was coming, the changes that would surely occur at the end of the century. He had seen it back in the 1870s, when they had come up against the shamateurs at Swinton, the disregard for the rules, the lack of understanding over the importance of playing the game fairly. They had allowed men the chance to redeem themselves without knowing the importance of work, of the system of rules and manners that bound the country together. People like his brother John had mistaken decent Christian charity, compassion and care for the poor, with acquiescing to the demands of the mob and the redistribution of the wealth that paid for that charity. He could try to warn them but he knew it was too late. They had won, and the new century wouldn't belong to the aldermen of Chorley, to Harry Hibbert or anyone else in the banquet hall.

He thought of the mob outside, imagined them waiting to hound them all. The socialists had come from Wigan, dirty-faced miners in the middle of the shift, telling his men that it was time to stop talking and start taking action. They had spoken about communism and the rights of the working man against the slavery and ignoble system of oppression keeping them in the chains of servitude. They said they were protecting their right to work but urged the rest of the men to rise up and take control of the means of production. Most of the Chorley pitmen were loyal enough to the family but at Blackrod they listened to the false prophets and went on strike to demand a number of vague and unrealistic concessions.

John had wanted to appease them, to send Mister Garstang along to listen to their grievances and attempt to settle things amicably. But Humphrey Whittle had gathered as many loyal workers as he could and tried to take over the pit, shutting out the mob so that work could continue without them. He'd waited for the mob in the shunting yard, next to the red-brick of the winding shed, surrounded by the strongest men from the family's businesses and a few strong Oddfellows and athletes. When they arrived, a seething mass of angry men, Whittle stood his ground, prepared to die like Leonidas with his Spartans at Thermopylae. The mob had shouted and threatened them with violence, then a brick was thrown. It smashed through the window of the winding shed, shattering the glass into a thousand shards. Enraged, Whittle had stepped forward and challenged the brick-thrower to chuck him around if he was man enough. Then the mob had backed down.

In the banquet hall, those close to Whittle watched him carefully, fearful that he would prove awkward, as he had been over the business with Shellard. He ignored them, speaking only when they spoke to him, and answering with only the briefest word before falling silent. He sipped at his wine, refusing offers of other glasses, and toyed with the meat and vegetables so as not to offend the cooks, who had not offended him. Seated across from him was his brother Leo, a guest who attracted considerable attention with his gentle humour and his wry observations about his customers in the market garden trade. Humphrey Whittle knew his brother was doing this to protect him, as he had protected Leo in the rough and tumble of the maul. He knew he didn't deserve Leo's kindness.

At opposite ends of the table were the Mayor, who had succumbed to the sauce and was only being kept awake by judicious prods under the table from the faithful Town Clerk Ramsbottom, and Harry Hibbert MP. The latter had turned the conversation around to a new investment opportunity Harry was backing in South Africa, despite the unrest there and in the House, where the Liberal policy of free trade was under attack from the protectionists of the other benches. Harry spoke of high yields, guaranteed returns and the wealth of all nations: he didn't mention anything of the difficulties in the House over economic policy and foreign affairs, except to dismiss the fears one person raised as the 'rhetoric of politicians'. He said this without any irony.

The banquet hall was in the new extension at the back of the building, opened at the start of the 1890s. On that occasion a craftsman from Yorkshire had tried to convince the aldermen of the town that they should invest in a table shaped like a horseshoe, so that no one would ever have their back to the guest of honour. He showed them the designs but they didn't understand what he was saying. Curved tables were an innovation even the businessmen of Chorley feared. No respectable Council had curved tables, except the Council of King Arthur and his knights; but that, they knew, was just a story. So the table was thoroughly traditional, being long and carved of oak. It contrasted with two huge tapestries on the long walls, which showed a diorama of factories, machines, engines, shops, pits, architects, engineers, craftsmen, mill-women, hospital wards and schools. Once, when the tapestries were being commissioned, someone had suggested that Whittle should have been on the tapestry, running across a football field with the Cup in the sky behind him. He had argued against this, saying the victory was the town's not his, that he was never a runner, that the football club had proved to be a transient thing, and rugby was an old-fashioned game unknown to the roughs who cheered on the association code. He was relieved he had won the argument, that he wasn't on the tapestry – he couldn't be a hero with Nellie dead, buried in the earth with her secrets.

He heard his name mentioned at the far end of the table. He glanced down past the empty trays and bowls and plates, past the crumpled napkins and the gravy stains, the glasses collected around each diner, and saw that it was Ramsbottom the Town Clerk talking about him with one of the waiters. He saw Ramsbottom point down the table at him, and the waiter nodded. Whittle looked away, as if he had not seen what was happening. He didn't want to let Ramsbottom see him looking and remember what had happened at the front of the council chamber. Was it right to honour the football player and forget the soldier who had fought for his country in Africa? But Africa was not Chorley, not Blackpool, and Ramsbottom was never a gentleman. Whittle shook his head. It was a troubling thought, made worse by his own guilt.

'Councillor Humphrey Whittle?' asked the waiter behind Whittle's chair.

Whittle turned to look at the man. He was not a regular town-hall worker. He was a young lad of about thirteen, a casual waiter drafted in to serve on such a grand occasion. Whittle sensed that the lad was afraid of him, which was pleasing.

'What is it, boy?'

'There's a young lady to see you outside, sir, said her name was Prudence, said as you'd know who she was,' said the waiter.

Whittle's eyes narrowed. The blood that had reddened his cheeks in the heat of the meal rushed away to his stomach. He felt sick, and gripped the side of the table to steady it and the rest of the room. The waiter looked at Whittle's pallid complexion and stepped backwards, in case he was in the way if Whittle was sick.

'Are you all right, sir?' he asked, trying not to smile at what he thought was the effect of the drink on Whittle.

Whittle ignored the pain in his shoulder. He nodded, shutting his eyes.

'I am all right, damn you, boy, stop bothering me,' he growled through gritted teeth.

'What shall I say to the young lady, sir?'

'Tell her I am not here,' replied Whittle. He fumbled in his pocket for some loose change and offered the young waiter a sixpence. The waiter took it, and left Whittle alone.

Prudence. He'd hoped never to see her again.

Of course, his wife had never understood his fear of the mob. She had lived a secluded life, away from the masses in the towns, and the only working-class people she met were servants and delivery boys. She'd asked Whittle why he felt the way he did yet still worked for the Poor Board, giving money to the needy and paying the bills of doctors who looked after children from the terraces. He'd tried to explain to her about duty and position, and the importance of opportunity over the slavery of the mob, but she said he was foolish to think a working man was different from his sick wife or starving child. Whittle had ignored her – he didn't expect any woman to understand politics and economics, they were too concerned with the immediate to have a firm, logical understanding of the broader picture. Whittle expected such irrelevancies from women, who talked about nothing but love and feeling while failing to appreciate the forces that shaped men and society.

Humphrey had never told his wife he loved her. Why had she never understood the reason for that?

They didn't allow women in the council chamber. They'd told Prudence that when she first arrived but when she'd asked about the public gallery they knew they didn't have an answer. She smiled at them and pretended to be a simple girl and they fell for her, forgetting the instructions they'd been given by Ramsbottom to guard against such an eventuality. She knew they would try to stop her, Whittle's friends, but the porters on duty at the entrance to the town hall were servants like herself, men easily distracted by a flash of her white teeth and the note of her laugh.

Prudence had watched Whittle face his ghosts in the council chamber. She had seen Nellie sitting next to Whittle in place of the Mayor, her thin face lined with worry and despair, her dark brown eyes gazing mournfully at the Cup. Prudence had looked for Nellie's reflection in the Cup but of course there wasn't one. When Whittle had looked up at her in the public gallery she had held his gaze, looking into his eyes as she had never done as a servant, facing him as an equal. They had both seen his wife's dead eyes, seen her blood dry and brown streaked across them. Prudence knew she could stare at anything after staring at them.

She saw Whittle falter, slipping into memories of the moment, heard him mutter something and drop the Cup in front of his friends, his brother, the men of the town. She had seen Nellie smile, as she surely would have done if she'd been there, mocking the pomposity of the occasion and Whittle's lack of courage to face his own failings. Then the ghost had disappeared, replaced by the bibulous Mayor fondling his gold chain of office.

Mrs Whittle had been more than Prudence's mistress. She had been a friend, a mother Prudence had never had in her crowded home. She hadn't had to work at the mill collecting shuttlecocks and repairing threads, or look after sick children in a tiny kitchen whilst wringing out damp clothes and washing dirty pots. When Prudence had been taken on she'd thought Mrs Whittle was a princess of some fairy land, who had rescued her from ogres and trolls and taken her away to a shining castle. Her real mother was pleased to see her leave the home and work for the Whittle household, proud that her daughter had found a decent job and glad of the extra income and space that entailed. Prudence knew her proper mother feared she would lose her, that Prudence would come to look upon her family as something less than herself. At first, Prudence tried to love her mother as she'd always done, but Mrs Whittle was more independent, more knowledgeable, more real. In becoming her maid Prudence had cast away her old life, and she found it hard to conjure up anything other than pity for her own mother. Her past life became as interesting and accessible as the subjects of an old painting hung up and forgotten about on the wall of a staircase. Mrs Whittle's death made Prudence's feelings for her even stronger. She was no longer the same Prudence who had listened to her parents fight over the cost of a pint of beer against the cost of a loaf of bread. She could never go back.

Now Prudence waited in the corridor outside the banquet hall, sitting on a wooden bench under a plain window overlooking the kitchen yard. Through this window she could hear the cooks and the council servants laughing, shouting, swearing over the hiss of steam and the metallic drumming of pans colliding. In front of her was a large panel door embossed with trailing leaves around its frame with brass handles that reflected light, dazzling her. Beyond the door she could hear the men of the town laughing at each other's jokes and shouting for more of this, more of that. The corridor itself was silent, draped in shadows as the gas lamps struggled to keep out the night. She wondered how many ghosts were in the darkness of the town hall, disturbed by the decision-making of the aldermen, enraged at the merriment they made as children went hungry in the next street.

She waited for the ghost to come out of that darkness wearing a light summer dress. She would smile and sit down on the bench next to Prudence, kissing her in a friendly manner, then she would tell Prudence that she wasn't really dead and they should go to live in Australia, far from Whittle and the shade of George Shellard. She thought that if she wanted to see Mrs Whittle so much then she would appear, brighter than the stars. Then she wondered whether Shellard would appear with her. She saw him standing at the door, trying to grasp the brass handle so he could go into the banquet hall and appear in front of Whittle.

She shook her head. The ghosts in the town hall remained in the shadows. The only things to move in the corridor were waiters, passing back and forth with their burdens. She smiled at her own joke: she would also wait, as they did, on Humphrey Whittle. It was a joke she'd heard Mrs Whittle say in the midst of one of her rows with him, when she told him that the time would come when a woman didn't have to wait on a man, no matter how much she loved him. Prudence didn't want to upset the ghost, but wait she had to do, for Mrs Whittle's sake.

The waiter came out of the banquet hall, grinning at her sheepishly. She knew he'd failed to get Whittle to come outside, that his emotions were in turmoil because he had failed to win her affection by completing the task she set him. She smiled at him through the black veil covering her face. He smiled back, perhaps unsure about why she was dressed all in black and fearful of offending her.

'I'm sorry, love, Councillor Whittle's... weren't in when ah looked, like, nob'dy knows where 'e were.'

'He told you to tell me he wasn't there, didn't he?' said Prudence.

The young waiter frowned. He started to speak but before he could ask his question Prudence answered it.

'You wouldn't be the first to be told that by Humphrey Whittle.'

6.

Ellen Moreton

HUMPHREY MET ELLEN MORETON at the club's wake, almost ten years after Chorley rugby football club had won the Cup.

Humphrey Whittle stopped playing football in 1882, the same year that Britain annexed Egypt, defeating the despot Arabi and protecting her vital trade interests in the Middle East and beyond to India. Chorley Football Club continued to survive another few seasons without Whittle, but its success was its own eventual downfall. Like Rome, which grew so big that it could no longer defend the expanse of its borders against the barbarians, the club forced its lesser rivals to fold and allowed association football to spread in their place. In the south of the county and over the hills in Yorkshire, the rugby code flourished, nurtured by unscrupulous entrepreneurs and missionaries in the slums who took the game to the poorest of working men. But Chorley became an oasis of rugby in a desert of association football supporters, and as the fixture list grew more unfamiliar and the best matches were turned down, the club lost its reason for existing. Whittle left, sensing the change coming in the industrious eighties, as did Harry, who contrived to get himself elected as the town's Member of Parliament.

By the early 1890s the club had been reborn as an association football club, attracting the working man who cared only for the spectacle and not the physical and spiritual development the game had offered. By then, they were already talking of the rugby code following the 'soccer' example and allowing men to make a living out of playing a game, of becoming a profession.

It was Lever's idea to hold a memorial service and wake for the club, ten years after the successful retrial of the electric lighting system. After they had failed the first time, Harry and Mister Bury had had a huge argument, which resulted in the latter offering to re-light another match as soon as possible. Swinton declined to make the journey up-county again, citing concern about their own safety following the farcical end of the last match, so the club made do with a scratch side of squad players and guests from the smaller teams in the outlying villages. Harry wanted to charge three pence on the gate but for once the rest of the committee got the better of him and opened the gate for free. This placated the journalists, who placated the town. The good atmosphere under the lights, even though in places the pitch was too dark to see, convinced Harry that the Cup idea would be a huge success, especially if Chorley were to win.

Humphrey never quite understood why Lever chose the tenth anniversary of the successful floodlit match to commemorate the club, although he suspected that Lever knew more about the Cup and Mister Fish, the developer and manager of Raikes Hall Gardens, than he should have done. Under the floodlights, taking the field as two scratch sides, they played with the same innocence with which they had first come together on the park under the watchful eyes of Harry Hibbert. Lever had the chance that night to captain a side, opposing Humphrey at every scrum and shouting himself hoarse with excitement. The lights did not illuminate the centre of the pitch, despite the guarantees of Mister Bury, and on one occasion the ball went into the crowd without any of the players noticing. Humphrey, face down in the middle of the scrum, had searched vainly for the ball amidst the feet and knees of the scrambling players, until Lever's laughter brought the match to a halt.

Later, in the banquet hall, he wondered about the choice he had made that had led to his meeting with Nellie. That, at least, was a decision he remembered making, one that had not been made for him. If others had done their best to contrive a meeting between a girl of suitable background and a young politician and leading man of the town's business community, to further his reputation and respectability, Humphrey preferred not to know.

Lever's wake for the club was held, by no great inspirational decision, in the *Rose and Crown*, which was given over in its entirety for the private party. All the men who had played for Chorley Football Club in its first six seasons of existence were invited, but the usual list of the town's influential and prosperous figures was deliberately ignored. Lever wanted the wake to be one for the players, not the town, and so Harry Hibbert wasn't informed until the last minute. Only Flash Jack suggested that they invite the association football players who traded under the Chorley name, on the grounds that they would sup a lot of ale. But once Lever had prised open his senile father's wallet and slipped Flash Jack a substantial retainer the pub was theirs to do with as they wished.

Ellen Moreton, Nellie to her friends, knew something was about to happen at the party. Lever, an old friend of her father, seemed to be keen to get her and her friends to attend, promising them that the rugby players were so honourable there would be no need, in this instance, for them to have a chaperone. He had charmed her mother so well that Nellie wouldn't have been surprised to see herself offered to Lever like a pagan princess to some foreign champion. However, she knew that Lever was married to a friend of hers, that he was as charming and warm in their private moments as he was on the public stage. If Lever promised to look after her then neither of her parents objected to her frequenting a public house associated with sportsmen, as long as the invitations to the party were exclusive.

Nellie thought about the men she was to meet to meet that night, how different they would be to her insipid father and foppish cousins. Her mother, she knew, would be shocked by the thoughts she was thinking, but she didn't care. She was twenty-four, not sixteen. She wanted to feel the touch of a strong hand on her breast, find some pleasure to loosen the corset of her life. All her mother ever talked about was respectability, as if the evolutionary drives of their ape ancestors could ever be overcome by prayers and pursed lips. She looked at Lever's back. He was a good catch, but she was sure there'd be more just like him.

Lever's party drove through the town centre in his horse-drawn car, an open-roofed affair painted on its black sides with yellow Oriental flowers and a Chinese dragon. The dragon stared out at the pedestrians, its demon face grinning and poking out its tongue with no shame at spinster women and clergymen, ruffians and street urchins, policemen and clerks. Lever was at the front, leaning into the wind and the reins as he urged his horses to pull them across the cobbles. The car was an extravagance that earned Lever as much scorn as respect, but he didn't care for people who criticised him.

Behind Lever Nellie sat with three other young women. Opposite her was Mrs Lever, dressed in the latest Parisian silks and carrying an umbrella more modish than practical. She held it with both black-gloved hands, delicately like a particularly fine piece of Venetian glassware. Next to Mrs Lever was Annie, Nellie's younger cousin, only just turned thirteen and on her first night out after Lever had told her mother it would be a good preparation for the following season. Finally, sitting next to Nellie, was another of her friends, a plain looking girl called Victoria. Her green dress was cut shockingly low, making Nellie envious and impressing the young men who were out on the street despite the cold drizzle.

Nellie didn't know much about football players. She knew Lever, of course, but he had always insisted that he was never a proper player, more of an enthusiastic dilettante who had ended up playing the game almost as an accident. She never knew what to believe from Lever but she was certain there was some truth in his eloquent defence. She had seen a few matches of both codes when she had gone with her father, though none with Chorley as one of the protagonists, and thought the men there had been brutish and rather rough in their manners, though at the same time they rather attracted her she had to admit. She had heard them shout and swear when the noise of the braying mob around the pitch had quietened down. Yet her father had insisted that the game was a game for gentlemen, and she couldn't deny that many of the people Lever said he had invited were rich, well-known and undoubtedly well-bred.

Nellie thought about them. She hoped something would happen. Unlike most of her friends she had no interest in astrology and stars. Her father had brought her up to be a woman of science, a woman of the 20th century. There was no space in their library for magic, masses and madness, as he'd always told her. The Age of Victoria would be remembered as the moment when mankind cast off its chains of superstition and learned how to see the world logically, rationally and objectively. As she grew older she realised his plea was a desperate one from an old man brought up to worship the Enlightenment in a decade of occult revivals and religious frenzies throughout the world. It was with some trepidation, then, that she examined the premonitions inside her, manifesting themselves as butterflies in her stomach.

If Nellie had not abandoned her own reason and questioned Lever's motives more cynically, she would have realised there was good sense for her to feel something was about to happen to all three of the unmarried women in Lever's car. He knew that not all of his old friends from the club had found themselves wives; and of those who had not, one in particular had ambitions that necessitated both a suitable wife and a very public, loving relationship.

The streets of Chorley were covered in a thin layer of rainwater, which seemed to clean the soot from the metal railings and the dirt from between the blackened cobbles. The gas lamps hissed and rumbled as the water leaked through the lead seals of the glass. Houses were dark, their windows and curtains shut tight against the cold, keeping in the light and warmth. Smoke caught in squalls of wind spiralled and curved down the alleys, passing over their car like burnt-wood phantoms. In the distance, beyond the low roofs of the houses, huge mills blacked out the grey and orange clouds. From a distance, with an unfavourable wind biting their ears, it was impossible to tell whether the mills were still working, or whether their engines were silent. Beyond the town centre, beyond the chiming clock of the town hall and the busy activity of the railway station, the number of people on the streets declined. They drove past the Dole Lane football ground, dark and empty, its wall covered in posters advertising soap, newspapers and comedians.

They passed Harry Hibbert, struggling along in the wind with his umbrella turned inside out by a gust of wind. His hat was bouncing away back towards the football ground, skimming across puddles. Lever didn't stop to hear what Harry was saying, not with the women in the back. He drove his horses on, tipping his own stiff hat at Harry and winking. A hundred yards ahead of Harry walked Humphrey Whittle, unaware that his mentor was behind him. They drove past Humphrey too, but not before Lever had slowed the horse to a trot so he could shout:

'Ho there, Councillor Whittle, I shall see you at Flash Jack's bar with a glass of hot toddy!'

Nellie looked out of the car at the dark shadow on the pavement, standing at the point between two gaslights where their light failed to reach. In the few seconds they were passing him by, she saw Humphrey for the first time in her life. She saw him glare up at Lever, angry that he was not being offered a lift, and saw in the darkness his eyes burning with a devilish fire. They drove on to the *Rose and Crown*.

'Who was that gentleman we passed just then?' asked Nellie. She had to shout above the rattle of the wheels and the racket of the hooves over the cobbles.

'Don't you know our great Member of Parliament, Mister Harry Hibbert?' shouted back Lever, not bothering to turn around.

'She means the other gentleman, stop toying with young Nell,' said Mrs Lever reproachfully.

'That was the captain, the caliph of the club, now a council member, a great public servant as well as a half-decent football player in his time, Mister Humphrey Norris Whittle,' answered Lever.

'Nell, be patient, we're not even there yet!' joked Victoria, gasping in false modesty.

Nellie smiled and looked at the glowing windows of the pub at the top of the street.

The back room of the *Rose and Crown* turned itself into a makeshift rugby pitch after they had cleared away the savouries and empty beer bottles, and most of the furniture. The tables and chairs were manhandled into the front bar, and the delicate ornaments were handed over after some of the women complained about drink and recklessness. Finally, the Mockett brothers, dressed alike in dark blue suits with chins covered in dark whiskers, lifted the old clock out into the corridor.

Lever had foreseen such a situation developing once the men had whetted their tonsils with a fair share of Flash Jack's cellar, and had brought with him a large, leather patched irregular shaped football. It was the ball they had played with on the occasion of the floodlit match, coloured by a web of white paint at the seams around the leather. When he pretended to find it behind Flash Jack's bar he had those who could still stand cheering with excitement.

'Well now, who's to play... Humphrey?' asked Lever.

Humphrey was standing by the door, where he had been observing the forced good humour and the polite conversation. He had endured talking with three of the old players, men who had played behind him in the scrum or in the backs in front of Leo, and not one had made anything of his life after they had lost the game of rugby to soccer. These, along with Leo and around a dozen not passed out or chatting with sweethearts, gathered quickly around Lever. Humphrey shook his head. He hadn't drunk except to be sociable – that side of the game had never appealed to him, and he knew it was something of which many of the Liberals disapproved. They had allowed Humphrey the public role because of his father, whom he had to accept as his patron even though the thought of owing him anything made his heart strain with anger. But he knew he was on probation, someone to be watched, tested for his perfection and his usefulness.

Lever shrugged his shoulders.

'Your loss, old boy.'

They began to divide themselves into two teams, one of seven and one of six, led by Lever and Leo respectively. Because the forwards had been the biggest drinkers only three of them were in a fit state to play, and these were apportioned so that Garstang made do for the other two, which was a fair match.

Humphrey watched them argue over the rules.

Across the room, Nellie sat with Annie and shared a cigarette with her. Most of the other women, who numbered around twenty, had politely removed themselves to the front bar when the first suggestion of an indoor football match had been aired. A few, including - to Nellie's mock disgust - Victoria, were in the intimate company of some of the football players. They were, thought Nellie, as debauched as the defenders of civilisation – at least those who wrote to the newspapers - said they were! The room's lamps had been extinguished by the rush of people and the close atmosphere of woodsmoke and tobacco. The men had removed their jackets and loosened their collars, and some had rolled up their sleeves like navvies working an embankment. Annie could not stop herself from giggling due to a combination of coarse manners and India Pale Ale, and coughed on the cigarette when she tried to inhale.

The makeshift match started, with Leo taking the ball into the middle of the room and falling into the arms of two of the opposition. He took them down onto the carpet and released the ball, which Lever tried to scoop up from the side of the play. Then Garstang lunged forward, pushing everyone back towards Victoria and her prize. She shrieked and the entire room enjoyed a laugh at her expense.

Nellie glanced across the room. Harry Hibbert had aroused himself from his slumbers by the fire and was calling for a penalty goal-kick. Leaning against the door frame with a cigar in his hand, though he hardly noticed it, was Humphrey Whittle. He was looking at her. She could see his eyes under his heavy brow. She smiled back, and in the briefest of moments licked her bottom lip with the tip of her tongue whilst staring straight into Humphrey's burning eyes.

Humphrey noticed her knowing look, her inviting smile. He glanced away, not wanting to encourage her. Then he thought otherwise, in an instant. She was young, and obviously respectable, unlike the women who had been attracted to him when he was a player. Yet he could sense that the respectability hid something wild. He felt his skin tingle. He looked back at her, and could see that she was impressed by the fact he wasn't taking part in the drunken exhibition of manliness put on by Lever and Leo. He raised one eyebrow. It was a trick of his face caused by the blow to the left eye he'd suffered during the Cup final. She smiled back, evidently amused by this, and turned to say something to her younger companion.

'Humphrey Whittle is staring at me, I think he's drunk,' whispered Nellie to Annie.

They both laughed, and Annie sneaked a quick glimpse of Humphrey. The match started anew with Lever passing the ball out to one of the Mockett brothers. He was then quickly tackled by Garstang, who was enjoying the game.

'I think he likes you... wouldn't it be strange, to be the wife of a politician!'

'Don't be so silly, Annie, he's only looking,' said Nellie. 'Why would I want to marry a man I don't know anyway?'

'Lever says he's a fine man, rich too,' answered Annie.

Lever paused in the middle of the maul, looking across at Annie. He smiled and put his head down under the cloud of smoke hanging over the room, pushing someone else to the floor.

'Really!' gasped Nellie.

She looked back up at Humphrey. He nodded and smiled. He considered her appearance – a fine womanly shape, healthy looking glow, and an attractive, angelic face framed by long brown curls. She considered his posture – she could sense he was arrogant, that he considered the pub and the match and the drinking far below him. She could see he was different to the other men, more noble somehow, yet full of passion. He reminded her of an iceberg, a silent, harmless object until circumstances brought it into contact with an unsuspecting ship. So enticing, so dangerous... too dangerous for a girl like Annie, but Nellie knew with Humphrey it would be a meeting of like souls. There would be bonfires, fireworks, flames, warmth.

When she knew he was watching, she let the strap of her dress fall, revealing the white curve of her shoulder. She fussed about pulling it up, and smiled coyly at him. He turned away, pretending there was nothing lustful in wanting to kiss her bare skin. He wanted her to take him away from the pub to some fairy forest, where they could live as Adam and Eve, free to shout and scream and make wanton love on a bed of flowers. Humphrey knew it was wrong to think of any woman that way, but he didn't care. He wanted her.

Later, as the night ended and Lever offered to take her home in his car despite the amount of beer he'd had, she found time to thank Humphrey for a pleasurable evening. He looked at her, surprised, but was clever enough to take her hand and kiss it softly. She shivered at the touch of his lips, and thought about his eyes all the way home. Humphrey walked back with Leo, looking up at the half-moon's light diffused through the clouds, and wondered how it was possible to lose one's self-control, one's own reason, over a simple thing as a smile.

7.

Raikes Hall Gardens

HUMPHREY HAD FIRST MET FISH – the King of the North of England Challenge Cup – after a meeting of the shareholders of Raikes Hall Gardens, of which the Whittle family was one of the most important. It had been Humphrey's idea to invest in the new industry - tourism - after Leo had told him of the expansion of Blackpool and the numbers of people who flocked there during the wake's days, when the mills and pits of Lancashire were shut to allow the workers to do whatever they wished.

Their father had sent Leo to take care of a financial problem at his market garden business on the Fylde coast, just down the road from Blackpool, which they had inherited by chance from a defaulting debtor. Leo was young and keen: he didn't seem to mind the travelling this necessitated, and he thrived on any opportunity to manage the family's affairs, which Humphrey thought very unbecoming of an owner and gentleman.

Leo told them about the money to be made along the golden coast, between the saltmarsh, the sand dunes, and the cold Irish Sea. Every day men laid down a new road in Blackpool, marking out land and building rows of houses, each brick placed in an effort to keep up with the madness of growth. Houses that had existed for more than ten years were considered old, as architects, builders and businessmen struggled to eke out more profit from the same pieces of land in sight of the sea. The aldermen of the town and those in the know said that by the end of the century Blackpool would cover the entire Fylde coast, its rows of pubs and houses stretching into the horizon, out of sight, to consume the towns and villages north and south. When Humphrey heard this he knew they had to invest in something in Blackpool, something which would be a certain success - and the Raikes Hall complex, the Garden of Eden at the centre of the town, was it. He didn't have to make any business inquiries: all he did was listen to the workers at their biggest pit just outside of Chorley talking about Raikes Hall and Blackpool as if it was the Promised Land.

Their father was initially sceptical. He wanted to know why the entrepreneurs of Blackpool thought that there was an infinite number of working-class families to fill the guest houses and enough money in their pockets to spend in the pubs and the cheap fish and oyster bars. He asked them how much holiday time a working man had, and what the people in Blackpool proposed to do when the workers were working.

Luckily it was a sunny day, and on the lawn at Primrose Cottage, between the pond and the orchard, the gardeners were sat eating their dinner with their backs naked against the sun's burning rays. Humphrey was with his father in the sitting room overlooking the lawn, surrounded by paintings of dead people unrelated to either side of Humphrey's parents. A clock modelled on Harrison's famous maritime chronometer Number 3 sat on the mantelpiece, innovation shrunk and copied in a multitude of shiny brass parts far smaller and more accurate than the primitive machinery of the previous century. Another clock, with its pendulum ticking in an irregular fashion, stood in the corner, informing them that despite the evidence of the high sun outside it was almost six o'clock.

The elder Whittle was sitting in a stout, plain wooden chair looking out of the window at his beloved orchard. He had placed the chair and its accompanying small drinks table in such a manner that it was impossible for anyone else to sit with him, so Humphrey stood behind the chair. He looked over his father's white hair at the gardeners, who had abandoned themselves to the sun not knowing they were being watched by their master.

'Father, look at how those men enjoy themselves on the grass, under the sun,' said Humphrey, gripping the top of his father's chair.

The elder Whittle rapped his knuckles on the chair's arm.

'Humphrey, boy, stop hiding and speak to me man to man. What trickery are you trying on me now, eh?'

Humphrey walked around the side of the chair, avoiding the table and its half-empty decanter of brandy. He smiled coldly at his father, trying not to despise him for the way he sat straight-backed against the stiff wood, his mouth thin-lipped like a man suffering with stomach cramps.

'Father, the working man spends most of his life in a pit, or a mill. Look at these men here, give them a bit of sun and some grass to lie on and they're happy, content. They will not strike or revolt.'

'They are happy, Humphrey, because I pay them enough, the blighters,' grumbled his father. 'Anyway, what are you going to do, eh? These men in Blackpool can't make the sun come out at their command, can they? They don't own the sun.'

'No, but they own the grass, the trees, the water,' answered Humphrey.

His father nodded. He wouldn't say Humphrey had made him change his mind, but the next day he told Leo to buy a minor stake in the Raikes Hall Gardens Company.

The Blackpool Lodge No. 1 was an inauspicious stone building between the steel arches of the central goods yard and the covered market. Like other Masonic lodges, it had a simple, unadorned stone face and an unmarked wooden door. Its position on the street, in the middle of a mixture of banks and solicitors' offices, allowed it even more anonymity. A passer-by, rushing from the gaudy pubs on the seafront to the train home, wouldn't have given it much notice, or, quite possibly, would have mistaken it for some kind of nonconformist chapel. In all respects but one it was the same as any other lodge in the country - unlike the others, it was brand new and purpose-built.

Carpet covered the black and white checkerboard floor of the main hall, which in turn was covered by rows of wooden seats. On these seats sat the shareholders of the Raikes Hall Gardens Company, denied the chance of seeing the sacred secrets of the Masons by a simple red curtain hanging behind the speaker's pulpit. Instead, those few who were not adepts of the ancient rites could only guess at their nature by examining the functionless pillars propping up the plaster roof, the repeating fivefold geometry of the structure and the mystical symbol of the square and compass glazed discreetly on every window.

Humphrey sat in the middle of the hall, as far away from the Masonic secrets as possible. Most of the people he knew, both in politics and business, were either masons or dependent on Masonic privileges to gain advantageous positions in their lives. It was a powerful and useful thing to be a mason, but Humphrey refused to join, even when Harry Hibbert took him to one side after a match against Manchester and offered him ancient and noble secrets. He had no objections to the masons, only to the most venerable and worshipful master of the Chorley Civic Lodge: his father. When John had reached the age of twenty-one their father had initiated him into the lowest rite of the Order, into a place more useful for a prospective man of business than any university. John, being rather simple and despite the warnings of vengeance and murder on the betrayer, quickly told Humphrey what had transpired. It was, he'd said, a bizarre and frightening ceremony, but one that finished with a splendid dinner and handshakes from the most powerful men of the town. Humphrey was obviously keen to reach his twenty-first birthday himself, so he could be led blindfolded by his father into the mystical pentagram. But it never happened, and when he dared to broach the subject, six months after his birthday, his father had told him that he wasn't a mason, and that if he was, he wouldn't bring an arrogant boy like Humphrey before the men of the Lodge.

It was humiliating, especially since his father said this in front of the entire family, in front of John the talkative mason and their younger siblings. That evening, full of rage, Humphrey had left Primrose Cottage and found the cheapest pub in the slums of Chorley, where he allowed himself to be provoked into a fight with some saloon-bar politician. He found his victim an easy match, and after knocking him unconscious out on the street he'd fled into the darkness. He stumbled his way into the unlit alleys behind the railway goods yard, where he knew poor women plied their trade to those who could pay. The place where he had found himself was a mean shed at the back of an empty shop, dank and dark except for the light in his eyes. The girl who had been there with him was young, as young as Jane had been when she'd died. He couldn't remember her face, only the white skin of her shoulders, the hair draped over them like the hair of a fairy queen. When he was with her, all he could think about was his father.

The next day he'd contacted a school friend who was an Oddfellow, and joined Chorley's Hall.

Now he was sitting in the Masonic hall listening to Mister John Fish, entrepreneur and creator of the Raikes Hall Gardens. Investing in him had given the Whittle family a good return – Leo clinched a contract to supply the gardens with turf, bedding flowers and fertiliser, ensuring a favourable deal that profited everyone. Humphrey was normally busy with assisting

John to run the surface operations at the Chorley pits, organising distribution, ensuring good sales returns and chasing unpaid bills, as well as keeping track of their ever expanding shares portfolio. But Fish had specifically asked for him, as the captain of 'the best football club in the world'. Humphrey thought that this was plain nonsense, an exaggeration which even Harry Hibbert wouldn't make about Chorley Football Club. But Leo had encouraged Humphrey to go, to listen to what Fish wanted to say, about a business opportunity for both the Whittle family and the football club. So he had gone to Blackpool, and listened to Fish as he finished his annual statement to the assembled shareholders.

Fish gripped the sides of the speaker's pulpit like an overly sincere parish vicar. He was a small-boned man, with a slight deposit of fat around his waist being the only sign of opulence and success. He was in his fifties, with a slight covering of sandy hair, which he tried in vain to sweep forward over his sweat-glistened brow. He smiled, even when there was no reason to do so. He was wearing an expensive grey suit with a burgundy silk cravat more suited to a wedding than a shareholders' meeting.

'And so to conclude, gentlemen, the financial year 1877 to 1878 was a profitable one for Raikes Hall Gardens, and as you've no doubt seen, we're packing the punters in right now... I can see the money rolling down the pipes into the safe right now, with the opening of t'monkey 'ouse I reckon on that the biggest problem we'll 'ave is making sure we don't get the punters and the monkeys mixed up,' joked Fish, the general manager and unofficial boss of Raikes Hall. The audience of shareholders laughed politely, and one or two started to clap. But Fish shook his hand, stopping them, before he told them the punchline to his music-hall joke. 'I've got no doubts about the credit of your monkeys, it's 'aving men in cages as attractions that's the problem.'

He finished, and the shareholders were finally allowed to applaud – if the joke wasn't funny, then the amount of dividend he'd given them was enough compensation for a poor end to his speech. Fish smiled and waved at them with false humility, then stepped down from the pulpit to talk to the biggest investors individually. He passed among them like a saint, gently shaking their hands and touching their shoulders in a most informal way. His whispered words seemed to satisfy each one, but he didn't stay with them for long. Ignoring the questions of some of the smaller investors he found the local press at the back of the hall and gave them each a prepared transcript of the proceedings, along with an off-the-cuff statement of how the Gardens would stage a world premiere of some kind in the winter. They tried to ask him what he meant by that but he shook his head and walked away, dismissing them like a mandarin dismissing servants. He walked towards Humphrey.

Humphrey saw Fish's face change like a clown's from showing scorn and disdain to overbearing gratitude and sincerity. It was a gesture he managed in an instant, the period of change being infinitesimal, the emotions causing the lines on his face to be as ephemeral as words etched on a sandy beach.

'Mister Humphrey Norris Whittle? I believe we're not introduced as yet, am Fish I am, John Fish, the big fish,' he said risibly, as he held out a limp hand for Humphrey to shake. Humphrey stood up, grasped the hand and squeezed hard, to see what Fish's response would be. The general manager of Raikes Hall didn't even wince, and continued to smile earnestly.

'Ah think we can do a deal, Whittle, you don't mind me calling you that, do you, only a man like you's bound to be going places soon.'

Humphrey released Fish's hand, and said, coldly:

'Mister Fish, if you are looking to gain investment from myself or my family, you will not get it by insincere flattery.'

Fish's smile became broader, more jocular. 'Whittle, am not a man who minces words, ah'll tell it straight, see what you think. How would you like Chorley to win the Northern Challenge Cup?'

Humphrey disliked the implications of Fish's question. Of course he wanted Chorley to win every match they played, but was Fish suggesting something else other than that desire, something as furtive as the handshakes he'd given on the way down from the podium? He considered what Fish had said, whilst Fish waited patiently for an answer, or, as was likely, a question to his question.

Eventually Humphrey put his arm out in the direction of the exit.

'I'm not quite sure what you're offering, Fish.'

'On my word, nowt fishy, my lad,' grinned Fish.

'I think we should discuss this elsewhere, Mister Fish, don't you? A Mason's Lodge is not the place for making schemes,' said Humphrey, attempting a joke. Fish had that strange effect.

They went to eat at a fish restaurant on the promenade, where they were served cod in batter with fried potato slices on china plates. Fish made great play of this, and engaged in a self-mocking banter that soon became tiresome for Humphrey. He listened, and ate his food, then could not contain himself any longer.

'Mister Fish, what are you talking about? What is this Northern Challenge Cup you mentioned? Have the Union brought in another novelty without telling us?' asked Humphrey, putting down his stainless steel knife and fork across his empty plate.

'Well, never mind that fer now, Whittle lad, let me ask you this. What did you make of that Cup they've just played for in Yorkshire? Not the trophy, mind, but the games,' said Fish, chewing on a large piece of soggy batter.

The Yorkshire Cup had been contested in the middle of the previous season, fought between the biggest clubs in the country. It had drawn crowds of thousands to watch each match in the sixteen team knock-out competition. At Heckmondwike, the tie against Hull had to be delayed due to the sheer size of the crowd, which had spilled onto the pitch. At Bradford, the semi-final against Halifax saw hundreds of people climbing over the walls to gain entry (Bradford's officials were less ruthless than Harry Hibbert, and didn't think to tar their walls). The final at the Holbeck ground in Leeds, though taking place in horrendous blizzards, saw over three thousand spectators brave the weather to see Halifax beat the favoured York side by a goal. The press in Lancashire had been dismissive of this act of Yorkshire frivolity, as had the Manchester Club - the unofficial mouthpiece of the Union in Lancashire, which drafted a motion condemning the Yorkshire collaboration with, and capitulation to, the unhealthy forces of professionalism. The Union in London had sent all manner of threatening letters to Yorkshire, to the local officials and the members of the clubs participating in the venture, questioning their motives and their finances. The Yorkshire clubs, feeling that they were more powerful than the compliant local officials, ignored the letters and warnings, and listened instead to the clamour from the spectators for more of the same.

'I see nothing wrong in competing for a cup prize, as long as the Union in London agrees to it. No one has actually shown the Tykes a rule that says they can't have a cup competition,' said Humphrey.

'Do you think they'll play for it again?' asked Fish.

'Why, of course, the gate takings must have been tremendous... the football was of the highest quality, so I've heard, although there are some rumours of foul play,' said Humphrey, thinking of the 'guest' players in some of the competing teams, and the suspicions of match-rigging and match payments, although he suspected that most of the rumours had come from the Yorkshire and Lancashire clubs who had condemned the idea of a cup competition in the first instance.

'Right, well let me tell you this. I won't tell you lies, I'm not that sort of businessman, my record stands for itself in t'middle of this bloody town,' said Fish. The profanity shocked Humphrey because although the word itself was nothing new to a football player, it was so out of place in the gentle tranquillity and formality of the restaurant. Fish continued.

'I 'ave a mind to stage a cup competition right 'ere in Blackpool, in Raikes Hall, between best teams in t'North of England.'

'In Raikes Hall?' asked Humphrey.

'Ah'll build a ground, charge 'em extra to gerrin, a knock-out competition this winter, during close season, see, make more brass from the punters, get them to Blackpool, not just for me but for Raikes Hall, Chorley'll be invited of course, and as a shareholder you'll get a good payback, and a good draw to get you to the final,' said Fish, grinning with his mouth full of his namesake. 'What d'yer say to that, Whittle lad?'

Humphrey didn't know what to say. He looked at the other diners, who were polite enough not to show they were listening.

'Well?' asked Fish.

Humphrey wondered about the finance of this adventure, the costs of preparing a playing field, the expenses the clubs would incur travelling to and from Blackpool, and the number of clubs Fish already had signed up to the Cup. It all sounded rather grand, but Humphrey could see quite a few problems in the plan. The Yorkshire clubs had their own cup to play for, the fixture lists were already drawn up for the following season, and there would be considerable opposition to the Cup from clubs, officials and the Union.

Yet the Cup offered a challenge, a prize. It was the Grail he'd been seeking. Humphrey was Parzifal, standing before the Fisher King, waiting to ask the right question. He knew what to say. He wanted the Cup. He wanted to prove himself worthy.

'Where do we sign up?' he asked.

He first saw the Cup at the beginning of the season, when no team except Chorley was aware of its existence and Fish was making plans to secure the provision of skilled craftsmen to build the ground at Raikes Hall. Fish had sent him a telegram telling him to proceed to Manchester, where the final purchase of the Cup was taking place. Because Fish wanted to keep the idea secret from the press and the inquisitors of the union, the Cup had been bought through a Raikes Hall intermediary, who was to hand it over in the relative seclusion of the Lodge in Fallowfield. This was some distance from the centre of the town, and away from the rugby football areas to the north and west.

Humphrey had gone secretly, missing a grudge match against the public schoolmen of Liverpool FC, who put Chorley on their fixture list out of a duty to test themselves, rather than any social necessity. The next day in church Harry had expressed his anger in words not usually heard in house of God, since this secrecy had meant Chorley fielding fourteen players and losing to the men from the Mersey by a touchdown, the score being three goals apiece. Humphrey had taken him aside then and told him about the beauty of the Cup, its inner radiance, its voice speaking to him of honour and purity. Harry hadn't understood, of course, but he knew the value of fifty guineas, the price Fish had paid.

The Fallowfield Lodge had been empty save for Fish and his intermediary, a sallow faced wretch in a cheap suit who had ink on his fingers. Fish introduced him as Duckett, the clerk to a Manchester firm of solicitors he would not name. Duckett seemed to object to Humphrey not knowing any of the secret signs, and fretted lest he escaped them and entered the private hall. But Humphrey had no intention to see their Masonic treasures: his eyes were for the Cup alone.

They had it on a table in the dining room, on a red velvet cloth. Flames from the fireplace were reflected across its polished sides, around the bowl flowers grew as if it had been touched by a Green Man. Fish had closed the heavy curtains, so that the Cup absorbed all the light, turning the mundane gas lamp and coal fire into sparkling stars of silver and gold. It didn't seem made to Humphrey – it was too perfect for any silversmith to have hammered and turned – unless its maker was some immortal who had sent it down from heaven for those who were pure enough to find it.

'Who made it?' asked Humphrey.

'That's the wrong question, Humphrey, lad, I say it's the wrong question. Ask another,' grinned Fish, hobbling over to the fire to warm his aching knees.

'Who's the Cup for?'

'Whoever wins it, lad,' answered Fish.

'It's fifty guineas, it is, 'ave yer seen t'Yorkshire Cup? Tha's just a tin pot compared to this un, this un's champion,' said Duckett plainly.

Humphrey looked at the Cup again. He thought of Frederick in the water, taken away because they were playing at being knights. Their father, too, the time he had watched him dash out the brains of a monkey he had bought in Liverpool as a pet, a substitute Frederick. His father couldn't have known this, he never told anyone the monkey was Frederick, a substitute smuggled in under monkey skin like a fairy changeling. His father had called it a pest, but Humphrey knew it was just a way of ensuring the patriarchal authority of Primrose Cottage.

'I want this Cup,' said Humphrey.

8.

The First Round of the North of England Challenge Cup

THE RAIKES HALL GARDEN COMPANY have presented a mag-
nificent Champions silver cup value fifty guineas, to be contested for by twenty-
four North of England football clubs. One match is to be played every
Saturday at Raikes Hall Gardens commencing October 19th, and the cup will
become the absolute property of the club winning the final match. In addition
gold medals will be presented to each player in the winning team and members
of the second team will each receive a silver medal. The draw to decide the
order of play in the first round and to fix the dates of matches will take place
at Raikes Hall on the 10th instant.

Fish read the *Fleetwood Chronicle* with some satisfaction. Rugby was the
new craze in Lancashire, more so than in the south where it was still played
by a handful of overgrown schoolboys. And in Yorkshire it was the
favoured sport of just about every working-man except in Sheffield, where
just to be different they played their own version of football. In the seven
years following the formation of the Rugby Football Union the game had
spread like the plague through the cotton mills and coal-pits. Now the clubs
fought with each other over who would play who, which clubs would be on
the respectable fixture cards and which would have to struggle to get a full
season's worth of fixtures. Fish was certain that the cup would change all
that, as the Yorkshire Cup was forcing the best clubs over there to think
about having a soccer-style league competition.

He'd had no idea how many clubs would respond to the letters he'd sent
out, and the advertisements he'd placed in various sporting and regional
newspapers. In the end, the predictions Humphrey Whittle had made about
problems attracting clubs, such as had happened in Yorkshire, had come

true. Not that Fish, or Whittle, or Harry Hibbert (once he was convinced of the drawing power of the Cup) minded this lack of interest. Fish had no qualms about telling the papers a lie or two about the size of the competition – what mattered most was that the North of England Challenge Cup was seen by the punters and the press to be a competition for and between northern rugby football clubs, whether or not clubs actually applied to enter it.

After the floodlit match Fish met with Humphrey and Harry Hibbert to discuss the mechanics of the cup-ties and which clubs were to enter the competition. Altogether, Fish had managed to persuade six clubs to enter, despite the opposition coming from the Union in London and the open letters to the press sent by Manchester and Liverpool rugby football clubs. Competition would, they argued, turn Lancashire footballers away from the handling code, which would be destroyed by the ill-mannered savages who were attracted to such baubles as the Cup like Zulus to a settler farm. Their use of such a metaphor at a time when men from Lancashire were fighting and dying on the plains of southern Africa was not lost on the learned public, who supported their stance. The rest of the football-following public, however, especially those who cared nothing for distant wars on the Empire's frontier, took up the Zulu cry as a taunt throughout the season and beyond, long after the Cup had been largely forgotten. When – sixteen years later - Whittle handed the Cup over in the council chamber to a veteran of the Zulu campaign it was not without remembering the rancour surrounding the letters in the leading columns of the press. As for the Yorkshire clubs, they were either of like mind, or preferred to make room on their fixture cards for their own lucrative cup matches.

As far as Fish was concerned, it was good riddance to bad rubbish if Manchester, Liverpool and the Yorkshire clubs chose not to play in the competition. Folk on the Fylde coast, unused to the handling code, knew nothing about which teams were favoured and which were reckoned the best – they only cared, he said, about what he told them.

More important were the six other clubs he'd managed to persuade to come, since they were local names from places people in Blackpool knew plenty about, and they had enough of a following to make a tidy profit at the gate. In addition to these there had been applications from another seven clubs, junior in rank and little more than park teams made up of fellows from churches, offices, railway and rifle companies and – in one case – a private lending library. Most of these he turned down - there'd be no money made from teams without supporters - promising them that they would be entitled to a reduced entry charge at the gate and they would be looked on favourably for inclusion in an expanded competition the following year.

After some careful planning, Fish settled on eight clubs for the competition, a mixture of complete beginners in the handling code, village sides and a strong senior team: Chorley Football Club. This suited Harry well, and he looked forward to receiving the Cup. Humphrey was unsure about this, about the legitimacy of any victory won by playing weaker opponents. Where was the sport? But at the same time he knew he had to win, he had to have the Cup, and that was worth more than playing a fair game and earning the respect of other footballers, other gentlemen. Like Fish said, it was an open invitation competition, and it wasn't the fault of Humphrey and Chorley that Manchester and Liverpool, and others like Swinton, had refused to take part. They were, Fish claimed, too scared to test their footballing prowess in meaningful competition – and in that respect, the smaller sides were showing far more courage and character by challenging Chorley and each other for the honours, to be called the best in the North of England.

When Humphrey was convinced of this, he took to planning the Cup with eager anticipation, and Fish found it far easier to convince him of the necessity to fix the draw.. It would be a simple matter to rig the fixtures to allow Chorley an easy build-up to the final. It wasn't as if they would be giving Chorley any real advantage, he explained, since at some stage they would have to play someone who had – through the process of the knock-out competition - beaten all the other winners whom Chorley hadn't played. Humphrey understood what Fish was saying, even if the exact details of the process seemed to elude Fish. If Chorley won the final, that was proof against any fixed draw that they were worthy champions.

The draw was fixed to enable Raikes Hall to generate as much gate revenue as possible. It was a business decision, which would benefit Humphrey and the Whittle family as major shareholders in the Raikes Hall Gardens Company. To that end, eight clubs had been chosen which would pair up easily in the first round to produce large crowds. Chorley, being the club with the largest number of supporters, would play Southport Olympic, with the least number, a match which would give Chorley an easy entry into the second round. Manchester Athletic were paired up with Walton from Liverpool, a match which Fish would advertise somewhat deceivingly as Manchester versus Liverpool. That it wasn't the Manchester FC versus the Liverpool FC was neither here nor there, according to Fish. The third tie was between two clubs from East Lancashire who were already great rivals with a small but loyal band of supporters and a growing sense of civic pride – Rossendale and Whitworth Rangers. Both teams were ones Fish had persuaded to play through his connections in the Masons, and the former in particular was associated with an important Lodge. The last tie was between two clubs from Preston, the nearest town to the Fylde coast: Olympic and North End. This local derby, Fish was convinced, was certain to attract thousands of paying customers to Raikes Hall from Preston, which was little more than a stone's throw away down the railway line, and was sure to whet the appetites of football supporters on the Fylde coast.

At one point in the discussion Humphrey was sent away to buy more cigars from a shop down the road towards Dole Lane. When he returned to the backroom he heard Harry asking the question:

'Now then, 'ow do wi know we're gunna win t'cup, then?'

And Fish replied:

'I'm a man of my word, Mister Hibbert. I'll make sure this other side loses all right.'

Humphrey knocked on the door and went through. Harry and Fish were smoking cigars by the fire. They looked at him with warm, friendly faces, their arms raised in a comradely salute. Humphrey smiled, relieved to be back in their company. Fish beckoned him over with an unlit cigar in his other hand and three brandies on the mantelpiece, ready to celebrate a successful cup competition with a toast to victory. It was only later, when he was in bed at Primrose Cottage haunted by memories of childhood beatings, that he dared to guess what was meant by Harry's question and Fish's answer.

Chorley v Southport Olympic
Leo Whittle, Crumblehulme, Lever, Brown, Gartside, Little,
Ingham, John Mockett, Spedding, Humphrey Whittle, Stock,

Garstang, Brindle, Booth, Joe Mockett.

Names, read out by Harry for the benefit of the Rugby Union official and the reporters presiding over the first match of the North of England Challenge Cup. It was a litany in Whittle's head, a list from Beowulf of the brave Danes and Geats in the Golden Hall of Hrothgar. The first match took place only three days after the second, and this time successful trial of the floodlights, so close to the night when electricity burned away the shadows that the guest of honour at the match was a somewhat bemused but relieved Mister Bury of Parker and Bury's electric company. Yet it felt like years had passed, even at the time, and this feeling was magnified as the memories of football faded, so that the Cup seemed to be something played in another age.

Unlike Beowulf, they did not have to confront Grendel. Mister Fish, the creator of the Challenge Cup, the magician who had conjured up the draw for the matches, had made sure of that.

Rain. Everything in Blackpool was drenched with rain. Black clouds of Biblical proportions heaved their way over the Irish Sea and collapsed over the grey sands and black terraces of Blackpool. The new houses built to the south of the town in the sand dunes sank slowly into the wet earth. The streets became streams, rushing down the imperceptible slope from the railway stations towards the new promenade and the empty guest houses. The streams washed away the muck from the holiday season, cleaning the town for the following summer as if the Aldermen had made a deal with God. The sea churned, washing up silt and black soot over the breakwaters. It was not a sea for fishermen.

Set back from the promenade, away from the empty front and the salty rain, the resort's pubs, freed from the burden of day-trippers from the mill towns, hid behind steamed-up windows. The few shops that remained open were empty except for their determined owners, clad in white aprons and straw boaters to sell meat, ironware, cloth, fruit, shoes and vegetables. Smoke drifted up from chimney after chimney, dissipating as the rainwater absorbed the particles on its way down to the ground. Nothing moved on the streets except the incessant trickle-trickle of the clogged-up gutters.

Blackpool was a dead town. And yet, at its heart, amidst the pagodas and willows of the Raikes Hall Gardens, beyond the speckled boating lake, the animals shivering in their cold pens, there was life. In the middle of its open fields and crafted woodland walkways, surrounded by ponds of goldfish slowly spreading out over adjacent picnic benches and children's swings, Raikes Hall's football ground hissed with excitement. At its gate, men in grey greatcoats made black by the rain were wreathed in damp clouds of breath and tobacco smoke as they waited to pay their way through the brand new wrought-iron turnstile. The warm smell of hot pies and tea mingled with that of dirty rain. The walls of the new football ground, tall and topped with black iron spikes, were made of bright red brick set against the grey grass and the black trees. Its grandstand rose above the wall, its huge tar-sealed wooden roof serving as a bulwark against the rain clouds.

Humphrey wiped the rain from his forehead, from his floppy hair, from his moustache. It was a hopeless gesture, but for a moment his eyes were clear of rain. He looked down the field, ignoring the shouts of encouragement from Harry Hibbert and the hushed anticipation of the crowd huddled under the roof of the grandstand. Somewhere behind him he heard Leo explaining something about tackling them into touch to the other fullback, Crumblehulme. Nearer, Lever was telling a joke about the Irishman who thought that a football was made out of people's feet. It wasn't funny, but Lever laughed, forcing Brown and Gartside to laugh. It was a strange sound, familiar enough in the back room of a pub but not on a waterlogged football pitch before kick off.

Ahead of Humphrey, beyond the place where Fish had optimistically whitewashed a centre line in the morning before the rain clouds burst open over the town, Southport Olympic readied themselves. Humphrey glared at them, hating them, seeing there the quack doctors who had convinced the elder Whittle that hydrotherapy was a proven method of removing the poisons that caused hysteria. They had failed, as Humphrey knew all too well, because Jane's affliction was not the result of something material, but something in her soul, a madness that affected all of them, except perhaps Leo. The blue shirts of Southport Olympic, newly made for the Cup from pure cotton bleached then dyed, had turned a deep blue, almost black, by the rain which seeped through to their bones. He hated them, as he hated the doctors, as he hated his father for locking Jane away as he'd locked Frederick away, for the beatings to try to ensure that none of the madness surfaced in his other sons.

More rain trickled down his brow to drip from the end of his eyelashes. Fletcher, the Southport captain, waved at someone in the crowd. His companions, the enemy, lined up behind their kicker, and Humphrey could see their faces. They were ugly, twisted demons, things that had never heard of the Redemption, creatures of the Enemy.

He exhaled, calmly. He was ready.

Their kicker, Johnson, stepped two paces back behind the muddy brown leather football.

'Play up, Chorley!' shouted Humphrey, clenching his fists.

'Up and at 'em, lads! Balaclava!' added Harry, who was standing on the grandstand side of the pitch with his yellow umpire's flag.

Every person in the stand, on the pitch, stopped breathing.

This was the moment Humphrey lived for.

Johnson booted the ball into the air, kicking it up in a little arc to land some way behind him in the hands of Southport's left three-quarter back, Lonsdale. The spectators exhaled, the sigh of pleasure rolling across the pitch like mist. Humphrey bellowed at the top of his voice, his incoherent rage hidden in the magnified cheers of the crowd. He ran up the field, his boots squelching with every step into the boggy grass, mud kicked up on the back of his black trousers. The ground shook as the nine Chorley forwards followed the ball, lunging down the pitch at the Southport players. Lonsdale held the ball up in the air, taunting the charging Chorley men, then punted it over their heads. Humphrey tried to stop running and slid into one of the Southport players, almost knocking him over.

The Southport player held Humphrey up, and grinned.

'Steady on there, old boy,' he said, patting Humphrey on the shoulder and looking down field where the ball had been hefted off the pitch and into a large puddle. 'Your feed-in at the scrimmage I believe.'

Leo listened to the crowd as he stood near the Chorley goal. The rain didn't touch him. He followed the movement of the ball as it was carried back onto the pitch for the scrum. He waited, like a whippet in a trap, savouring every moment, every movement.

Humphrey looked to the Southport umpire, who was on the empty side of the field holding an umbrella over his head, which the wind was trying to drag away. The Southport umpire splashed his way through puddles to where the scrimmage was about to take place. Men breathed, steam coming from their backs where shirts stuck to skin. Harry stayed where he was in the shelter of the stand, refusing to join the thirty men on the morass. Behind him, the stand was full but there wasn't anybody around the other three sides, except two young urchins playing under the far wall.

Humphrey walked to where the scrimmage was being set, and settled into his place at the open side of the scrum, ready to peel off and knock the opposition to the ground. Ignoring the rain, heedless of the muck that had already stained Ingham's white shirt, he put his head down. The comforting smell of man's sweat, starched collars and old carbolic overwhelmed him. Chorley favoured a human triangle in the scrum, all pushing up against the central man, who would hack for the ball and use his hands and knees to force the enemy back. Against Southport Olympic, this meant Ingham, one of the Mockett brothers and Spedding being the men in the middle, with Stock and Garstang serving as a foundation in the next row behind. The other four forwards pushed where they could, changing places as tactics dictated, moving to prop up a weak point or splintering away to reform the scrum elsewhere. The other Mockett brother, however, a regular in the side, nearly always added his weight to the base of the scrum, grappling the forwards in the second row (invariably including Garstang, the keystone of Chorley's scrum) as he ground his legs into the grass and pushed.

They settled against Southport Olympic, who had three rows of three, a regular formation which gave them more muscle but fewer options if the scrimmage came loose. The half-backs and the three-quarters of both sides trailed away on the open side, ready to receive the ball and make a running move.

'Play up, Chorley! For the Cup!' shouted Humphrey, putting his shoulder down and pushing against Ingham's back with all his strength, pushing him up against Southport Olympic as every forward squeezed the scrimmage. Each man shouted and groaned and pushed, as if they were trying to compact the men in the front row into the size and shape of one man. Humphrey slapped Stock on the arm.

'For the Cup!'

'For the Cup!' roared Stock.

'For the Cup!' repeated Garstang.

'FOR THE CUP!' shouted the Chorley forwards, pushing ever harder.

The ball was thrown into the middle of the scrum between the men, and legs hacked out for it and other legs. Humphrey relaxed then jumped forward, squashing his own men. On the other side of the scrum Brindle slipped on the grass and the scrum wheeled around. Chorley's forwards were pushed backwards, and the Southport formation collapsed. In the middle, Fletcher managed to pick up the ball from the mud, cradle it to his chest and jump out of the way of Humphrey's grasping hand. He ran straight across the field, cheered on by his team. He made ten yards before Little brought him down from behind, tackling his legs like a lion on a wildebeest. The ball went loose, skidding across the grass, and Gartside picked it up with his spade-like hands. The crowd cheered him on as he ran free with only the Southport full-backs to dodge. Lever had the sense to run with him, staying close to the wing so he could listen to the enraptured cries of delight from the men - and especially the women - up in the grandstand. Feet clattered across the grass as the Southport backs struggled to get close.

'I say, Gartside, pass the ball before you're tackled, man!' ordered Lever, who wanted to make a try for goal himself, to be the first man to score in the Cup.

Gartside passed without looking, and the ball shot behind where Lever was running to hit a man standing on the steps that led to the grandstand seats.

Down the pitch, where the forwards were picking themselves up off the ground, Humphrey shook his head and cursed. They had to win, he had to win. If Gartside couldn't pass then he'd have to find another club to play for.

'Come on, Chorley, concentrate on the game! For the Cup, for the Cup!' he bellowed as the players made their way down the pitch, wiping the muddy rain from their faces. He reached Gartside, who was apologising to Lever. Humphrey glared at him but said nothing.

The ball came back into play with a throw-in. The forwards converged on where it bounced, pushing and kicking and shoving. Harry, who was the umpire at the near side, nodded and clapped. Behind him, in the wooden benches rising up into the darkness of the top row of the stand, the crowd joined in the applause, urging the players on. Humphrey looked up and saw Fish, standing against one of the stanchions, smoking his pipe and frowning. In front of him, Mister Bury was trying to tell Councillor Lever about something, but the old man was on the edge of his seat and roaring the name of Chorley with pride reddening his hairy face. Humphrey smiled. He put his head into the loose scrimmage, knocked over one of the Southport players with the palm of his hand, and stood on a blue-shirted arm stretching out for the ball. He heaved and strained until the drops of rain on his face turned to sweat, and thought only about winning the Cup.

The game was confusing, unpredictable, a collage of unruly scrums and mauls and kicking jousts that would turn without warning into mad dashes down the field. This was the famililar game, but there was something else that Leo noticed from the back. The crowd watched every scrum, waiting for the ball like children waiting for the first snowfall in winter. The players, instead of smiling and talking to their rivals, looked away into the distance, concentrating on some elusive gap in the clouds. It was as if everyone was suffering from some sort of fever.

Southport Olympic's right-hand full-back tried to pick up the ball skidding towards him but it bounced off his forearm into a pool of water. Mutters of bad luck from the crowd turned to cheers as Chorley players rushed over the ball, hiding it between their dirty workman's boots. Southport forwards ran back, swearing like navvies, faces red and twisted. They lined up for a scrimmage but were knocked back by the Chorley players, whose legs were like engine pistons. The defensive line collapsed but Stock lost control of the ball, kicking it instead of dribbling it forward. Men fell into the puddle or were stamped on by Chorley's forwards. Humphrey charged into the middle of the loose scrum, knocking Southport from the ball and making a gap through which Stock, the ball now in his hand, squeezed over the line for a try near the far side. The Chorley players cheered and clapped, and after Harry conferred with his fellow umpire the try was confirmed.

The crowd clapped politely.

'Well played, Stock,' grinned Humphrey.

The teams lined up for the goal attempt. The Southport side stood under their goals, ready to charge Leo Whittle, who was to be the kicker. On the line where the try had been made, Lever had the ball ready to kick out to Leo, who would then attempt to go for goal. The other Chorley players stood next to Leo.

'Humphrey, how fast can you run?' asked Leo, looking at the angle and distance he had to kick.

Humphrey shrugged his shoulders.

'Why do you ask?'

'If I kick off target, they might not expect it… if I aimed for a spot nearer to the goal and you ran for a try the conversion would be easy,' said Leo.

'You mean, deliberately not kick for goal?' frowned Humphrey.

'Why not? It'd be hard to get a goal with this blasted weather,' said Leo. He looked at his brother with an urgent, childish frown, wiping mud over the polish of his boots so that the ball wouldn't slip when kicked.

The umpires waved their flags and Lever booted the ball towards Leo. Humphrey looked at his brother, astounded at the suggestion, but he nodded anyway. Leo caught the ball, placed it, and kicked it wide of the mark, just where he wanted it to go. Humphrey ran after it, grinning at the stupefied faces on the Southport players under the goals. It bounced once then slowed down, its momentum being lost to the mud, then slid to a halt just over the Southport line. Their full-backs ran up the line and got to the ball, just ahead of Humphrey, before dribbling away up the field. Humphrey chased after them and hacked the ball away, back to Leo, who had another attempt from the field. He did the same thing again, and this time Humphrey had the advantage over the full-backs. He ran past them with a smile as wide as his face and retrieved the ball for a try.

Harry Hibbert, standing behind the posts, smiled at the Southport umpire.

'That's not fair,' the umpire complained.

'Not Leo's fault if he can't kick, is it, eh? I 'ardly think the Union's got owt to pin on the lad for that, that's initiative that is!' laughed Harry.

Lever converted the try into a goal, and the umpires called for a change of ends, despite it being only one quarter of the way, or twenty minutes, give or take a few seconds, into the match. The wind and rain made it hard for the team running against the weather, so they'd agreed to swap ends more frequently.

Humphrey dribbled with the ball up the field, avoiding the tackles made by the blundering Southport forwards. He reached the quarter flag in Southport's half and lost control. The ball went forward and Fletcher, the

Southport captain, tried to pick it up. It slipped out of his hands and a scrimmage formed. After a few seconds of pushing, Humphrey found the ball at his feet and hacked it away, allowing Gartside to make a run for another try at goal.

'This time,' he told Leo as they lined up ready for the kick, 'just get it over the crossbar.'

Leo laughed. The others looked at him, as if it was the mark of madness to be merry in the middle of a match. He missed the kick, the ball blowing with the wind out beyond the field, above the rain, and into the Chinese gardens. When it was recovered the game turned into one long scrimmage, which moved slowly up and down the field as neither side managed to get the ball passed out to the backs. Whenever someone had the ball it was grappled out of his hands, or kicked away by heavy boots that then rattled his shins. Humphrey and Lever encouraged the forwards, clapping out time like a beater on a slave galley. Garstang picked up the ball in the middle of the scrum and handled it back to the second Mockett, who somehow punted it out over their heads to land in front of the Southport three-quarters. They stared at it, as if it was a star fallen from the heavens, and Lever ran forward to kick it over the line for Little. He then made the goal, to the delight of the crowd who cheered and bayed for more.

Humphrey listened to the crowd. They were cheering Chorley, they were cheering him. Even though they were only a few hundred huddled under the grandstand to shelter from the rain they made the noise of thousands packed into the Circus Maximus. The grey light and the dark clouds did not affect them. They were enthralled, entranced by the football Chorley were playing. They knew Chorley couldn't lose, just as the Southport players, bent over with their hands on their knees, covered in mud and bruises, knew they could not win. Two goals and two tries built a formidable redoubt for Chorley, one which Southport's tired and miserable players couldn't breach.

'Half time!' cried both umpires, looking at their watches and to the captains for approval. The Southport players trudged off the pitch to shelter from the rain under the roof of the grandstand. Some of the Chorley players started to follow them but Humphrey called them back. They were heroes. They didn't need to hide from the rain like mere men.

'Gather round here, chaps,' said Humphrey, squatting down next to the abandoned ball. They did so, huffing and puffing big clouds of damp breath that were quickly dispersed by the wind. Lever sat down on the ball, and used his handkerchief to wipe away the mud on his face. When he had done he carefully shook it and folded it back into his shirt pocket. Humphrey looked at each one of them, proud that they had played their best.

'I think we've got this game in the bag, their scrimmaging is the worst I've seen this season.'

'We're only halfway through, though, Humphrey, best not treat them like schoolboys,' said Leo. 'I've read of teams coming back in the second half a different side.'

'We'd spot that, surely,' said Lever, smiling.

'They're rubbish, they are, Mister Whittle's right,' said Garstang, furrowing his heavy brow and ignoring the blood coming out of his nose where someone had punched him in the last scrimmage. He winked. 'I dint feel nowt when 'e 'it me.'

'Well let's not overstretch ourselves, we're going to win this Cup, you know,' smiled Humphrey. 'Let's enjoy ourselves, what?'

Chorley held off Southport in the next two quarters, but failed to make a goal themselves. In desperation Southport threw the ball in long arcs from one part of the field to the other like Yorkshiremen, though they couldn't catch and run effectively. Leo made a try-saving tackle, lining the attacker up against the grandstand and knocking the wind out of him, and on another occasion he was forced to touch down behind his line by the Southport forwards. But the afternoon soon turned to evening, hastened by the rain, and the mood of the crowd turned cold as they thought of their homes and a warm fire. This mood spread from the stand to the players, who started to jog instead of run, and who pushed half-heartedly in the scrum. When the umpires called time the Chorley team cheered, but the applause was muted.

Nevertheless, Chorley were through to the next round.

Chorley's victory over Southport Olympic was the first match of the Cup, one which dispelled any troubling thoughts from Humphrey's mind. Fish complained about the apathy of people in Blackpool, then complained about the weather, blaming a whole pantheon of gods for spoiling what should have been a moment in history for Raikes Hall. When the press tried to get a comment from him he shouted at them for being little more than leeches, and warned them that he could have them sacked if they quoted him. Harry, who took a longer view of things than Fish, told the reporters it was the first step towards a full, national football competition, a deed that showed northern business sense and modern thinking was needed to overcome the prejudices and backward traditions of the old Tories who ran the game. He had the reporters scribbling when he told them that he would make sure, as an aspiring politician who believed in liberty, that the dark forces of prejudice and metropolitan snobbery would not stop the men of the north of England challenging each other for the Cup. Humphrey admired his friend for his audacity, for turning a football match into a political issue. Harry seemed pleased with himself - the reporters would have a story, he had scored a political point, and they had ensured the next match would have more publicity than the first.

Walton v Manchester Athletic

The second match of the first round, that between Walton and Manchester Athletic, was a played a week later. Fish ignored the advice of the Raikes Hall lawyers and printed posters and flyers for every pub in Blackpool and Fleetwood advertising 'the most thrilling football teams in the North, from LIVERPOOL and MANCHESTER, meeting to decide who will be crowned the Caliphs of the Rugby Football Union, only at Raikes Hall Gardens', with no indication that the two teams meeting were not the famed football clubs from those two cities. When he was asked, he told the truth, but he hadn't become the General Manager of the north's most famous holiday destination without knowing there was no point – and, more important, no profit – in telling the truth unprompted. By the end of the week he was a happy man, looking forward to a full house, with interest being shown by businesses and sportsmen across the county.

The Whittle family was having difficulties at the market gardens on the Fylde Coast. Three days before the second match the elder Whittle received a telegram from their site manager explaining that the men were threatening to strike unless they were paid some kind of retainer over the bleak winter months, when most of them were surplus to requirements. Humphrey, who watched his father reading the telegram over the breakfast table, was impressed by the speed of the message. He looked at Leo – who had just visited the market gardens - struggling to break into a boiled egg at the other end of the long table and hoped that this would be the moment when Leo stopped being the prodigal son, when his father would realise that Leo was not the better man of the Whittle sons.

The elder Whittle read out the telegram, ushering their manservant out of the room and ordering him to shut the doors. When he had finished, he put the scrap of paper on the tablecloth next to the silver tea pot, and shook his head.

'Not good,' he said, tapping his cup with a spoon as if he was a schoolmaster bringing the children to attention. 'This is not good, boys, not good at all. I blame the French, damned spoilt everything just when we were making progress.'

'Father?' frowned Leo, who had expected the blame to fall on him.

'The revolution, Leo, how can we be expected to build a civilisation to be proud of when the mob just wants to tear everything down?' said Humphrey smugly, proud that he had listened to the old aldermen and party members who attended their father like viziers around an Ottoman sultan. 'Isn't that right, father?'

Their father nodded grudgingly.

'Leo, remember what I told you? These people would have us all reduced to their level, fighting over loaves of bread, burning everything, our paintings, our carpets, things we've earned through our own 'ard graft. Give them an inch and mind or they'll take a yard, and before you know it they'll have the shirt of yer back an' all. Now what's all this about?'

Humphrey held back his anger – he had been right, and what praise had he had? Nothing, only a quick acknowledgement. But he listened to Leo's story. There was one man called Lindsey who had been going to reading lessons organised by some socialist movement. Leo hadn't minded because bettering oneself was a way of becoming a gentleman, an opportunity they were trying to make possible through the board schools and the various Christian organisations. Humphrey guessed that the socialists used these reading lessons to feed the man's mind with their sedition and slander, their hatred of wealth and civilisation. When Leo said he thought some of the things the man had learnt were perfectly reasonable he clenched the side of his chair, ready to pounce. But Leo continued to tell of the demands the man started to make, and the way he used other, simpler men to stand up to the management.

'I'm not surprised this Lindsey's making strike demands now that yer in Chorley, Leo, my boy,' said their father, once Leo had finished. 'These fellows are all the same, cowards all of 'em, they prefer to slink around like foxes... none has the courage to stand up himself and face his betters like a man. Now, something must be done, and fast. Humphrey? Didn't I hear Harry Hibbert say he was planning to travel over to Blackpool with you to watch this cup competition of yours?'

Humphrey nodded. Chorley could do without him for one week – he had to be at Raikes Hall to watch the other teams, to know them like he knew his own team, so that he could respect them and at the same time know their weaknesses. Harry was also foregoing the pleasure of an away match at the other end of the county in hilly Oldham, to arrange some business deals with John Fish and some of the grandees of Blackpool.

'I can go, father, the football's not important,' shrugged Leo.

'Don't be absurd!' shouted their father. 'You're the most important fellow on the pitch, Leo, they say none can tackle like you. Humphrey here's just another big fellow in the scrum, but you're the fellow protecting the flanks, eh, boy? Most important. No, Humphrey's going to Blackpool anyway, so he can go and sort out this Lindsey blackguard.'

The elder Whittle's commandment was final.

Humphrey arrived at the Whittle market gardens near Lytham St Anne's on the morning of the match between Walton and Manchester Athletic. He had arrived at Blackpool with Harry on the train from Chorley, and since his business coincided with the match they took a trap out to the market gardens together. Although the Fylde coast was rapidly being submerged under cheap houses and new roads, away from the dunes and the beach one could quite easily find huge fields stretching away towards the sky, enclosed by small dark green and brown hedgerows. Between the fields tiny cottages and huge manors broke up the flat landscape, marked only by rising smoke from chimneys. Where the towns of the Fylde coast touched this countryside low villas and industrial farms had been built, branching off curving lanes and next to streams fighting their way to the sea. Around these trees were planted to shield the ever-present horizon from view, to make the world go away for those who worked and lived there. It was to one of these farms, with a back field covered in four long greenhouses of iron and glass, that Humphrey and Harry travelled.

They left the trap and the hired driver waiting at the gates, and walked through to the courtyard. The business was on an old farm, and its medieval buildings, covered in whitewash, surrounded the yard. The stables and the barn had been turned into a warehouse, with a shop where the labourers' cottages had been. The farmhouse served as a kitchen and wash-house for the men, and as an office for the foreman and site manager.

Standing on the step of the farmhouse was a man in a crumpled, soil-stained brown suit. It was of good quality cotton, implying that he had got it second-hand from one of the charity shops. The man took off his battered bowler hat and nodded.

'What can we do fer you gents?' he asked with a cheery smile.

'I am Humphrey Whittle, Mister Whittle's son, where is the site manager?' Humphrey replied, looking at the man with undisguised animosity. He had not told anyone that he was travelling over, in case the site manager was sympathetic to the rabble.

'Gone off to Blackpool, sayz thurz a football match ovver thurr,' the man answered. He looked to Harry for some support, but Harry glanced away at the greenhouses that could just be seen through an archway in the barn. 'Gone in 'is own time, 'appen.'

'Very well. Where is Lindsey?' asked Humphrey.

'Bob Lindsey? In second 'ot-'ouse, wi' watering can,' the man answered.

Leaving Harry with the man, Humphrey left the yard and went into the back field. It was about the size of a football pitch, with enough room to push a wheelbarrow between the four long greenhouses. He reached the second one and opened the door, reeling back as a wave of warm, damp air rushed out. He looked inside, and in between the tomato plants he saw a thin, bearded man carefully dripping water over the leaves with a watering can.

Humphrey had an idea to sort the man out, and see the site manager disciplined for neglecting his responsibilities. He smiled, and cupped his mouth with his gloved hands, and shouted:

'You there! Lindsey! Come here at once, will you?'

Lindsey looked across at Humphrey with an insolent face. But he did as he was ordered and walked between the tables and the plant beds to look up fearlessly at Humphrey. He didn't take off his cap, and carried on holding the water can, as if he was impatient to get back to his work. It was impudence, but Humphrey knew how to deal with it.

'Lindsey, isn't it?' he asked.

'Maybe, who are thee?' asked Lindsey suspiciously. He looked more carefully at Humphrey, seeing the family resemblance. 'Taking over from Leo Whittle, then?'

'Leo can't be here today. I am Humphrey Whittle, his older brother.'

'Fine, what's tha want?'

'Lindsey, you know perfectly well why I am here. You're the cause of these outrageous demands, that is perfectly clear.'

'So? Man's got rights, you know,' smiled Lindsey defiantly.

Humphrey took a deep breath. The greenhouse was making him sweat. He had worn clothes suitable for an autumn afternoon watching the football with other businessmen. Lindsey could see how uncomfortable he was getting. Humphrey had no choice. The talk of rights frightened him - it reminded him of Frederick, of their father forcing them all to behave the way he wanted them. He'd had no rights then, and he'd hated his father for it. Was that all Lindsey wanted?

'You talk about rights, but I have rights, too. This is our business and we run it our way. My father worked damned hard to get where he is today, he... well, you should know your place, man. You must stop these demands at once. They will be the ruin of the business then where would you be, without a job?'

'I reckon you couldn't survive without us. Who do you think does the graft? You? Your bloody lapdog of a site manager? Nice work he does, skiving off on a Sat'day afternoon to watch a football match,' smirked Lindsey. 'A monkey could do the job better.'

Lindsey's comments reminded Humphrey of the monkey he'd bought in Liverpool, which had bitten his sister, and his father's anger. The monkey reminded him of Frederick. It had had his cheeky grin, his self-pitying eyes, his foul temper. Had it reminded his father of Frederick? Had the fact that it bit their sister reminded their father of Jane, suffering from her attacks of hysteria, sent from one doctor to another in an attempt to drive away the demons in her stormy soul? He thought of Frederick, locked away in the poor hospital like a destitute tuberculosis victim, suffering his palsy alone.

He was angry at Lindsey. What did he know of suffering? Of anything? And yet the man was evidently clever, even if that was due to some native sense rather than formal education. Lindsey had to be shown the order of things, the meaning of man's struggle. He had to be taught a lesson.

The talk of the football match reminded Humphrey he had to be there, and he glanced at his watch. It was unbearably hot, so hot that Lindsey seemed to be melting in front of him, disappearing into the sweating greenery leaving only his perpetual sneer. Humphrey had to get to Raikes Hall in time for the kick off.

'Lindsey, do you consider yourself better than a monkey?' asked Humphrey.

Lindsey grinned.

'Sometimes I think I'd like to be a monkey, swinging on a tree all day with no one to tell me what to do. It seems to me, see, that monkeys have a better time of it than most of us. What can you get out of this life? You're just as trapped by the old man as the rest of us.'

Humphrey knew what he could get out of life. The Cup. Nothing else mattered to him, not even the other football matches that season. They counted for nothing. He stirred, feeling the sweat pouring down his back.

'I've a good mind to throw you onto a football pitch to see how you fare, you runt!'

'Football?' frowned Lindsey. 'I don't see how running away from someone is something to applaud.'

This was too much for Humphrey. Quickly, and without warning, he grabbed Lindsey by the lapels and shoved him up against a supporting post. The watering can clattered to the floor.

'You see, Lindsey? Football is a play, a play about life... it is, to use Darwin's words, the survival of the fittest,' growled Humphrey.

'You're wrong. That were Tom Huxley,' gasped Lindsey as he struggled to escape Humphrey's firm grip.

Humphrey felt the rage rushing through him, darkening the corners of his vision. Lindsey was a demon of some kind, taunting him through a red mist. It wasn't right. Lindsey had to be stopped: he had to be punished. Humphrey saw Lindsey now as a monkey. He felt his hands wrap around Lindsey's throat, he heard Lindsey gasping for air. Humphrey's fingers tightened. Why wouldn't Lindsey shut up? Humphrey's head started to pound, like a furnace hammer. It was too hot. He needed fresh air. He needed to get to the match.

'Mister Whittle, sir!' someone else shouted. Humphrey looked around and saw two other workers standing at the end of the bedding row. He looked back at Lindsey then relaxed his fingers, allowing the man to fall. The spell was broken. Lindsey was coughing and retching, but Humphrey felt no pity, only elation that he had dealt with Lindsey in a way the man would never forget. It had felt right.

He brushed down his coat, then turned to the other two workers.

'See that Lindsey is removed from the premises, and let everyone know what happened to him. I don't want to return.'

They nodded, and he left to watch the football match.

That afternoon Raikes Hall – blessed with a gentle wind and clouds that were broken by a weak sun – was full. The gardens were thick with elderly shopkeepers and clerks pushed around in bathchairs, families having picnics, young couples walking in front of their chaperones, children playing at sports and games involving hoops, ropes, balls, sticks, and nannies looking after babies. Amidst these mingling generations, to the delight of Fish and the other shareholders, were football supporters of every class and both sexes. They came in groups straight from work with their wage in their pockets, wearing rosettes of their own teams' colours - and not just those of Walton and Manchester Athletic, for Blackpool's workers were drawn from towns and villages across the north of England, and home was still where these men and women owed their loyalty. A few of the club's devoted supporters had made the trek north, but neither club had a huge following among the lower classes. Along with these workers came the town's middle-classes and the middle-class supporters of the two clubs, eager to better themselves by being seen at the game, jostling with each other for a good seat, envying each other's clothes. Then, finally, the town's rulers, aldermen and their wives arrived in carriages, wearing fine bespoke suits and Paris dresses, to sit with the directors and their friends who had come from the two competing clubs.

The stand at Raikes Hall groaned under the collective weight of the supporters. The air was enriched by strong, perfumed tobacco and the perfumes of women. The centre of the stand was a collage of well-fed men, sombre suits, gold watches, chatting women, frills, gloves, furled umbrellas and crumpled dresses. In the cheap seats, railway sleepers used as benches, men made coarse jokes and argued the odds with Fish's unofficial bookmakers. Older men and women pushed and shoved to get to their seats, helped along by drink and strong language. Around the pitch the rest of the supporters packed into the ground leaned on a white fence, a long row of flat caps and raincoats.

At the front of the stand, on a reserved bench in the middle of the crowd, Humphrey sat down after shaking hands with the other guests. Behind him Harry was explaining the rules of rugby football to Fish, who didn't seem to understand the difference between it and the dribbling code. At the quarter flag on the far side of the pitch, he spotted the market garden's site manager, a yellow-faced man with hair down to his collar.

The teams ran onto the pitch, and the subsequent claps and cheers saved Humphrey from having to dwell on his actions earlier that day.

The Walton team, despite the importance of the match, had neglected to tell Fish they were two men short. There were enough football players in the crowd of over two thousand to find two to wear a green Walton jersey – but since no one had been told, they started the game with thirteen players, which Humphrey thought was a most unusual and absurd number for a rugby football match. At the front of the stand, Fish's bookmakers were changing their odds and men were arguing over how the lack of forwards would affect the outcome of the match.

Heedless of this debate, the Walton team kicked off as the bells of the nearby church chimed the hour of three. Both teams had agreed to a referee, a player from a junior side in Cheshire, and he puffed on a pipe throughout the match as he did his best to keep out of their way. His presence, though, was well-received by the crowd, who listened as he explained what had happened every time the play stopped due to a try, a touchdown or the ball going dead out of touch.

Immediately after the kick-off, things started to go wrong for Walton, who conceded a touchdown due to the Athletic's quick chase of the ball upfield and their determined marking. In the scrimmaging, Manchester Athletic had the services of a number of strong men on loan from other junior teams from the city, and this, combined with the two-man advantage, saw them win most of the scrums. Their captain Unsworth broke away from one scrum with the ball at his feet and dribbled sixty yards, before

Jones then Sutton took it up to run the rest of the way to the Walton goal. In desperation Walton touched down for the second time behind their goals. But as soon as the ball went back to Athletic, Jones made an impressive run between the Walton tacklers to score a try, an act of skill that had everyone except the Walton directors up on their feet applauding.

When Humphrey sat down, after Manchester Athletic failed to convert the try into a goal, he turned to Fish and asked him what he thought of the match. Fish shrugged, saying:

'We've earned a few bob, Humphrey, that's the best part of it.'

The teams changed ends, and with the wind at their backs Walton managed to make some ground in the scrimmaging, pushing Manchester off the ball and making slow ground forwards. Harrison took the ball in his hands and went clear to the quarter flag, before he was tackled in front of Humphrey's site manager. The ball went loose and another Walton player, the three-quarter back Parry, picked it up and dashed under the posts for a try. The crowd clapped in appreciation, sensing that Walton, being two men short, needed as much encouragement as possible. The travelling Walton supporters called for silence as Waters readied himself to kick the goal, and the crowd hushed except in those places where men had bets on Athletic. The goal was made, and the crowd cheered, excited by the tense competition the game had become.

The kick-off led to a scrum near the Walton line, which was soon won by Athletic after an enormous push. The Athletic backs cheered on their comrades as Walton's forwards fell away and lost their footing. Then the ball was caught by someone's boot and hacked away towards the front of the Walton posts. Gresty for Manchester was the first to it and he ran straight before changing course for the corner, fooling his chasers. Just as the line was below his feet the Walton full-backs moved in and brought him down in a ground-shaking tackle around his shoulders. He dropped the ball just in front of the line, and a scrum was claimed by the Walton captain.

The scrimmage was fierce, and the forwards soon lost sight of the ball as they grappled like bulls locking horns. Splintering away from the scrimmage, a maul developed between Gresty of Manchester and two of the Walton players on the Walton line. The other players stood back, exhausted, watching the three men struggle for the ball in a tangle of hands and elbows. The two umpires came over to the maul, and started to cheer their men on by waving their hats in the air. The referee was talking to the Walton full-backs.

Suddenly the Manchester Athletic captain, prompted by a nod from his umpire, raised his hands and cheered. The other Athletic players clapped, and shouted they had a try. The players in the maul fell away from each other and the ball, which settled on the grass behind the Walton line. The Walton captain, who had been in the maul, shook his head and pointed to his own hand, declaring a touchdown at the most, and his umpire nodded and shouted 'no try!'. The crowd cheered when the try was announced by the Athletic umpire, then cheered as the try was declared void by the Walton umpire.

Humphrey frowned as the players started to argue amongst themselves. The referee was surrounded by Manchester's forwards, and quickly came to a decision favouring them. The Walton players protested, and fists were clenched. The Walton captain was pushed, and half of the players started to fight before the umpires and a few men from the crowd pulled them apart.

By now the crowd was muttering and arguing and hissing their disapproval. Fish was shouting at the club directors, telling them to sort it out before he lost his temper. On the pitch, Manchester were lining up for an attempt at goal, smiling smugly at the flustered Walton players. A fight started at the front of the stand between two rival supporters, and some men started to usher their wives away fearing a riot.

The Walton captain called his men together, and then declared to the crowd that they were not going to carry on unless the decision was rescinded. They walked off the pitch, cheered by some, booed by others, and the club directors in the stand started to argue among themselves. Both club's declared themselves the winners – Walton on the evidence of their goal, Manchester Athletic on account of the fact they had stayed on the pitch. The crowd, angry and confused, spilled over the fence onto the ground, where some of the Athletic players were pushed and punched. The rest of the crowd joined in the arguments, declaring for one team or another. Fish cried for help, and Harry found three players from the Preston North End club to usher them both to safety.

Humphrey stayed in the stand, brooding over what had happened.

Nobody could decide who'd won the match. Both sides said they'd won, and looked to Fish to make a decision. Fish didn't understand the problem, and suggested the teams ask an expert on football. The problem needed the attention of someone of importance who would satisfy both teams, since the result of the match decided who would go through to the next stage of the Cup. It wasn't a normal match where the toss of a coin could settle the argument. So the decision went to the Union in London, who had never needed to make a decision before.

Fish was confident they'd make the decision for Christmas. The match between Walton and Manchester Athletic didn't deter him from promoting his spectacle. The other first round fixtures could be played without waiting for the Union to finish its endless debates over the result of the second match and the legality of the whole competition. Talk of clubs going on strike and refusing to meet their fixtures with the clubs in the Cup proved to be just the talk of a strange alliance of obstinate reactionaries and wild-eyed revolutionaries. A few personal visits by Harry Hibbert and Humphrey Whittle, on behalf of the Raikes Hall Company, reassured the small clubs that no one was about to strike them off their fixture card. Fish convinced everyone that since the union was judging the outcome of the second match, they had set a precedent accepting the official nature of the cup competition. Whether he convinced himself was another matter entirely, and what few friends he had made sure they kept out of his way, and people in Blackpool claimed they could hear his high-pitched cries of anguish from one end of the Fylde Coast to the other.

Rossendale v Whitworth and the Preston Derby

The last two matches of the first round, however, passed with both good crowds and without any further disputes. Rossendale, who had only just been formed, showed the strength of their Masonic backers by fielding a side rumoured to have been picked from the best footballers north of Manchester. Whitworth, who had previously claimed two of the Rossendale men as their own, were hard pressed to match their opponents – technically their juniors – and although they had possession of the ball at most of the scrimmages they were unable to match Rossendale's solitary goal with one of their own.

The match was played in front of the biggest crowd of the competition so far, mainly local people who had taken advantage of a fine, unusually mild autumn day to sample the new sport and see what all the fuss was about. They cheered as soon as Rossendale's big forward Wright booted the ball into the clouds, then cheered again as Leach made a clean catch for Whitworth at the other end. Seizing his chance, Leach ran down the side of the pitch, holding the ball ready to kick ahead of him as if it was a bomb of some kind. Then he collided with one of Rossendale's backs and the ball was hacked away over the far wall to splash into the lake between surprised boaters and lovers.

After this daring display of running football, both sides slowed the game down by keeping the scrimmage wheeling around in the centre of the field. Whitworth managed to force Rossendale into touching down in-goal after a collective dribble, but the Rossendale captain Scheidler showed his athletic skill by running free from a scrum and dodging the tacklers until he set his side up for a try at goal. This was kicked with a resounding smack of leather, and the ball rebounded off the Rossendale umpire over the crossbar. The Whitworth players objected to this intervention by their rivals' own umpire, but a referee was on hand at the side to decide in favour of the goal.

Whitworth tried again and again to level the score, but to no avail. Although they forced Rossendale to make three touchdowns and one touch-in-goal, pressing them back beyond their goal and leaving them no room, they failed to convert their three tries into the elusive goals they needed. By the end, their anguish was evident to all in the crowd, who sympathised with their occasional and colourful cries of despair. When Warburton, a Whitworth back, found himself in front of the Rossendale goal an audible gasp of anticipation rose. He dropped the ball to kick it, but the ball rebounded from the bottom of the post into the grateful hands of a Rossendale defender. Seeing this, Warburton fell to his knees and looked at the ground dejectedly, though he waved a hand at the crowd to show his thanks for their muted applause. The Whirtworth forwards continued to heave with all their might over the loose ball, hacking and kicking to try and get possession, but time was called soon afterwards.

Some of the Blackpool crowd were perplexed that Whitworth had lost after all their effort, but luckily Fish had printed a guide to the rules, which he hawked in the moments when the ball was dead. It was inaccurate and based on a conversation he'd had with Harry, whose grasp of the subtleties of the game was hardly better than Fish's. Nonetheless it sold better than the hot pies at the pie-stall, and served as an explanation to the press who inquired after the match about who had won and whether anyone was taking the decision to their solicitor.

December came and finally the last match of the round was played in a bitter Siberian wind between the two Preston clubs. It was a proper 'derby' match, with both sides keen to pummel the stuffing out of one another like housewives spring-cleaning cushions. A cold chill had descended from the sea, putting off a good portion of those who had watched the previous match. The Preston element of the crowd, however, was fiercely partisan and the atmosphere was tense, though softened in places by the neutral football fans who made jokes whenever the arguments were about to turn into fights. North End's team was disorganised, and too many players were willing to give orders but not take them. They squabbled among themselves as to who should kick, and who should pass. Olympic, on the other hand, kept the ball in the scrimmage as much as they could, and steadily pushed their way across the field. It was a grim, dour match, with the one side making mistakes and losing the ball, and the other refusing to let the crowd see anything except the slow movement of the scrum. Scuffles broke out at the edges of mauls and after every tackle, so that a good part of the time was spent settling quarrels. As the sky went dark the game was settled by Olympic obtaining a try for goal, which then sailed high over one of the posts, so that it was impossible for either umpire to judge how it had flown. This 'poster', however, proved sufficient in giving them the laurels, and North End had to be content with being the second-best team in Preston.

The North End club chairman complained afterwards about the unfair nature of the Cup, and the over-enthusiasm of the Olympic's players. He was an ex-player from the early days of the game, when it was the domain of a tiny number of ex-public schoolboys and teachers. He carried himself with an arrogant swagger, letting his large frame speak for itself and looking contemptuous whenever he was forced to speak with a lesser being. Since he assumed he was from the finest class in England, and had suffered the best education in the world, he was contemptuous of nearly everyone he ever met - but most of all he reserved his ire for the keen businessmen with little proper education and certainly no time at college in their curriculum vitae, men who seemed to dominate Lancashire and football, men like Harry Hibbert. It was no surprise for those close to the Lancashire game that he soon after switched his club to the association code, which at that time was still controlled by Old Etonians.

After the match the press inquired of Fish as to the date of the finals. He promised them that the 1878 Northern Challenge Cup Competition would be over before the end of the year, and if it wasn't he would allow them to drag him over hot coals. He told them that he'd heard informally from a source close to the committee passing judgement on the second match that they would be coming to a decision by the middle of the month, which meant the finals could go ahead as planned around the Christmas holiday. He suggested that Preston Olympic would give Chorley a good challenge, which to some of the journalists was somewhat presumptuous since they thought the draw was yet to be made. But he ignored their questions on the matter, and promised he'd have a plate of Christmas pudding for each of them at the final on the 28th December.

9.

The Wasteland and the Passion

ONE DAY BEFORE THE FINAL was supposed to take place, Harry Hibbert admitted defeat on the matter and scratched it from the fixture list, cursing the Union for its lack of business sense and John Fish for failing to take full responsibility for the affair. The last letter he'd received from Fish had assured him that a decision was about to be made and they could go ahead with engraving the trophy with the name of the winning side, which of course they already knew. Harry had done so since the trophy was in his keeping following the debacle of the second match, when Fish had feared some irate customer would break into his offices in Blackpool and take the Cup for himself.

The winter was the coldest one Harry Hibbert had known. He wasn't a man to complain about the cold, as he would often say once he was safely enthroned in a chair next to a warm fire with a hot toddy in his hand. As far as he was concerned it was a test of a man's character and those who couldn't face a freezing gale or a snow blizzard were either effete or lazy, metropolitan types. Nonetheless, it was as if the Nordic gods had declared the Ragnarok, the End of the World, and were riding across the north of England on chariots of ice, breathing cold winds that sucked the warmth out of every living thing. Snow at Christmas was a pleasant thing, but the winter of 1878 brought with it only slashing rain and gusts of freezing air that stabbed their way through layers of clothing to cut into bones.

It wasn't a natural winter, people were saying. Harry agreed, especially when his feet turned blue with the first signs of frostbite. He had his hands full with charitable work, trying to overcome the worst Jack Frost could offer, distributing hot broth and blankets made from offcuts to the destitute. It was unpleasant work sitting on a committee and judging one man's misfortunes over another, but it was essential to ensure that only the needy were cared for and not those who could look after themselves. He sat alongside the elder Whittle, the chairman, who saw the Poor Board as a way of weeding out the workshy and feeding those who were willing to work. Weeding and feeding, he would remind his fellow altruists. Even Harry - who believed unquestioningly in the value of free trade and the market - was disturbed by the man's single-mindedness on the subject of welfare.

The football club, with free weekends either side of the Christmas holiday when the finals should have been held, organised a rifle-shooting competition and a raffle in aid of the Poor Board, which although well-received by the public was little consolation for the players. Some, such as the student doctor Marsh went off to play for other teams. Marsh ended up guesting with Gartside for a club in the shadow of the Pennines amidst rumours of duck roasts being offered on top of generous travelling expenses. Others such as Lever and Garstang joined the first teams of junior clubs in the Chorley and Horwich area, where their appearance was treated as nothing more than a chance to snatch a victory in the keenly contested Christmas derby fixtures.

Humphrey spent the Christmas break fuming over the audacity of Lindsey, blotting out the man's face as he ground his boots into the grass, or seeing it on the side of a ball as he kicked it with all his might for Leo to catch. The break from football gave him a chance to train his body, improve it in the manner the missionary taught them, stretching each muscle and working it until he could feel it no more. He found it useful to focus his attention on the meaning of Christmas, dwelling on the gospels as he ran up and down the gardens of Primrose Cottage. Leo joined him in some of the exercises, but only as long as there was a football involved. Needless to say, Humphrey disapproved of Leo's attitude: they needed to be strong, otherwise they would grow weak and die. Or if they didn't die, then they would grow sick like Frederick and Jane, and never recover.

On the day when the final was due to take place, Harry received a letter from John Fish. He was down in London, visiting one of the Union's committee members and had it on good authority that a decision on the result of the second match would be made public in a matter of days. There was no word about the legality of the Cup itself, which remained an issue that the Union couldn't agree on without upsetting either the strong Yorkshire clubs or the university colleges. The compromise, it seemed, was to delay a decision on the matter indefinitely. Nor was there any word of the mounting debts which Raikes Hall had accrued while men from the Whittle market gardens kept the football ground in good condition, ready for a match at short notice. Fish didn't believe in making apologies. The Cup, he told Harry, would go ahead, and Chorley would get the trophy for which they'd worked so hard. This did at least cheer Harry, and he spent the new year in the snug of the *Rose and Crown* discussing his plans for the club - long tours and new stands - with Humphrey.

The following week they were due to play Broughton Rangers, a team from Manchester who had refused to play in the Cup for fear of losing their status in the eyes of their close rivals from the city's main football club. At Dole Lane, the rain and cold winds had turned the ground into a flour-speckled skating rink, and Harry had Mister Ditchfield borrow the brass and glass paraffin heaters from the town hall to try to thaw out the hard tufts of grass and the biggest puddles in the middle of the pitch where the scrimmages had formed small trenches. The team gathered at the pub on the Thursday before the match and were reassured by Harry that the game would be on, and posters went up suggesting the same on every corner in the town centre. He had made a deal with a farmer who laid out straw where the heaters had turned the ice to slush. The straw served as a blanket to insulate those areas and stop them from freezing over in the middle of the night.

After he had spoken to the players, Marsh came up to him with a friendly, innocent smile on his face. He sat down in the snug with Harry, who ushered Humphrey away to buy him a bottle of pale ale. When they were alone, Marsh looked up to make sure there were enough people talking, then whispered:

'And what about if the match ain't on? Do I still get what's owed me?'

Humphrey heard Marsh from the bar, picking out the student's voice amidst the clamour of calls and coarse jokes. He listened to Harry reply that there would be something after dinner even if the match was called off. He knew what that meant, but he didn't want to confront Harry. He didn't want to upset the club and his friend, and find out something he didn't want to know. He told himself he'd misheard both of them, or perhaps misunderstood what was being said. The accusations about the Cup and its impurity were beginning to affect them all, and he had allowed them to shape his own perceptions. He shook his head - Marsh had to be talking of something other than money.

Despite the precautions, Chorley's friendly match against Broughton Rangers was one of the first victims of that winter's great freeze. It started to snow at around mid-day on the Saturday of the match, covering the brown ice that had stuck to the streets of the town. On the roof of the town hall, snow drifts appeared between gargoyles and lead piping. The town-hall clock stopped, its clockwork gears frozen. The street traders and beggars who cluttered the market square had hobbled off to get warm in gin shops in the alleys by the train track. The entrance to the train station was hot and smoky, its high roof blackened by soot. Urchins were huddled in the corners fighting over sweets and pennies, savouring the hot air from the steam engines outside and the coal braziers on either side of the ticket office. Flakes of snow caught by the wind were flicked into the entrance to die a quick death, melting as they met the draughts of smoke and steam.

In the entrance of the train station, Harry looked out at the swirling gusts of snow and smacked his lips in disgust. There was still no telegram at the station's telegram office. The street was obscured by the snow and the snow's dark clouds. Sulphur and coke hung in the air, forcing people to put handkerchiefs over their mouths. Down the road towards Preston, near the edge of town, Dole Lane had disappeared under the snow, its stand a strange clash of white space and shadows. Mister Ditchfield pushed the gate shut and fumbled through thick gloves to lock the icy padlock. The only sound was that of the warm revelry up the lane behind the steamed-up windows of the *Rose and Crown*. With brandy and porter warming their bellies, the club's directors and players watched the weather and were glad they were inside the pub. Out of the town, at Primrose Cottage, Humphrey watched the snow falling on the trees in the garden and clenched his fists impatiently.

For a brief moment Chorley was a contrast of clean white spaces and black shadows, the broken cobbles and damaged slates smoothed over by a delicate stroke of snowflakes. Then the ash being spewed out by hundreds of chimneys, finding the sky lower than normal, fell quickly back down amidst the snow, speckling the drifts and turning them into sleeping dalmatians.

Less than a week after the cancelled Broughton Rangers match, Harry received two urgent telegrams. One was from the club secretary at Widnes, who was having to apologise in advance for withdrawing from a match they were due to play against Chorley. Their pitch was frozen by the same cold spell that had settled on the north of Lancashire, and because so many players had injured themselves in the previous weekend's matches they were forced to accept public opinion and cancel all matches until there was a thaw. Harry was disgusted at this attitude, but it wasn't unexpected: the papers, including those in Chorley, had allowed a discordant note to appear in their coverage of football, condemning clubs for putting their players at risk on hard pitches.

The second telegram was from John Fish, who was still in London. The Union had decided that Walton had forfeited the match when they'd left the field before the finish, so Manchester Athletic won by default. The Cup had its finalists at last - but the small matter of the weather was still to be resolved.

Harry and Humphrey met Fish at the gates of the Raikes Hall Gardens. His stay in London had left him unprepared for the cold winds blowing across the Irish Sea and swirling in the wake of the Lake District, and he was shivering and cursing every icy touch. Like the two Chorleymen he was wearing a heavy greatcoat, a thick woollen scarf, gloves and a balaclava, so that the three of them looked like veterans from the Crimean War. Although it wasn't snowing and the sun made occasional appearances from behind windswept low cloud, the temperature was freakishly cold. Small clouds of breath clung to Fish's balaclava, his nose was red and a drop of watery phlegm on the end of it threatened to turn to ice.

'Quite nippy, eh? Someone forgot to pay the coalman, eh?' joked Fish uncertainly. He swiftly moved on, in case they started a conversation he had no hope of following. 'Well then, down to business, don't you think? I trust everything is ship-shape regarding the Cup?'

'Just a few minor problems, Fish, such as the lack of the finals and the small matter of it being 1879 not 1878, mere trifles,' replied Harry.

'Of course,' grinned Fish, choosing not to notice the sarcastic tone of Harry's voice. He gestured with his hand inside the Gardens. 'Although I dare say we will have a grand final, one to be proud of, as soon as we choose the finalists.'

'You don't choose the finalists, Mister Fish, if anyone chooses it's the players, out on the pitch,' said Humphrey.

Fish smiled, then put his shoulder to the gates. Ice crunched and with a shattering noise the gates freed themselves and were slowly pushed inwards, shovelling up the thin layer of hard snow that lay on the ground. Beyond the gates the gardens were black and desolate: the trees were like shadows, the lawns were grey and the streams were frozen. Someone had put rocksalt down on the main path through the gardens, leaving a brown and black scar on the untouched snow.

'Well, let me show you chaps something, then we can discuss who plays who in the finals.'

'Oh? What is there to discuss?' asked Humphrey.

'Come on, Humphrey, you knew all about this beforehand, and don't pretend yer've 'ad a knock on that 'ead of yours, neither,' said Harry, taking Humphrey's arm and trying to pull him into the Gardens with Fish. 'Them as don't ask any questions don't get no answers, isn't that right, Mister Fish?'

'Of course, Mister Hibbert,' said Fish, nodding his head with approval. 'We could always scratch Chorley from the Cup if you're not happy with the arrangements we've made. It's not as if we're cheating now, is it? More ensuring it's profitable, like.'

'Mister Fish!' exclaimed Harry, glancing around the street. The few people who were out trying to stay upright on the slippy cobbles were not stopping to listen.

'Well, you agreed, Humphrey, it's the same with the market, isn't it?' said Fish.

'Oh come now! The market is unrestrained by anything except competition! The market is free! That's surely a principle of human life!' argued Harry, losing sight of the aim of their conversation.

'Please, Mister Hibbert, I know all that, but a good businessman makes sure that the market is always in his favour. How else do you make decisions unless you have some knowledge of the workings of other companies, their profits and losses? I'm a gambling man, Mister Hibbert, but I won't back odds I haven't had a go at fixing,' said Fish. 'Now we're all agreed that Chorley should win the Cup. Am I right? Do you want to lose? Humphrey? Do you want to lose? Lose the Cup?'

Humphrey saw that the deal was done. His fears about Harry had been confirmed – he and Fish were working to ensure a Chorley victory, whether it was deserved or not. He wanted nothing more than the Cup, the prize. Did it matter that he used all the means at his disposal to get that victory? Would the victory be somehow less real if it wasn't won on the pitch? And what was the difference between fixing the draw, having a quiet word with the other side, and paying someone like Marsh to play? Fish was right – there was no difference. No one would know the victory was anything less than a true one.

But he would know. He didn't want to be given the Cup. He wanted it more than anything because he knew it would win him the respect of his father, his town, his peers. But he wanted it through winning it, so that he wouldn't have to lie. He owed it to himself to stay pure, or else the Cup wouldn't be his. He saw nothing wrong in fixing the draw, but once the two teams were on the pitch it was fifteen against fifteen, man against man. He could see that Fish wouldn't and couldn't understand what sport was about.

'I want to win, Fish, and mark my words I will win. But I will not cheat,' answered Humphrey. 'If you want to do what you did last time with the draw then fine, you know I've nothing against that. But nothing more, understand?'

Harry was silent. He shrugged his shoulders and looked at Fish, who smiled earnestly at Humphrey.

'I'm a man of m'word - there'll be no fixing… how could we do that anyway? If all footballers are like you it'd be an 'ard job just to get them to listen, never mind to accept our suggestions.'

'Don't worry about it, Humphrey, just concentrate on each match as it comes, eh? I reckon a good do against that Preston side'll serve us well,' said Harry, winking at Fish. 'Get it over with as quick as possible, right, Mister Fish?'

Fish stopped smiling, and ushered them into the park.

'Ah, now that's what I wanted to see you about. Come with me.'

They followed him through the frozen gardens. The boating lake had frozen solid, crushing the rowing boats and the weak supports of the willow-pattern bridges. The zoo was silent and the cages empty. The football stand, when they came to it, was creaking under the weight of the snow and ice on the roof. The gates and the turnstile were impossible to move without attacking them with a kettle of hot water. The pitch, from what they could see of it through the gate, was covered in a thin sheet of ice with just a few tufts of grass sticking above it like islands in the sea. And the goalposts nearest to the gate had fallen over.

'I thought your lot were looking after it, Humphrey,' frowned Harry.

'We had to lay people off because of the weather...'

'Well, whoever's to blame, there'll be no football played on this pitch until the spring,' said Fish.

'But what about the Cup?' asked Humphrey.

Fish smiled, and opened his hands in an apologetic manner.

'The only cup anyone's going to be playing for round 'ere is an ice-skating cup.'

The Semi-Finals

Fish claimed that the winter freeze was to their advantage, and when he announced that the Cup was to continue he also declared - with no sense of modesty or irony - that the freeze was a sign that powers even higher than John Fish wanted the final to end at the Easter holiday. The Passion of Christ, declared Fish, would be nothing to the passion of the football players. The reporters loved this minor blasphemy, and thanks to their mild condemnations of Fish's comparisons, everyone knew that the Northern Challenge Cup Finals were set to kick-off on the first of March.

Humphrey was more circumspect, and stayed within the bounds of taste, by suggesting the footballers would be worshipping Christ by following the example of His physical exertions against the Devil in the desert of Judea. Christ, said Humphrey before he went out to play against Preston Olympic, would have been a footballer if he'd been born an Englishman.

Chorley showed no mercy to Preston Olympic, who were defeated as thoroughly as the tribes of Canaan by Joshua.

Humphrey excelled himself, careless of injury, playing the full eighty minutes of the match as if he was indestructable. He exhorted his fellows in the scrimmage to push the Olympic side all the way back down the Preston Road and off the Fylde Coast, forcing them to give up the ball and the game. Initially, with the advantage of the ball in their hands, Preston Olympic's backs managed to take the game into the Chorley half of the pitch. They threw the heavy ball as if it was the size and weight of an apple, passing back to a man in support as soon as the Chorley defenders came in for the tackle. The two half-backs played with Chorley like this for a good few minutes, frustrating Humphrey, who considered too much passing of the ball a sign of a soft and pampered upbringing. Like his fellows in the Chorley forwards, who were forced to chase the ball like children after a spinning-top, Humphrey believed the true nature of the game was in the matching of brute force against brute force. And although he tackled the men to the ground, rubbing their faces into the grass for good measure, they were soon back on their feet and calling for the ball. But their speed was not matched by dexterity, and having slipped, their half-back Dennison was covered in eager Chorleymen hacking for the ball. When a scrum was called the Preston pack found themselves outweighed and slipping backwards. Humphrey cheered as he heard the crunch of a nose being crushed by his carefully placed knee. The Preston line collapsed, overpowered by the size of the Chorley pack, and to the crowd's disappointment they chose to concede touchdown after touchdown rather than stand up and fight.

In the centre of the pitch, Humphrey relaxed his shoulders and smiled at his men.

'We're up against women, chaps! Let's make them hurt!' he growled, slapping Garstang's mighty back. 'Damn the cowards for not playing up!'

Leo listened to the sound of men being pushed to the floor, the dull thuds and groans that made his own bones ache in sympathy. Whilst one of their full-backs fell on the ball on his own line to concede a touchdown to Chorley, the other was being helped off the field by their umpire with blood running from his scalp. That would need a splash of spirit and a tot of whisky. He heard the Preston captain asking Humphrey whether he would lay off a bit and be sporting. Leo didn't have to hear to know what Humphrey's answer would be.

It was an easy match for Chorley, playing as they were like devils.

By the halfway point, a long, staggering dribble with the ball by one of the Mockett brothers had given Chorley a try at goal, though the kick at goal had failed. However, with the restart of hostilities Humphrey barged his way across the field, throwing off tacklers with a shrug of his shoulders, to set his side up for another goal. Again Lever failed to make the kick, but Olympic had, as Harry explained to his guests in the stand, lost the stomach for it. They were forced to defend for the rest of the match, trying to save themselves from too much damage and resorting to grabbing hold of Chorley's shirt-collars to slow them down. They managed to rip off Humphrey's collar and bruise his neck, but their tired arms couldn't stop Brindle and one of the Mockett brothers making tries successfully converted by Lever.

Chorley won by two goals and two tries to none, with eleven touchdowns to their credit. The crowd cheered every Chorley move, and Humphrey found himself the rather uncomfortable focus of female attention for some weeks afterwards. They would smile at him, beg for favours, reach out in a crowded street to touch the back of his coat. It amused his friends, though he would do his best to make the women disappear. Whenever he went for a walk from Primrose Cottage into the fields and back along the railway line to the centre of town he was mobbed by excited folk keen to say they had had a word with their once and future king. These encounters, although difficult when they happened, always proved warming once they were over. It was good to be adored.

When time was eventually declared, the fourteen Olympic players left standing sighed in relief. They were thoroughly dishevelled, and limped off the pitch with their heads low as soon as they had shook the hands of the victorious Chorley men. At the end of the season they switched to association football, and the Chorley team knew in their hearts it was because the Preston men were too scared to face them ever again.

The second semi-final was played in front of a small crowd of a few hundred, which was boosted by the presence of the Chorley team and its officials who were the official guests of Raikes Hall. The atmosphere was muted except where the Chorley players, flush with bottles of Scotch, sang rousing songs to entertain and shock the women. Some gentlemen of the press sitting in front of the stand speculated that the 'whitewash' given Preston by Chorley had put off the neutral spectators of the Fylde coast, who were used to seeing more even spectacles at sporting contests. John Fish blamed the reporters for questioning in the papers whether the final itself was a foregone conclusion, following Chorley's superhuman performance in the first semi-final. He called them troublemakers to their faces and refused to comment on the size of the crowd, leaving them bemused and desperately seeking a shareholder for copy. Humphrey had been about to mention that the Whittles had a stake in Raikes Hall before

Harry explained about pecuniary interests and potential conflicts. The press, explained Harry, would always make connections on the flimsiest of evidence, relying more on speculation and inference than deductive logic. A good politician always kept quiet about such matters in case someone mistakenly assumed something - having a shareholder playing for one of the teams in the Cup would, said Harry, lead some to think that such a team was inevitably favoured.

Harry said this without showing any acknowledgement of its hypocrisy. Humphrey kept quiet. The only thing a reporter would find - knowing the conflict of interests and the history of the Cup - would be the truth. The example Harry had mentioned was too true to be comforting.

It was fortunate that the crowd was so low, because the second semi-final was a game appreciated more by the players than the spectators, who cared not for the mysteries of physical contact out of sight of all but the expert's eye. Although the Chorley men found much in the fiendish scrimmaging and kicking of both teams to keep them enthralled, the lack of any open play encouraged the crowd to find something else to do whilst the scrums shook the ground. The impatient shouts of the half-backs, who followed the scrum waiting for the ball to roll clear, echoed around the ground. Rossendale, led by their young captain Frank Scheidler, proved to be the heavier of the two sides, and this gave them a slight advantage in the scrum. They employed a three man front row, with the other forwards moving around to keep this line firm. Athletic were forced to match them and the scrimmage remained in the same place for minutes on end as both sides heaved and kicked and pushed in an attempt to gain the ball. For the three-quarter backs, there was little to do except borrow the odd cigarette from the crowd and talk to the umpires. They watched their fellows stumble from one part of the field to the other, neither side able to free the ball from the human slag-heap of the scrum. For the players who hacked at each other it was a manly battle, but one which was by necessity a private affair. Their backs were turned to the spectators, their eyes only on the muddle of boots and the fleeting glimpses of brown leather between them. When the ball did come free it was quickly booted off the field, as if it had no right to be there.

After the usual half-time interval the weight began to tell on Manchester Athletic who, although they had the wind in their favour, were penned in on their own half for most of the time. Their shoulders dropped and their legs slipped. Rossendale, sensing the weakening of their rivals, doubled their efforts at every scrum, pushing forwards until they were in a position to kick the ball down towards the Athletic line. It was a slow, methodical war of attrition.

In the grandstand people lost interest. They started to talk to each other in quiet voices about the weather (which was fine), the price of tea (which was very low) and the situation in the southern reaches of Africa (which was very grave). Humphrey found this indifference to the matching of men's strengths infuriating, and after hearing two men offer their opinions on the best mutton in Blackpool he couldn't stop from shouting at them to watch the game - or else he would box their ears. The Chorley players and the club officials laughed heartily but there were a few mutters of shame from others in the crowd.

It seemed as if neither side was capable of making a try for goal, and as the afternoon grew dim the umpires consulted on whether or not to call for a draw, which would then be decided on the touchdowns marked up against each side in the few times either one had threatened the other's line. Fish was despairing at the prospect of a football match with no goals, and took up a position on the far side of the pitch so that he could shout coarse words of encouragement at whoever had the ball. His offer of a jug of ale for the man who scored a goal was heard by the nearest umpire, who politely but firmly reminded him that the rules of the Union forbade any cash incentive or payment in kind. Fish started to say something about the rules of the Union - and where the umpire could put them - when without warning Scheidler had the ball in his hands clear of the confused mass of forwards and raced between the Manchester full-backs.

The crowd cheered with relief as he put the ball down with a gentle press of his small hand to keep it in place on the grass. His fellow players rushed towards him to shake that hand and congratulate him. The handful of Rossendale supporters clapped and waved their home-made rattles, deafening the respectable folk sitting nearby who were more restrained in their celebrations. Humphrey leaned forward to observe Scheidler, to better understand how the man moved, admiring his new enemy.

With the time up and the crowd restless, Rossendale's full-back Barker failed to kick the goal. But the try was enough to save Fish an awkward moment with the Union, and ensure that Rossendale were through to the final. The teams clapped each other off the pitch, and Humphrey watched Scheidler walk back to the cart that would take the Rossendale players to their hotel. Scheidler climbed up at the back, helped up a limping forward, then glanced back at the grandstand.

Humphrey knew Scheidler was looking for him, trying to get the measure of him. He turned away to stare out across the red-brick suburbs of Blackpool. They would meet soon enough.

10.

The Wedding

ELLEN MORETON BECAME NELLIE WHITTLE on the 29th of June, 1889, barely a year after she had first seen Humphrey on the street heading towards the party at the *Rose and Crown*. Humphrey was thirty-seven, twelve years older than her. Somehow she'd expected him to want their wedding reception to be held in the same place, a romantic gesture tinged with nostalgia and manliness. But she soon realised that he wouldn't think it proper for a man of his standing to behave like a common worker, celebrating with beer instead of fine French wines. The wedding was an essential part of Humphrey's long campaign to replace Harry Hibbert as the town's Member of Parliament, and as such the details of the wedding became as important as the wedding itself. Humphrey could eat out on the tales from the football pitch, and charm the electorate by talking about those days, but they wouldn't win him the approval of the old men who controlled the council and the party. Everything had to be just right, so that these men would approve of him, and whisper their approval to the eager reporters from the local press. When Nellie realised this, she realised also that she had a part to play in furthering Humphrey Whittle's political career, a part for which she had been chosen in the same way Humphrey chose the wedding guests. Stock and Garstang, for example, the working-men from the team, although welcome at the reception, were not invited to the church.

The reception, after some careful planning, was held at Primrose Cottage, which was decorated with garlands of white flowers, pink roses, long ribbons of pale green, cream and white. The motif chosen was that of the Garden of Eden - exotic plants from the colonies filled every corner and alcove in Ming-dynasty stylised pottery, creeping vines and bushes were turned into columns and archways inside the house, and the beds on either side of the lawns were bursting with bright blue and red foxgloves, roses, tulips and huge varieties of a sky-blue chrysanthemum. In the dark green privet hedges and the branches of fruit trees in the orchard were hung Chinese lanterns, ready to illuminate the evening like leaf-tangled stars.

The elder Whittle, face crumpled, hair white, wanted no part to play in the planning, other than ensuring there was a plentiful supply of sherry and port to help him sleep off the dinner of roast duck and Yorkshire pudding. His insistence that a true Englishman cared nothing for fancy foreign ideas such as the difference between an *aperitif* and a *digestif* was, said the younger aldermen, another sign of the senility of the town's father. In the council chamber the elder Whittle had taken to snoring loudly through speeches and complaining about a Russian hussar who seemed to stand just on the edge of his vision, saluting with his sword whenever a resolution was passed. This hussar, it transpired, followed the elder Whittle home, where he had been found in the orchard, the cupboards and the garden borders. The elder Whittle refused to listen to reason when he was found urging the head gardener to beat the hussar out of his hiding place in the laurel bushes. His insistence that extra sherry and port had to be bought was a relief to the Whittle family, who feared the Garden of Eden would have too many serpents in the fruit trees, waiting for the old patriarch, if he was still awake.

It was, thought Humphrey, typical of his father: as soon as he had announced his engagement to Nell, his father had lost the capacity to congratulate him. Humphrey had hoped that for once his father would be proud, would stand shoulder to shoulder with him at the front of the church with a manly tear of pride glistening in his eye. But they were losing the elder Whittle, losing him in the same way they had lost Jane - sent to the hydrotherapists to drench the hysteria with freezing water - and palsy-riddled Frederick. Humphrey knew if he wasn't careful the demons would catch him too.

The actual wedding was the responsibility of the Moreton family, who were long established landowners with smallholdings across Lancashire and Cheshire. Mister Moreton spent his time signing letters of contract for his managers, reading scientific journals and collecting butterflies, which he displayed in glass cases in every room of the Moreton home. His wife, abandoned in favour of dead insects, lived a free and fruitful life running charitable hospitals for the poor. Although the marriage vows remained strong, Nellie's parents spent very little time with each other. They nodded politely at one another like strangers whenever they happened to meet by chance on the staircase. Nevertheless, they had somehow managed to raise a family of five daughters, of whom two tended towards the taxonomic way of life, and three to the practical. Nellie considered herself to be firmly in the latter camp, and although she loved her father she would object to anyone who suggested there was a Darwinian similarity between them.

There was little difficulty for the Whittle family in persuading the learned and erudite Mister Moreton that it was the most rational solution for the wedding to take place in Chorley, away from the Moreton's sacred ground. There was still some value in the elder Whittle's standing in the Lodge, which gave him a measure of support in gently twisting Mister Moreton's arm, even if his fellows in the Craft did their best to stop him attending official engagements lest the hussar appeared. Chorley was where Humphrey was known, so Chorley was where Humphrey was to have his wedding. His mother, who had become a spiritualist in the hope of speaking to Jane, wanted it to be held at one of her halls, but it was only proper that they were wed in a normal, respectable Anglican church.

Mister Moreton, ignoring the entreaties of wife and family, chose a church outside Chorley's centre, close to Primrose Cottage and the farmlands stretching away to Preston and beyond to the fells. It was a modest early modern church with a mock-Norman tower resting on real foundations. Its parish vicar – a good friend of the retired Reverend Smith – was a believer in the High Church, and promised a solemn occasion worthy of the names of both families. The bells rang, the choir sang, the churchyard was blessed with an old yew tree and freshly cut grass. Mister Moreton inspected the red and brown butterflies resting on the gravestones whilst his wife and daughters fussed over the florist and the arrangements for all the guests. The vicar worried that he would disappoint on the day, in front of Chorley's gentry, and never reach the hallowed ranks of the bishopric.

The day of the wedding came, a warm if not hot Saturday in the middle of August, when the dry earth scent of the wheat fields mingled with burnt herbs to make eyes sting and noses run. The florists finished decorating Primrose Cottage, the carriages and the cloistered chamber of the church. The first guests arrived at the church to be ushered to their pews by Nellie's nephews, or to stroll pleasantly across the deep green grass of the paupers' graves. The vicar, robed in white and black with a purple vestment, whispered frantically to the master of the choir and the verger, worrying about things over which he had no control. At the back of the church, in a pew by the doors placed there for the most wretched of parishioners, the Reverend Smith, he who had tried to exorcise the evil sprits in Jane's mind, waited like an official from the football union to judge the vicar's performance.

Inside, the church was bigger than it appeared from the outside, the designers having used a combination of Gothic arches, flying buttresses and false alcoves to make the sacred space as big as possible. The cross of the building was squashed, so that the nave was a large, broad space, and the chapels on either side of the altar were small and of little importance - in one a small font, in the other a commemoration of the men who had paid for the building. Behind the altar and the small lectern hung the colours of local regiments that had fought in the Crimea and in Africa, bright red and blue flags ablaze with gold thread. These and the tubs of flowers arranged at the ends of each pew brightened up what was otherwise an airy but grey interior - the stained glass windows were cheap imitations of windows to be found in Lancaster, and failed to illuminate the wooden pews with the full spectrum of the rainbow.

At Primrose Cottage, Humphrey was dressed and ready to leave a good ten minutes before the rest of his entourage emerged onto the driveway. His grey morning suit was topped by a stiff grey top hat with white band and a mahogany cane tipped with a gold handle. Closer inspection of the gold handle would have revealed it to be in the shape of a new rugby football, a fat egg of leather panels stitched together, though of course in his day they had played with a round ball. He had trimmed back his moustache and his sideburns, along with his hair, which had such a severe cut that it was impossible to see under his hat's brim.

He paced up and down, pausing only to take his fob watch out from his pocket and curse at the moving hands. In front of him, on the lawn stretching down towards the orchard, men were rigging up a red and white canvas tent, where the wedding guests would eat, drink and dance in honour of the new Mr and Mrs Whittle. The thought of it made his stomach twist into knots. He had to be married, he had found a wife, done everything they expected of him, respectability, responsibility. But how could he love her? He'd tried to find that emotion, tried to love her, but her touch only reminded him of the touch of others, cheap and worthless like a music-hall song. How could his love be pure when the memory of each shameful moment still stirred him, their meaning as clear to him as the writing on the wall in the Book?

He shook his head, shaking away the dark clouds placed there by that other Humphrey Whittle, the one whom he imagined to be a malevolent spirit dwelling inside his head, who struggled for control of the machine that was his body. His soul was clean, he had committed no sin – it was this other one he blamed, the one that whispered foul and lustful suggestions when he lost his way in municipal papers and service contracts.

Leo bounded down the few steps in front of the porch, dressed in a morning suit cut from the same cloth as Humphrey's. He wore his hat at a jaunty angle like a football cap, and had a buttonhole blooming with a red rose. He smiled, smiling at the sun in the trees, the men on the lawn, the maids staring out of the window, his brother. He saw a small rock on the edge of the drive and tapped it forward with the inside of his foot, allowing it to turn over and bounce upwards, before he punted it hard and straight down the gravel to the open gates of Primrose Cottage. It was an association football kick, aimed low below the bar for a goal. Humphrey knew his brother played 'soccer' for a respectable side in Blackpool, close to the market gardens they owned. It had beaten rugby football across the north of England – Humphrey was glad of that, even though he never liked soccer, because it was some kind of revenge on the horrible Tykes who had ruined the spirit of rugby, muddying the clean waters of the spring of athleticism by their arrogance and ill manners. He knew the Union men in London encouraged soccer in Yorkshire as a means of ruining those who were doing their utmost to ruin rugby. There was natural justice in seeing board schools turning to soccer, betraying their own kind who had betrayed the handling code's virtues.

He thought of the men running the rugby game in Yorkshire, and of John Fish at Raikes Hall Gardens. Since the Cup matches, which had taken place a little over ten years before Humphrey's wedding day, Fish had tried his hand at staging exhibition matches of both rugby and soccer, though the powerhouses of both games had long ago moved away from northern

Lancashire, away from Chorley. Rugby had become a game played across oceans, spreading with good manners and modern fashions to the southern colonies. The professionals had helped this growth, of course, with their insidious and secretive ways. Everyone knew that the English tourists who had gone to Australia the year before were paid men, miners and mill-workers with their sham amateur superiors. Humphrey couldn't see anything to cheer about just because rugby was now played in all English parts of the globe. It was no longer his game.

He saw Frederick in the water. He thought of the first match they'd played in Blackpool, the rain and the sense of disappointment, the face of Fish as he told Humphrey how the draw would place Chorley in a favourable position. He thought of Jane, how Nellie reminded him of his dead sister. He thought of Frederick, dreaming of knights and jousts in the sanatorium. He wouldn't be at the wedding, no one in the town could see him, not without ruining Humphrey's political career and making the Whittle's stock worthless.

His father was excused his madness – they called it eccentricity.

'Humphrey, cheer up, wedding's today, isn't it?' asked Leo in the clipped way that was becoming fashionable among the brightest things. He spoke that way naturally, confident in his manner, unafraid of any scolding from their father or some stray schoolmaster.

Humphrey grinned. It was an empty gesture. Leo laughed. It happened to everyone, it was written.

'Nerves, Humphrey, nothing odd there. Where's Lever?'

'I thought he was with you,' said Humphrey.

'Just like old times, eh, Humphrey? The three of us, the triumvirate of Chorley,' smiled Leo. 'See the conquering heroes come, remember that?'

'Leo, I can't get married,' said Humphrey.

Leo smiled. 'Of course, brother. No one can, but they do.'

Lever appeared from the side of Primrose Cottage, dressed in a more expensive, flashy morning suit, which seemed to turn red and green at every crease as he moved, as if he had covered it in one of the dyes from his factory. He was clean-shaven, so much so that he appeared equally to be a boy and girl, without so much as a bristle or wrinkle on his face. He carried his hat in a glove-clad hand, and cooled himself with an Oriental fan decorated with the peacocks from which the fan had supposedly been made. He used this inconspicuously whilst Leo and Humphrey, buttoned up and neatly pressed, slowly roasted.

His shoes glistened where he had waxed them, shining like black diamonds.

'Have no fear, the best man is here, the ring is in my...' started Lever, tapping his waist pocket. He paused and let his face drop in feigned surprise. The two Whittle brothers laughed at his feeble attempt to fool them, and forgot what Humphrey had said. Lever shrugged his shoulders. 'Well, worth a try at least. Oh, don't suppose you'd know what that means now, would you, Leo? Any ill feelings from our stag, Mister Whittle?'

Humphrey shook his head. They'd gone to the *Rose and Crown*, drank with the men, enjoyed rough jokes and the company of drunken women, some of whom Humphrey knew to be whores hired by Lever as a spice for the stag. Humphrey had avoided their lewd attentions all through the night, then used the lascivious hints as an excuse to leave the pub before the night ended. He had left Lever with his nose in the pot, surrounded by rough-faced footballers, singing a ditty about some Mayor's daughter. As for Leo, he had remained sober all night, despite matching his fellow full-back Crumblehulme pint for pint.

'I feel like I am about to go out and face Broughton Rangers,' answered Humphrey.

'Surely not!' exclaimed Lever, nudging Humphrey's left shoulder playfully. 'How could you compare the wonder of a summer's day like this, your wedding, man, with that bunch of disreputable coves. They pay their players now, you know, it's common knowledge, pay them like servants. Those Maoris that toured last winter, they were all on the payroll, you know.'

Leo smiled. He had gone with the Mockett brothers to watch the Maoris, hoping to see a tribe of black fellows throwing a rugby ball around. The novelty had been spoiled by the fact that most of them were in fact as English as Dickens, but the matches had been exciting to watch. The Leigh ground had been packed with men straight from the morning shifts, who cheered on the New Zealanders as much as their local boys. It was all so different to the days when he had visited the ground as a Chorley player. The stands were new, as was the terracing at either end. And the game itself was faster, more open, played with an extra three-quarter and only one full-back after the Welsh fashion. He had watched with amazement as the Leigh side, along with a Chorley man called Coop, had scored two tries and a goal without a Maori reply. It had given him some satisfaction that Coop, whose pass resulted in the second Leigh try, had worked in a Whittle pit until a Leigh director had found him a surface position.

'They were nothing like we were in our prime, you know,' said Leo.

'Surely today's like the Cup, what?' continued Lever, ignoring Leo and responding to Humphrey. 'And a fine prize she is, too, our Miss Moreton, make a man a fine wife.'

Humphrey tried to love her, as he loved the Cup.

Before the reception, before the drink and honeymoon, there had to be the wedding.

Nellie was dressed all in white, save for a sky blue garter hidden under the drifts of taffeta and silk. The pins in her hair, holding it into tight tails attached to her veil, with ringlets teased over her ears and cheeks, were old, bought from a pawn shop in the centre of Chester by her sister. The chain about her neck and its emerald enamel locket was borrowed from Victoria, a good luck charm from the gypsies to ensure good health and prosperity to all who wore it with a pure heart. Apart from the dress, which was covered in translucent shawls flecked with silver flowers, the only new item she wore were her pale cream shoes, built up at the heel to make her taller.

She stepped down from the carriage, taking her father's hand. The bells of the church clattered and clanked, being rung by enthusiastic but musically lacking campanologists from the local society. The path up through the graveyard was carpeted by pink rose petals, strewn there by her bridesmaids, who went ahead of her to wait in the cool shadow of the porch. Her father grinned and stroked his scholar's thick beard, which had grown for no other reason than a lack of attention to mundane matters.

'Bless me, those are fine flowers... they remind me of...'

'Butterflies, father, the ones in the third case from the library door, the second row, they're all pink, aren't they?' said Nellie, interrupting her father impishly.

He harrumphed, failing to hide his loving smile under his yellow-stained whiskers.

They walked up the petal-dressed path, followed by the chief bridesmaids, three cousins eight years old, wearing pale red velvet dresses, white shawls and flowers in their hair. In their hands they held little posies of violets, which they gripped alongside the ends of Nellie's white train. The other bridesmaids joined the end of the procession, Nellie's friends and sisters, sylvan in clinging dresses of dark green and brown scarves.

She walked slowly, measuring each step, testing the reaction of the earth against the pressure of her feet. She felt the stone of the path, the greasiness of softly turned rolls of petal under her soles. Birds sang in the trees – the yew in the graveyard and the silver birches bent over the Church lane. Nellie felt tears on her cheeks, evaporating under the watchful eye of the sun to leave faint trails over her blusher. After they'd first met she knew they were destined to be with each other, had always been joined in spirit, two lovers who had known each other for all time. He was her Othello, a mysterious, silent, brooding lover. He was a standing stone on a silent moor, motionless at the eye of a winter storm, carved with secret hieroglyphs that hid its true purpose. She knew she was the one who would read Humphrey, find the secrets carved on his heart like symbols inside the Pyramids. She felt the places where he had touched her burning with those touches, reminders of walks in the park and evenings in society. She thought of the smile on his face when they'd found their perfect house in the middle of the town, how he'd said they would be better away from Primrose Cottage in a place where they could be alone together.

Birds sang, like angels. They entered the porch, and Mister Moreton nodded at the usher holding the door open. Inside, she could see rows of men and women, dressed in fine clothes and respectable suits. The ones at the back turned around, and this movement passed down towards the altar like a wave on the surface of the sea. She saw the vicar, clutching a book close to his vestments, looking nervously upwards.

In the church, Humphrey felt her arrive and glanced around. He looked down the aisle, and saw her step into the church, led by a bemused-looking Mister Moreton. Somewhere in the church the pipes of the organ wheezed into life and played a passing rendition of 'Here Comes the Bride'. Mrs Moreton started to weep at the sight of her daughter, which disturbed Humphrey. He looked at Lever, who winked, then at Leo in the first pew, next to the space reserved for the Russian hussar. Leo put his thumbs up.

Humphrey looked at his father, who was staring into the distance, seeing other places, listening to other conversations. He patted the space where the hussar's thigh would have been, ignoring the hushed pleadings of

Mrs Whittle. Humphrey looked away, across his family's pews, searching for Frederick. He was alive – why hadn't they invited him? Why was one madman deemed acceptable but two judged too risqué? He wanted Freddy to be there, to watch with pride, to see that his worthless life was more than made up for by his brother's beautiful bride.

He heard the vicar cough politely. He realised he was staring at the wedding guests and turned back to face the front, away from Nellie, who was nearing the front. He could smell the scent of her perfume, a rich fragrance of roses, jasmine and Oriental musks. The vicar smiled, relieved that the preliminaries were over. Lever patted Humphrey on the back, as if he was about to put his shoulder into the scrum and push the opposition away from the football. Humphrey wanted Nellie.

He turned to look at her. She smiled under her veil. He had expected her to be nervous, prim and withdrawn, a virgin. Her smile was warm, needing. He grinned back at her, his heart pounding. He wanted her more than any whore he'd taken in a foul and desperate mood. She was a pagan goddess, incarnate, stirring up unholy humours in his soul. He could feel the hand of the Devil around him, mocking the sanctity of the altar and the words the vicar was saying, out there in the world of politics and football pitches.

She felt him stirring, saw the passion in his eyes. She wanted to kiss him, touch him, take him to bed. She imagined him, naked.

They left the church behind, living the future in their minds. Humphrey glanced backwards, to see if anyone had noticed their behaviour. The pews were still there, the people were still there, listening to the words coming out of the vicar's mouth. And there, on the front pew between Leo and their father, sat the hussar, a huge Russian with a curved sword and a long Tartar moustache.

Humphrey looked away, then back again. The hussar had gone, back into his father's head where he belonged. He frowned, realised he was feeling faint, then remembered how to breathe. He shook his head, trying to bring himself round like he'd done on the pitch whenever someone had knocked him on the head.

He looked at the vicar. He had said something, and was looking at Humphrey. Lever moved an inch forward and nudged him. Nellie looked at him – as did everyone else. He knew what the vicar had said. He could see

Nellie's face, apprehension and impatience.

He smiled.

'I do,' he said.

11.

The Farmer's Cob

IT WAS LATER THAT SHE MET GEORGE SHELLARD: when Humphrey, jealous of Lever and seeking to improve his image, wished to buy a horse for a new carriage. At first she had objected to the idea, having watched their stocks lose their value as the nation's strength was eclipsed by Germany. She suggested that they could buy a bicycle with Dunlop's pneumatic tyres and new braking system, which were all the rage in America – but Humphrey thought such a faddish contraption of cogs and frames was unsuitable for a Briton of any class.

In buying a horse and carriage Humphrey had to employ a groom to look after the stable. After they had married Humphrey and Nellie had lived a while in Primrose Cottage until their home in the centre of town – a Georgian townhouse behind the town hall called Derwent Lodge – was repaired and brought up to the standard expected of a town councillor. Humphrey's intentions had always been obvious, even though he hadn't discussed them with Nellie, for Derwent Lodge's old stables were completely renovated. These were set at the back of Derwent Lodge, a four-storey terrace house, through a gate that led out onto the street under the servants' quarters. There was also a small back alley, leading away from the yard through the properties of the adjoining houses in the direction of the centre of town. When they had bought the house Nellie had expected the old stable to be turned into a wash house for the servants and a private studio, where she would improve her painting without getting in anyone's way. Humphrey had not objected when she raised the idea, and when she saw that his promises of private space had been broken they had their first argument.

Nellie said they didn't need a horse, that they could walk just as easily around the town, or hire men and horses for longer journeys. The Whittle family had enough carriages of their own for Humphrey to use for his work when out inspecting mines and meeting clients.

Initially, Humphrey had ignored her. As far as he was concerned it was his house, and she was his wife, suffering as she gave birth to his babies, and she had to accept what he said. But to his despair he realised she had no intention of obeying his every word, and was as rebellious as a Jacobin woman on the barricades of Paris with the Prussians in the suburbs. He had read in the papers about such women in London, or in America, educated girls with ideas above their place, who wanted to invade and take over all that men had made in the name of civilisation – commerce, universities, government, even sport. It frightened Humphrey; he feared these women were deluded by the aims of the Enlightenment, bereft of sound scientific facts about the differences between the sexes, and raising arguments which would in turn be used by the mob to overturn the natural order as it had almost done in the middle of the century.

When she continued to question him about their finances and the cost of hiring a hand to keep a horse, Humphrey saw her turn into a red-faced, bloody-nosed football player taunting him in the middle of the scrum about his manhood. He shouted at her as loud as he could, scaring the servants and their respectable neighbours as he tried to drown out her rebellious and contradictory words. And still she didn't obey him, still she didn't act like his mother had acted towards his father. Enraged, he had listened to her talk of bicycles with revulsion. He gave her warning to be quiet, then hit her as he would hit a man acting in a slovenly manner in a pithead office.

She said nothing when she was hit. He told her to go and look after the children, even though he knew the sound of their crying put her in a black mood. Shocked, she allowed him to leave and make arrangements for the purchase of a horse and groom. The latter was arranged through the butler of the Moreton family, who had worked with a man considered to be reliable who lived in Chorley town. This man's name was George Shellard – he was a reformed petty thief with a love of horses running through his veins that made Humphrey suspect there was something Romany about him. Humphrey was suspicious of the man's record with the law but Chorley's magistrates were convinced the man had 'learnt his lesson' and by marrying and starting a family showed that even the most baseless of wretch could improve himself. Shellard was in his forties, and was working as a stable hand for an old coaching inn that had survived the building of the railway between Chorley and the towns to the south and west. The offer of the post of groom and double his existing weekly wage was offered to Shellard via the intermediary of the Moreton butler. When he found out who his employer was going to be, George Shellard accepted the job immediately.

An argument over the fair price for a farmer's cob led Humphrey Whittle to his doom. Perhaps he would still have found out about the affair between his wife and George Shellard even if the cob was never bought, would still have reacted with all the anger and despair he felt for his own impotence, his own failings. Perhaps he would have ignored the scandal as he ignored those other things in his life, locked them away so that they would never be mentioned in polite circles. He considered these questions as he sat in the banquet hall, alone amidst the drunken revelry and bawdy humour, knowing Prudence was waiting outside. He considered them, and rejected them.

If not the cob, then something else would have alerted him, and he knew Nellie knew this too. She knew all along there would be no fairy-tale ending, no escape from the evil prince in the arms of the bold champion. It wasn't for love that she slept with Shellard. She didn't expect the world to change – it was a message he failed to read, a truth he knew but couldn't do anything about. That truth was the hardest of truths for Whittle to accept, and he knew it was the truth Prudence was waiting to tell him.

George Shellard didn't believe in handing over his money to his wife for house-keeping. What other men did Shellard considered weak, effeminate, a betrayal of man to that lesser kind. He earned his money and it was his to do with as he pleased, and if she wanted more than he was willing to spend on her then she would have to take a job and pay it out of her own wages. Of course, he was more than happy to take her money, since he was the man of the house, and had certain standards to maintain. What was hers was his and he had the law on his side, and the law of the Bible, to prove it. He'd protected her, given her a home – the least she could do was accept the rule of his belt now and then. He didn't like hitting her but he knew if he relented he'd no longer be a man, and the memory of frightening taunts, of football players sneering at his weak body, made him fear that most of all.

He finished combing what was left of his red hair over the bald patch at the front of his head. He was envious of his friends who still had a full head of hair, and he had a cupboard shelf stacked with bottles of various ointments, pastes and oils that were guaranteed to restore a man's hair to its youthful growth. None of them worked, and he knew each one was as fraudulent as the other, but he still bought them, hoping one day the miracle cure would reach Chorley and turn back the years for him. His wife said he had a high forehead, trying to placate him, but he thought that sounded even worse, as if he had some kind of strange deformity of the head suited for a circus sideshow.

He looked at himself in the mirror and smiled. The strands of hair were stuck in place by the cream on his comb. Satisfied, he put on his bowler hat, straightened his cravat and picked up his keys from the sideboard. He heard his wife moving about in the kitchen, wringing the wet clothes through the mangle. He sniffed and left the house without telling her when he was going to be back. He had his wage from Humphrey Whittle weighing down his trouser pocket and he wasn't going to leave the pub until a good portion of it had been converted into porter.

Humphrey Whittle came back from a meeting in a foul mood. The Tories were cat-calling over the Irish question and the state of the balance of trade, asking whether they were happy to let honest businessmen in Chorley be outpriced by foreigners who could well be the nation's enemies by the end of the century. Humphrey had stood up and condemned them for allowing the politics of the papers to hinder the business of creating a town which would be the envy of the north with something for all its citizens rich or poor. Of course the Tory motion was quickly defeated by moving a procedure to take the vote without further debate, but the good nature that had existed in his first years on the council had been replaced by a dishonest and dishonourable clamour. He didn't blame the Tories for this, for many on his side such as Lever were becoming just as fraught in their municipal work. There was, he thought, a dark cloud threatening to destroy the gains made over the century and reduce towns and factories to ruins as empty as those of Ancient Greece, surrounded by degraded natives and superstitious Turks.

At a time when men of learning and honour needed to have a united front against the growing threat of social disorder, unionism and communistic living, his colleagues were allowing themselves to be riven by dissent. Harry had told him it was the same in the House, that important policy debates were reduced to the level of an association football match, with ungentlemanly players being cheered on in an ugly manner by either side.

Humphrey wanted to have a civilised meal at Derwent Lodge then retire to his own room, where he could read the accounts of the family mines and prepare a speech for a gathering of local party officials in the railwaymen's club. He didn't want to see the children, who were too young to engage in any meaningful, purposeful lessons, and he wanted to avoid Nellie and her irrational, womanly moods. She demanded his attention at the most inconvenient times, and expressed her boredom at her domestic situation as if she was a man housebound by some unfortunate ailment. He couldn't understand why she wasn't content to run the house and do the things women did when they married; and it wasn't as if she was lonely, surrounded as she was by the servants and her maids.

He climbed the steps up to the front door of Derwent Lodge, furling his umbrella as he reached the safety of its porch. As he fastened the umbrella's clips the door was opened, but not by one of the servants. Instead, Nellie herself stood there with the smell of gin sticking to her black dress and shawl. She looked at him, her eyes red with uncontrolled emotion, hot with alcohol. Humphrey sighed and tried to push past her, but she blocked his way with an outstretched arm. Shocked by her insolence, he stepped back, dropping his shoulder as if he was about to join a scrimmage.

'Goodness sake, Nellie, get out of the way,' said Humphrey, looking at her.

She shrugged her shoulders. Behind her, he could see her young maid Prudence waiting patiently in the shadows, her reflection dark in the mirror surrounded by light from the wall lamps. Nellie smiled, and Humphrey realised she was drunk. He sniffed ostentatiously.

'You've been drinking again, woman, a fine example for the children.'

'I'm not drunk, if that's what you're thinking,' replied Nellie, 'though I've had a few, do you blame me? Humphrey, I want you...'

'What?' frowned Humphrey nervously. He didn't like it when she made demands of him; he knew he was weak and liable to give in only to hate himself for enjoying those moments of unreserved, wild passion. He could see that Prudence was listening.

'Let me in, Nellie, I've had a busy evening and it's cold out here.'

'Humphrey, please hold me,' whispered Nellie.

He ignored her and pushed his way past into the hallway. He glared at Prudence and she glanced down at a letter on the sidetable before retreating into the corridor outside the kitchens. He picked up the letter as Nellie slammed the door. It was from her friend Victoria, a note telling her that her mother had passed away in her sleep in the family home without anyone noticing until the next morning. It meant both her parents were dead. Humphrey's head started to pound and he looked desperately at Nellie, trying to say something. His sinews stretched as he struggled to express his sorrow, his sympathy.

Nellie saw the letter in his hands.

'Oh, Humphrey...' she said, tears in her eyes, 'for once, just this once, please, just hold me, I can't believe she's gone... oh Humphrey, please I don't want us to end up like that, I don't want to die without you being there...'

She walked towards him, and he felt his temperature rising. First the Tories, then this! He thought about the deaths he had known, the moment he had considered Frederick to be dead, the relief when his father died, putting to rest the Russian hussar and the Turkish horde that followed him in his final days. With his father dead Humphrey Whittle no longer felt every day was a test, and he grabbed the chance to take the old man's place on the Poor Board, putting himself around the town to prepare for the time when Harry stepped down as Member of Parliament for Chorley. He thought of having to watch Nellie die, being reminded of his own mortality, his own weakness.

'What a ghoulish thought,' shuddered Humphrey, thinking aloud.

'A ghoulish thought!' exclaimed Nellie, staring at Humphrey, hating him and loving him, not knowing whether to let his big hands clasp her waist and pull her to his shoulder, or whether to pick up the nearest heavy ornament and throw it at his stupid, insensitive, unnecessarily stoic face. She wiped the hot tears from her cheeks and backed away from him.

'A ghoulish thought!' she repeated, crying and gripping the carved veneer of the sideboard, letting her fingers trace the vines. 'How could you say such a thing!'

He straightened up and shut the door behind him. Calmly, he placed his hat and coat on the stand in the corner and put his umbrella in the brass case underneath. He took off his scarf and wrapped it up before placing it in his coat pocket, then removed his leather gloves. He placed these and his keys in a glass bowl on the sideboard next to the letter rack. Behind Prudence, Shellard's stable boy and one of the scrubbers had appeared at the kitchen door. He felt he could open his mouth and scream so loud that the house would fall down, then he would take a deep breath and suck in everything and everyone so that he wouldn't have be troubled anymore.

Nellie looked at her husband's face, the eyes flashing with spite and hatred. She could sense the rage trying to squeeze through his skin, pierce his cheeks. He reminded her of a volcano, Krakatoa, ready to explode and engulf everything with lava and tidal waves. She instinctively flinched away from him.

'Don't you dare hit me, not in front of the servants, by God!' she cried. 'Don't you dare hit me!'

'You're hysterical,' said Humphrey, moving towards her, blocking out the light of the lamps with his shoulders.

'Wouldn't you be?' asked Nellie.

Humphrey thought of his own parents. He thought about what the Missionary had told them about demeanour and deportment. He had seen a man die on the rugby pitch in the middle of the scrum, his liver crushed by the weight of the men above him. Everyone had been shocked to find him spitting blood and sucking down his last lungfuls of air, but no one had lost their mind about it. The match was stopped but the game, the eternal game, went ever onwards.

'I can't believe you have to think about it, Humphrey. You're not a man, you're a devil, a fiend, a changeling... why even poor Freddy's more normal than you!' cried Nellie in a mocking tone, turning her grief away from thoughts of her mother.

Humphrey saw his poor, palsy-ridden brother locked up in the charity hospital, muttering over and over about jousting with fabulous knights. He hated Nellie for reminding him of his brother and everything associated with his family. He bellowed something indecipherable, a curse, like an engine letting off steam before its ground its wheels away from the station.

He aimed for her wet cheek and hit her with the palm of his hand, feeling the bones of his knuckles jar and catch against her pale, soft skin. He didn't hold back, even though he had the time to do so. He put all his strength into knocking her down, driving her down and out of his way, out of his mind with the rest of the demons. For good measure he raised his fists against Prudence and the others, warning them to stay away from Nellie, who was crumpled on the floor weeping and pressing her hand against the red mark blossoming on her cheek.

He looked at her, suddenly realising what he had done. He felt sick, and put his hand under his arm, clutching it tightly in his sweating armpit. He stepped past her and paused, trying to think of a way in which he could apologise. But the servants were still there, and he knew he couldn't. He couldn't show weakness. He wouldn't allow his feelings for her get in the way of his power in the house. She was only a woman. She was his wife. He couldn't apologise.

He walked past the open door to his study, went up the wide stairs and around towards his bedroom, then locked himself in. He didn't want to see anyone who would remind him of his actions: he didn't want to be near her if the demons returned. In the darkness of his room he sat down on the bed, rubbed his hand, and allowed a few tears to fall silently down his face, knowing no one could see them.

Downstairs, Prudence helped Nellie to her feet. She was concerned for her mistress, scared that her master would come back down the stairs and beat her as well as his wife. She looked at the other servants but they had already disappeared back into the kitchens, to spread the gossip to everyone else. They considered Prudence to be a snob, a turncoat, someone living above her allotted place in life. She had no real friends - she knew they were all jealous of the intimacies she shared with Nellie. If Whittle came back down to beat her she knew she'd get no protection from the others.

'Shall I get some ointment? Balm?' asked Prudence, holding Nellie's hand and stroking her bare arm lovingly.

Nellie wiped the tears from Prudence's face, and smiled, as if there were none on hers. The mark where Humphrey had hit her was dark and shiny, turning yellow at the edges where it spread like a spider's legs over her cheekbone towards her ear. Tears glistened over it.

'Leave it, dear Prudence, my love, I'm not ashamed... I'm not ashamed... why should I be for mourning my mum? Why can't he say how he feels?'

'I don't know, miss,' said Prudence quietly.

Nellie laughed, and grasped Prudence by the head to kiss her hair.

'Oh, Prudence, dear! I love you... what do I care about Humphrey Whittle? The animal!'

'I don't know about that,' mumbled Prudence, feeling Nellie's heartbeat against her cheek, the smell of her perfume mingled with gin.

Nellie smiled, letting Prudence step back and retain her maid's composure.

'You're free for the evening, Prudence, forget about all this, make sure you don't have nightmares.'

'Free? But what about the bridge this evening?' asked Prudence.

'It's cancelled. Tell Hobbs to send my apologies. I'm going out.'

'Where to, miss?'

'To drink a drink for my mum as far away from Humphrey Whittle as possible,' said Nellie. She smiled at the thought, then before Prudence could ask any more questions she was helping Nellie to put on her fur coat and closing the door behind her.

Outside, Nellie breathed in the sulphurous coal smoke and stepped out into the dimly lit street heedless of the rain. Before she'd had the children she'd never needed drink. But it was only a substitute for what she wanted. It was Humphrey's fault for hating her body, refusing her the touch she knew would drive away the melancholy. It was his fault, then, that she'd find it elsewhere.

In the snug of *The Inkerman Tavern* Shellard grinned with delight as he admired his night's takings. When there was a market on during the day it meant more simple people from the countryside to be divested of their wages by a clever card-sharp like Shellard. They were always the same, full of bluster and beer, and Shellard's friendly smile and a few jokes were enough to distract their attention from the nailmarks and sleights of hand that were the marks of his trade. He left them when they ran out of money or patience, moving on to the next pub in case someone caught on to the loaded hands he shuffled. He had six pounds on the table, a good haul and enough to keep him going until the next opportunity came along.

He raised his pint to toast himself, and started to drink it like a child drinks milk.

Nellie opened the door of the pub, pushing it hard as the wind howled through to disturb the candle flames. The barman, an old soldier with a limp and a missing finger, looked up from serving three dusty, thirsty miners. A party around the fire continued to chat and laugh and sing snippets of songs but their eyes were drawn to Nellie as she walked hesitantly across the floorboards to the bar. She had hiccups, and tried to hide them by coughing. Thick smoke clung to the rafters, making the plaster yellow. Her eyes started to stream with water, and the mark on her face reddened with the combination of cold rain and hot air. She felt everyone looking at her, but refused to be frightened. The gin and a few measures of rum along the way had given her the confidence to face even the most fearsome ogre of her childhood dreams.

She coughed, this time to attract the attention of the barman. He glanced up sullenly, and continued to pull on the beer engine pumping porter up for the miners.

'It's all right, Fred, she's wi' me, like.'

Nellie felt someone behind her, close to her back. She heard his voice and turned around.

Shellard smiled at her. She smiled back. She had seen Shellard in the back yard of the house a number of times in the few weeks he'd been employed there in charge of the stables. He was almost twice her age and ugly in a brutish way, displaying his virility with every swagger. She knew he could give her what Humphrey couldn't. He had always said hello to her, and had sent his apologies up when two of the boys had a fight over the affections of a young girl. She had seen him look at Humphrey's back with a flash of animosity in his eyes, that had gone when he'd realised he was being watched by her from her bedroom window.

He grinned and bent to kiss her hand, a familiarity that would have been quite out of place at Derwent Lodge, but one which had Nellie laughing like a girl.

'Mister Shellard!' she exclaimed. 'What would people think of me?'

'Them in this place are all no good, anyhow, it don't matter two farthings what this lot think,' said Shellard, his grin crooked and wide. 'And call me George, please, I don't stand on formalities, me. Fancy a drink, ma'am? I've got brass aplenty.'

'I'll have whatever you're having, then,' said Nellie, thrilled that Shellard was treating her like any other woman he might have met in a pub. When she had seen him she was worried that he would take her back, but she could sense that wasn't about to happen. He had a nerve! she thought, enjoying his attention. She smiled and dropped her eyes flirtatiously, as she thought about ways to spite Humphrey, to make him love her again: it wouldn't be the first time she'd found another man to comfort her. 'And if I'm to call you George, then you must call me Nellie, we'll have none of that formality.'

Shellard couldn't help leering at her, admiring the heave of her breasts as if he was inspecting the shanks of a horse. He still remembered Humphrey Whittle the footballer, humiliating him in front of his friends, being so aloof and confident of his own superiority. He'd heard Councillor Whittle harping on about social justice and bettering oneself, pointing to his own success without mentioning the riches of Primrose Cottage.

He'd improve things for himself by taking some of Humphrey's riches, if he guessed right about Nellie's thoughts. He put his arm around Nellie's shoulders, pressing on a little too firmly for friendship, a little more each time to see how far she'd let him go, and ordered another two pints of porter. She smiled, letting his fingers stay there, brushing hers against his as he picked up the glasses.

A part of her despised what she was doing, but Shellard's animal nature was too strong to ignore. He wasn't the sort of man to collect butterflies. He was a beast. She needed him.

Later that night Shellard and Nellie entered the stables behind Derwent Lodge, whispering to the horses there to be quiet. The lights of the servants' quarters still blazed out, casting shadows as people walked between the lamps and the windows, but they couldn't hear anyone speaking. In one of the empty stalls Shellard had collected a bed of hay, which Nellie collapsed onto before unfastening the pins and buttons of her clothes. Shellard looked at her, and bent down to kiss her neck, her swollen cheek, her lips, touching. She touched his lips, kissed him back. She wanted him. In the darkness, warmed by the heat of the horses and the kitchen fires, Nellie thought of Humphrey and pulled Shellard down to her, fumbling for him, pulling him inside her as he groaned and sighed and pushed her deeper into the hay.

'I want a cob, George, I want my freedom. Get me a cob so I can ride around the town by myself,' said Nellie, after they had made love in the privacy of her rooms. They knew that Humphrey was away all day at the service and the hospital, and with it being a Sunday most of the servants had gone to their families for the day.

Prudence remained to mind Nellie. She sat outside her rooms, watching the people moving through the street, fighting against the wind, dressed in their finest. No one said anything: they moved in silence with their heads down, determined to reach the shelter of home. Prudence listened to Nellie and George making love, their loud whispers, sighs and moans muffled by urgency and fear. She didn't like being privy to their secrets, a go-between carrying messages from Derwent Lodge to Parson's Brow, having to avoid the angry glare of Shellard's wife and the sniggering faces of the Whittle servants. She tried to be discreet, keeping her face like a canvas without any paint, mindlessly obeying as if she were an unthinking automaton driven by clockwork through Chorley's cobbled streets. But she could hear people whispering to each other as she left the rundown terraced cottage where the Shellard family lived, she could hear them making jokes about his infidelity and his long-suffering wife. And in the town she could sense with shame the minds active with imagination and scandal, the gossip she never quite heard.

In bed, Shellard pulled the blanket over his naked body, ashamed of his pot belly and the wrinkles under his arms. He breathed in and pushed his chest out like a child playing soldiers, worried that Nellie would see him for what he was. He nodded his head and stroked her shoulder, pulling her closer towards him so he could savour the prize of her warm flesh, made sweeter by the knowledge he was cuckolding Humphrey Whittle.

'I'll get thee a cob, all right, my love.'

Nellie smiled and stroked the grey hairs on Shellard's chest. It was a strong chest, a pirate's chest, hairy and manly and smelling of horses and pipe smoke. She let her dark hairs fall over those grey hairs, becoming entangled in the wire. She kissed his cheek as rough as a grinding stone, thinking of the demands he made of her and the excitement she felt in complying. When he touched her she knew she was his, and it made her want him more.

'Get me a good cob, though, George, don't worry about the price.

151

Humphrey can afford it,' she said, kissing his ear, promising him more if he would only do the thing she asked of him.

'He'll afford it all right,' grinned Shellard, knowing she liked him to be the rogue. 'I'll turn a fine profit for miself on this un.'

'Then if you do you must give me a share of your profits,' said Nellie, excited at the idea of tricking her husband out of money like a common criminal.

'Tha's wanting to rip off that husband of yours?' asked Shellard.

Nellie thought about Humphrey, what she felt for him and still did. But those feelings were distant, like the plot of a book she'd read last year, or an old painting she'd put on the fire to rid herself of childish notions. Shellard was real - he smelt real, he felt real, an undeniable mass in her bed pulling her towards him like a star attracting comets.

She nodded her head, rubbing against him.

'Yes, let's rip him off, then, as long as I get my cob. It's about time you earned some money instead of getting it from me all the time, you devil.'

Shellard laughed, so loud that Prudence jumped up fearing that the people in the street could hear him.

'You'll get your cob,' he said, 'and we'll have a fine purse for it.'

Throughout November and into the cold rains that marked the onset of winter, Shellard made plans to get Nellie a cob and make some money into the bargain. He didn't mind sharing with her the profit he made from overcharging Humphrey - that was only a small amount, and was standard practice for grooms when buying horses for their employers. But he didn't tell her about the other arrangements he made, the opportunity to make more out of the deal than even she could have guessed.

Humphrey agreed to sending Shellard in search of the cob, glad that it meant he was away from Derwent Lodge and from Chorley, where nothing went unnoticed. Nellie couldn't go to the horse markets in Liverpool and up in the Forest of Bowland and the Lakes, she had no excuse to be in such a man's place, which satisfied Humphrey. He left Shellard to make the arrangements, not wanting to share the same air as the man for longer than necessary. Shellard acted subservient and respectful throughout, not giving anything away, not revealing anything that would incite Humphrey to seek his vengeance and quench the fires that burned inside his soul.

Prudence watched Nellie waiting. She sat on the edge of seats, bit her nails like a scolded child and shouted at the children. She poured large measures of gin in the morning if the postman never called, and when he did she would ensure Prudence was there to take the letters addressed in Shellard's grubby hand straight up to her room. Nellie laughed to herself, flaunted the letters in front of Prudence and spoke about proving a point. She was confident when the letters came, but Prudence also saw her crying when she was with the children, kissing their heads and whispering Humphrey's name. They stopped arguing, and Nellie seemed over anxious to please Humphrey, chatting to him in a nervous voice about the affairs of the council or old football players she had met in the street.

Prudence was frightened. She could see Humphrey was turning into something horrible, a seething mass of snakes churning up his insides. She could see that Nellie was trying to tell him something but he would not, or could not, listen. Winter came and Shellard appeared briefly to demand payment for a cob he'd placed in the stables. Humphrey paid without looking in the accounts or checking to see what a fair price was. Nellie talked about the cob eagerly, telling Humphrey what Shellard had told her about it - how it had come from a farmer called Bond, how Shellard insisted it was the best cob north of Cheshire and south of Scotland.

Prudence heard everything, saw everything. Christmas came and neither Humphrey nor Nellie seemed to notice its passing. The children became quarrelsome. Shellard appeared again, smiling at Nellie in an open and lecherous manner. Humphrey retreated into the company of his old footballing friends at the *Rose and Crown*, remembering and reinventing the glories of the past. They came to the house when Nellie was out - Prudence heard them talking about revolution, about rugby clubs turning into breeding grounds for unrest, plagued by professionalism. Nellie no longer asked Prudence to wait for her, and went out in her trap to learn from Shellard how to handle the cob, only to come back with tears in her eyes.

Prudence sat outside the master's study and listened as he berated Nellie for failing to keep the house accounts in good order. Nellie defended herself by saying it was only a shilling but Whittle argued that twenty bob made a pound and a pound was more than many people had for a week. Prudence knew where the shilling had gone – she'd been short and it was her nephew's christening, she had to get something for the little baby. Nellie had given her a shilling. She heard Nellie laugh at Whittle.

'And how many of these poor wretches are poor on your account?' asked Nellie, her voice loud, clear and confident. Prudence smiled when she heard Nellie speak, it was how she imagined God would speak, if He was, as some daring people·claimed, actually a woman.

The passage outside the master's study was lit only by an old oil lamp, its measly share of light lighting only the sphere of space around it. In the winter a cold flow of air crossed the passage from the door up the stairs, eddying about the feet of anyone careless enough to stay there. As a servant Prudence had to wait on Nellie no matter the weather. If Nellie wanted to go outside and roll around in the snow then Prudence had to join her. The housekeeper and Nellie's maid were quite insistent that Prudence, Nellie's personal girl, should always be with Nellie unless she specifically told her to stay. Prudence knew the other servants laughed at her, and said she was no better than a lapdog, but she didn't care. She loved Nellie.

She heard the master's heavy chair scrape back on the floorboards, his boots clumping across the room. Whittle said something, incoherent, strangulated, and Nellie laughed again. Whittle stopped walking.

'Put that down, Nell, or it'll be the death of yer, I swear, you whore.'

'I'm your whore, is that all I am?' said Nellie, taunting him. Prudence wasn't shocked by the words, she had grown accustomed to Whittle referring to his wife in that way, and Nellie responding in kind. She listened, wishing she had the courage to open the door and confront Whittle herself, stand protectively between him and her mistress, suffer the blows instead of her and carry the bruises with pride. 'Better a whore than a bastard.'

'You step over the mark, Nell, I've been told you're a cheap roll in the hay,' growled Whittle. 'You are mine. You are my wife. Think about what you're doing, Nell, think what you're throwing away.'

'I'm not yours, not yours to keep, to put on display like this thing.'

'You are my wife. I command, you obey... so put it down or by God I'll thrash you to within an inch of your life.'

Prudence realised Nellie had picked something up in the study.

'How can I be wife and whore?'

'Damn you, Nell! You're my bloody wife!'

'Then why do you see those girls down t'railway?'

Whittle growled, like a bear, as if the English language didn't have the words to express the confluence of his anger and despair. Finally, the sounds that came out of his mouth were recognisable, a word, a question, a plea: 'Shellard?'

'Do you love me, Humphrey?'

Silence.

'Do you love me?' she asked again.

There was no answer. Seconds later Prudence heard a sonorous clatter, as Nellie dropped the thing she'd picked up in the middle of the argument. It was a heavy, metallic thing. Prudence knew there was only one thing in Whittle's study of that nature, one thing he kept dear in his heart: the Cup. The door was wrenched open and Nellie raced out, her face puffed up and red. She ran past Prudence, and out of the front door in a swirl of snowflakes, not even pausing to put on her fur coat. Whittle appeared at the door of his study and stared out of the open door into the dark blizzard, his eyes red like the devil's. In his hands he was holding the Cup, caressing its curves. He glanced down at Prudence, and pulled her roughly to her feet.

She thought he was going to kiss her, to drag her into the study, throw her down in front of the fire and use her like the whores they'd mentioned. But instead, with tears rolling down his cheeks, he pushed her towards the door.

'Go find her, bring her back,' he pleaded, fondling the Cup and the dent in its side close to the image of the Raikes Hall grandstand.

When Prudence found Nellie out on the street she was laughing hysterically. She had bought a bottle of gin from the gin shop and had drunk half of it in the municipal park, sat on a bench in the snow. She was shivering, and her long brown hair was loose and glistened with frost. Prudence had with her Nellie's fur coat, and put it around her without her saying anything. She had another swig of the gin bottle, which shone green in her white hands. Prudence could smell the alcohol everywhere, its fumes clinging to the falling snow flakes like smoke from a chimney.

Prudence sat down next to Nellie and put her arm around her shoulders. Through the fur coat she could feel Nellie's frozen muscles and cold skin. She could see the steam coming away as the fur combined with the heat of her body and melted the ice. Her own breath mingled with Nellie's, creating swirling spirals and circles that lasted a second before the snow dragged them away.

'Come home, mistress, you'll catch yer death of cold, it's freezing out,' said Prudence, shivering herself. The park's lawns were grey, flecked with black soot, spoilt by Nellie's feet. The trees groaned with snow on their bare branches, the wood creating an illusion of shadows and depth through which the dim lights of the town could be seen.

Nellie looked into the distance. Prudence followed her gaze, hoping to see someone like Councillor Lever, Nellie's friend, appear through the maelstrom. Dark patches where the snow relented turned into friendly faces and policeman saviours with whistles and cloaks. There was nothing real.

'I wanted to marry him, Prudence, don't you see? I made that decision, not him, not my dad, not my mum no one else, only me.'

Prudence nodded. How could she say anything?

'You should've seen it, the colours of the flowers, the Garden of Eden... I thought that he had got the Lord Himself to make the sun shine for our wedding, but I was wrong, I was wrong to marry him. I knew then he didn't love me, not proper like, like that... I never thought I'd get married like mum and dad, bless them, living in different rooms. I wanted it to be proper, real like, I wanted him to love me, I want him to love me, why won't he, Prudence? Why? Why is he scared of loving me?'

Nellie started to cry. Prudence shrugged her shoulders.

'Don't know, ma'am,' she whispered.

The year was ending.

The sun hid in the morning, fearful to come out from behind the black clouds.

12.

An Encounter In A Hospital

WHEN SHELLARD WAS SENT AWAY at the end of 1892, Humphrey saw Frederick. As part of his duties as a councillor, inherited from his father, Humphrey chaired the Chorley Hospital Board. It was a public duty and an important municipal board, one which he served with all the solemnity and gravity it deserved. He did not flinch from facing the poor and destitute coughing up coal dust, weeping with pain and dying of all manner of diseases and ailments. Nevertheless, he despised those duties for the necessary contact it forced him to have with the hospital, the place where Frederick was incarcerated, abandoned by the expensive doctors in the sanatoria he'd been sent to as a child.

During the season of goodwill, which for the aldermen of Chorley started soon after the November bonfires, a tradition had grown for the members of the Board to visit the children in the hospital and distribute penny sweets and pocket bibles, to give them succour and faith. This early Christmas brought joy to the children and enabled the aldermen to prepare for their own private festivities with a clear conscience. These presents were distributed in the middle of November, on the first available Sunday after bonfire night, after a grand service reflecting on charity held in the Anglican church and - afterwards, for the nonconformists - in the secular ground of the council's town hall. Humphrey didn't like this tradition because he knew once he was in the hospital, some goodly doctor would ask him whether he wished to see his brother, and he could never refuse without appearing callous, too callous to stand for the House of Commons.

He met Frederick with his elder brother John, one of the trustees of the Board as the direct inheritor of the family's fortune. It was John's idea - he didn't need to be prompted by the conscience of some meaning-well spirit of Christmas. John, as simple as Humphrey was single-minded, had never

157

considered his own culpability that day in the orchard, when their game had led to Frederick almost drowning and their father divesting himself of all responsibility for looking after his sickened son. John had grown fat on the family's fortunes, proving to be a capable if unimaginative administrator of their affairs. Humphrey knew John would never start seeing Russian hussars saluting him in every dark corner, would never succumb to the demons, though that stability seemed to have deprived him of all the creativity and insight their father had used to turn a farthing into a five-pound note.

John was waiting for Humphrey at the far end of the busy children's ward with a handkerchief held up to his mouth. Humphrey, being more tactful, ignored the stench of dirt, decaying flesh and antiseptic spray. Careful to distribute the Bibles to each child in turn, he left the others to hand out the penny sweets and joined John to climb the steps towards the barred room where they kept Frederick and the other incurable cripples - the tragic flotsam and jetsam of human life.

'It will be good to see Frederick again, don't you think, Humphrey?' grinned John.

Humphrey didn't answer him.

Things changed at Primrose Cottage after they'd taken Frederick away. No one would mention his name, and although the young Humphrey asked his mother what had happened she would not tell him. Mister Whittle pretended not to hear Humphrey, except when he lost his patience and hit out with his rolled-up newspaper. Humphrey suspected they had sold Frederick to the knacker's yard. He knew that was where people sent the horses when they got old or were hurt, and he'd heard the maids crying about Frederick in the same way women cried about horses when one fell at the races. It was all John's fault that it had happened. Humphrey had tried explaining that to Jane, but she hadn't noticed him. Her eyes had been glazed and distant, and when he poked her to see if she was all right she just smiled back at him. He told his mother about this and she said Jane had to stop moping about the house or they'd have to call in the doctor.

In the weeks following Frederick's disappearance Jane started to withdraw from all family life. At first no one noticed. Then it became a matter of argument between their parents over how to deal with their shadow-like daughter. The elder Whittle said that Jane was hysterical and she had to learn that women got nowhere in the world by throwing enormous sulks. Mrs Whittle said that Jane was seeking attention, but that she was concerned Jane's grief was eating her up like a dark, malevolent worm inside her. The Whittle boys heard this from under their beds, where they had built dens, and wondered amongst themselves what game Jane was playing. John claimed she was planning to run away and free Frederick from the pirates who had kidnapped him, which to Humphrey sounded like utter nonsense, especially since he knew Frederick had gone to the knacker's yard to be turned into glue. Humphrey tried to get the answer from Jane, but after the incident at the stream she didn't play with the boys, and would rarely leave her room. So he'd come to the conclusion that she had been bewitched by a travelling gypsy woman he claimed to have seen hiding in the orchard when they'd had the fight over the stream.

Spring had turned into summer. The fields around Primrose Cottage became golden oceans, populated by mice and stoats and rabbits. The apple trees were covered in green leaves and the branches hung low with fruit. The windows of the house were flung open and the sound of people talking and clocks ticking spilled out into the garden and mingled with the endless bird-songs. For the boys, the summer offered freedom from the house to which they had been bound since the incident at the stream. The elder Whittle supplied them with a leather covered ball to throw and kick, and a bat and ball for cricket, which they played on the lawn and in the meadows between Primrose Cottage and the black houses of the town. The excitement of fresh air and blue skies was more immediate than the worry over their brother, who they remembered only as a passing thing like some hedgehog found in the garden.

Jane did not leave the house. They saw less of her than ever before. When Humphrey asked their father what was wrong with Jane their father had shrugged his shoulders. The men in the stables said women were different to men and suffered from strange passions and moods. When he spoke, his father said she was an irresponsible young woman beginning that descent from reason which afflicted all the weaker sex. Humphrey hadn't understood this but knew then that women were not the same as men – not as good as men. From that day he listened keenly to what his father said.

Only when the gardener's apprentices' loud and clear voices echoed up the stairs Jane would emerge from her shadows and look at them as if she was seeing the sun for the first time after a thunderstorm. When these boys went away on jobs with the chief gardener she would retire back to her room, or sit in the darkest part of the parlour drawing pictures of trees without leaves out of charcoal.

Humphrey had heard his mother talking with one of her black-dressed friends about spirits and devils, and how to get rid of them. The old woman had told his mother that young girls of a certain age were always more prone to be possessed by the demons beyond the pale. Humphrey wasn't sure what that meant, but he was clever enough to realise they were talking about Jane. It wasn't an easy task, he knew, to get rid of demons. They said at school that demons could only be got rid of by writing their name backwards in your own blood at the stroke of midnight on a murderer's grave. He couldn't imagine his father letting Jane go into a graveyard in the middle of the night – besides which, the old woman hadn't said which particular demons were inside Jane.

Their mother called in a local clergyman to investigate Jane. Humphrey didn't know what was said but Jane's condition worsened, which only seemed to confirm the suspicions raised by Mrs Whittle's companion. Their father disapproved and they all heard a huge argument between the two men with their mother crying in the middle of them. All they knew was that she was wanton, disobedient, and almost certainly influenced by some dark spirit.

Jane had been sent away for good when their father had found her in bed with one of the gardeners, one of the boys who had made her smile. She had become so much of a recluse that her indecent behaviour went unnoticed by everyone in Primrose Cottage, whether servant or family. She was fourteen, and had already been away on a number of occasions to doctors who diagnosed various forms of hysteria and unbalanced humours inside her. It was, they claimed, a fairly common thing for a girl making the change to a woman but something that most girls managed to grow out of without becoming a bother. Mister Whittle had tried everything – the rod, the lash, a controlled diet – but she looked at him with sheer hatred whenever he'd finished. She was out of his control, and always asked where Frederick was when they came down for a family dinner.

Her affair with the gardener was proof that she couldn't be expected to behave herself in respectable company. What man would marry a girl who had lost her maidenhood to a common worker? The chance discovery was, Humphrey realised later, nothing of the sort: another gardener, jealous of the first, had warned Mister Whittle of his daughter's fiendish behaviour, and had been rewarded with an overseer's job in one of the mines. The gardener they found in bed with Jane was whipped soundly by Mister Whittle then dismissed without a reference.

As for Jane, she was obviously wrong in the head, and was locked away in the care of a procession of doctors and quacks who tried an assortment of potions, pills, regimens and treatments until she weakened and died in a blast of cold water.

The nurses had washed Frederick and dressed him in a plain brown suit made of shoddy cloth. They had combed his wispy, neglected hair and shaved him of his hermit's beard. They hadn't given him a pair of shoes, and his twisted feet were bare and black with muck. His eyesight had failed as the palsy spread - he wore a black eye-patch over one blind eye and his other was yellow and cloudy. Saliva dribbled out of the side of his mouth and sores clustered about his lips, his nose, his fingers. They had seated him in a stationary bath chair, cosseted by clean blankets and leather straps, in a dark room facing away from the pale November daylight, lit by a solitary gas lamp.

Humphrey looked at the bent, humped shape of his brother and felt sick. He couldn't bear watching Frederick's fingers and feet twitching to some random music only Frederick seemed to hear. He hated his father for leaving Frederick, for not telling them what had happened to him, for letting him turn into the forlorn being in the hospital. He feared that one day he would become like Frederick, and the palsy would turn him into a creature dependent on the goodwill of others, his strength and wits eaten away by the disease. Frederick was an evolutionary mistake, thought Humphrey, a reminder of how fickle things were, how lucky that it was Frederick - not Humphrey - Whittle who had almost drowned in the stream. And seeing Frederick reminded him of Jane, who had blurred in his memory so that he saw her as he imagined Nellie had been as a girl, as Nellie became more like Jane with her mood swings and her unfathomable female ways.

John offered Frederick a sweet, a boiled humbug intended for the children downstairs. Frederick grinned and tried to take it, but the nurses had strapped his arms down. So John slowly and deliberately brought it to

Frederick's drooling mouth to push it between his full lips.

Frederick coughed as the sweet lodged at the back of his mouth, and John stepped back nervously.

'I say, John, don't choke the poor wretch, what did you give him that for?' frowned Humphrey, looking warily at his younger brother. For a second he thought if only it was Leo in the chair, not Frederick, but he soon dismissed that frightening thought. They watched Frederick trying to crunch the sweet, struggling to stop himself from suffocating. Neither of them knew what to do, other than to watch. Eventually, Frederick spat the sticky shards of sweet out in a thick mucus that dribbled over his suit. Humphrey shook his head.

'Really, what a frightful thing! John, look what you made him do!'

'I thought a sweet'd be nice for the lad,' John said with a shrug of his shoulders.

Frederick looked up at them both, and tried to say something. They ignored him.

'Well look what you've made him do, now, what a dreadful embarrassment he'll be when the nurses come back to clear him up,' Humphrey complained, taking a cigarette out of his coat pocket and lighting it by removing the cover of the gas lamp and putting it to the flame. 'I don't know why we keep him here, we don't need any more scandal, not after father and that Russian hussar of his.'

John frowned at Humphrey, and thought about the rumour he had heard that day before the service in the town hall. He knew Humphrey and Nellie were having trouble, despite the two children, but he'd heard that it was far worse, that it was Humphrey's own manhood, his respectability, that was under question. John went pale just thinking about the nature of Nellie's affair, which went to the root of all evil in the world according to what they'd been told at school: the sin of lust and temptation.

'I say, John, got something on your mind?' asked Humphrey. 'You look like you were about to say something, what is it?'

'Nothing, Humphrey, just thinking... you know, about this and that, nothing important. Shall we go? Frederick's spooking me.'

Frederick looked up at his two brothers, trying, trying so hard to understand what was going on, why they weren't playing at knights in his castle. What wits he had had were drained out of him in his first years in the care of the doctors, who locked him away with the other lost causes. He tried to concentrate, think about what he wanted to say to these two people, who he knew were his brothers, but he couldn't think, the words weren't there. Humphrey left John behind to say farewell and find the nurses. He knew what John had been about to say, he knew what was going on. He had heard the people talking in whispers go quiet as he passed, heard their giggles and snorts of uncouth humour. But he denied it. As long as he didn't know, as long as he didn't have the proof in his own hands, before his own eyes, he refused to accept the truth of his own failure.

13.

A Matter of Public Knowledge

HUMPHREY KNEW ABOUT THE AFFAIR. As a politician, it was necessary to know everything that was happening in the constituency, to know of brides, babies and lovers. Harry knew too, because he was more of a politician than Humphrey Whittle, and wasn't afraid of asking the roughest men the most scandalous questions in an attempt to find something out about the corrupt and lascivious ways of his political enemies. Whittle knew before the fraud trial that she was seeing Shellard, before he'd sent Shellard away in an attempt to find a cob and remove his evil influence from Nellie. He knew she considered her husband to be a failure, as if she'd been possessed by the angry spirit of his father, who had grown more and more disappointed with life as he passed away from it into a world of ghosts. However, he just could not speak to Nellie, he couldn't say the things he'd wanted to tell her without his chest tightening, squeezing the words into the fire of his belly where they served as a fuel for his anger, his despair at his own failures, his inability to win her affections. She was a real woman, unlike the whores he'd used who would give him all the affection he wanted for a silver coin. She frightened him more than any working-class rugby player in the middle of a scrum. She frightened him more than the socialists who were plotting to take over the country and hang people like him by the neck from street-lamps. His fear was an irrational one, yet there'd been the rumours of her walking hand-in-hand with Shellard, rumours that had given that fear some credence.

All he'd needed was some proof - he'd thought he would be satisfied that all he feared was true. But one year after it was all over, in the banquet hall, Whittle knew he could never be satisfied, not until the final days of blood and fire when all his works would be judged. Then, he knew, he would be accounted for, and all his fears would be weighed in the balance against his sins - and would be found in the Devil's favour.

Ten years before Nellie, fourteen or so years before the affair, there was the Cup. Although in the years since those matches that object had lost much of its lustre, and he had failed to live up to the ideals moulded into the metals from which it was made, he could remember the time when he was happy. It was ephemeral, a brief glimpse of some earthly paradise; the happiness was a measure of his own selfishness, his yearning to own the Cup, and the memory of it was a mixture of foolish nostalgia and forgetfulness. But it had happened. They had played for the Cup to make Chorley famous, and he had been on the pitch at Raikes Hall with only the prize of the Cup as a purpose. He had been happy, if only until the moment when the game stopped and the real world of his father and Fish started anew.

The club was gone, lost to association football barely six years after the cup matches, lost to men who cared nothing for Humphrey Whittle and the spirit of rugby. Raikes Hall had closed the winter before he gave the Cup away, despite a string of novelties promoted by Mister Fish throughout the 1880s. It had struggled to compete in a town where novelty was all and ten years was a lifetime. John Fish had gone, leaving no trace of his passing. All Whittle had left was the memory of the Cup, like the memory of Nellie, a reminder of what may have been and never was.

Outside, in the corridor, Prudence waited. She knew Nellie had had money of her own following the death of her father then that of her mother. Nellie didn't need to take Humphrey's money, squander his profits on favours for her lover. There were other reasons, thought Prudence, as she waited for Whittle in the cool and dark insides of the town hall. She'd told Prudence that she would show Humphrey that there were more important things than money, and that was why she did what she did. Prudence had never worked out what Nellie had meant, what she had been trying to achieve. How would she show money wasn't important by taking it? And what lesson was there to be learned? What was it that Nellie wanted to prove to him? What was the thing that was more important than money? Prudence could think of a lot of things, but she couldn't see how Whittle could fathom them by Nellie's actions alone.

A waiter went past her, carrying in his white-gloved hands a silver platter with a steaming pudding. A perfume of fruits and sugar filled the corridor and little clouds curled up into the dark arches in the high roof. The waiter balanced the platter on one arm and opened the door, using his hip to nudge his way through into the noisy banquet. Prudence's stomach rumbled, echoing in the corridor after the door shut. She hadn't eaten properly since Nellie had died - the plumpness of her face had been eaten away in place of meals, leaving her with a gaunt complexion. She thought of the satisfaction she'd felt when Humphrey had dropped the Cup, and suddenly realised she was very hungry.

It was New Year's Eve, 1892.

Humphrey recalled the wild feelings of being a pagan hero as he waited for the affair to be discovered. He was sitting in the *Rose and Crown*, watching his friends come and go through the day, making merry whenever their backs were turned to him. He didn't like alcohol - there was something in its constituency that disagreed with him, something other than the intoxicating element. He never reached that plateau of esoteric happiness that others reached when drinking, never found the secrets others claimed to have found there. All it gave him was a bad head, pain behind his eyes and an inability to forget his failings. And yet there was nothing else he could try, nothing he could do to ease the agony of waiting for something to happen. There was, too, that envy of Shellard deep in his heart, and a desire to prove that he could do better at being Shellard than Shellard. Would Nellie then come back to him, forget her dalliance with Shellard and see whatever she saw in him in her own husband? Humphrey thought it was possible, so he continued to drink, saying little to the ex-footballers with whom he had surrounded himself.

It was the end of the year. He remembered the time fourteen years ago when the team had sat together in that same pub waiting for John Fish to bring news about the result of the Walton-Manchester game. Time had flowed on in its inexorable, inevitable way towards the future, the new century, yet to Humphrey it seemed as if along the way he had been left behind. Around him, people like the Mockett brothers were singing songs about the day Chorley conquered the world and for a horrible moment Humphrey thought that somehow he'd lost himself in the past. But it was the beer befuddling his brain, that was the simple truth of it, only a simple chemical reaction. He had nothing to fear.

Shellard heard the news from one of his gambling pals - how Humphrey Whittle was about to be taken to court over the crooked deal to buy the Liverpool cob. Cook, the crook he'd conned, had made the necessary arrangements with his solicitor and they were coming to Chorley to see if they could settle like gentlemen and start the new year afresh. One of the things they were bound to discuss was the relationship he had with Nellie, since that was instrumental in the crooked deal. Most of the town already knew he was having an affair with Nellie but solicitors and courts made it all official, proved the rumours. It didn't take him long to reach a decision - he'd had enough of his ugly, complaining wife and his demanding children; he fancied he could have a nice time with a rich, good-looking woman like Nellie.

'I'm off,' he told his wife as she worked wet clothes through the mangle.

He didn't wait to hear her reply. He put on his coat and left through the front door, rubbing his hands together to keep them warm. The walk across town felt good. The day shifts were coming to an end and people were rushing about on the icy roads heedless of the danger. The sky was dark and the council workers were busy lighting lamps. Small groups of dirty men drifted towards pubs, families still rosy with Christmas went to visit each other, and over everyone the ghost of Old Father Time moved in the snow clouds and over the bare trees. Shellard liked New Year's Eve, the way it made people think of their past mistakes and their hopes for the future. It made men more willing to take a chance on that future, to see some hope in the turn of a card - he could always see in the new year with a fat wallet of other people's dreams. Then at midnight there was always some drunken woman fed up with her husband looking for something different, something new, something with which to shock the neighbours - and he would go home sated.

Except, he thought, *not tonight*. That night he knew he wouldn't be going home.

He unlocked the snicket gate at the back of Derwent Lodge and went in the back through the tradesman's entrance. He saw a light on in the kitchens but no other. Suspicious, he checked the stables to see if the cob was still there, to make sure Nellie hadn't conned him in the same way he'd conned everyone else. But it was in its stable, munching at some hay the stableboys had put out for it, staring unconcerned back at Shellard. Its coat glistened where his lad had groomed it. Shellard grinned and lit a cigarette. The cob was unaware of what had happened to it, the switch Shellard had made between two cobs and the profit he'd made selling it twice over. It only knew that it had gone from one stable to the other where the food was the same.

He left the stable and rapped on the back door four times, their signal. He didn't like coming unannounced but there was always risk in any adventure. If Whittle answered the door he'd think of something. But he felt lucky: he would have bet money that the only person in the house on New Year's Eve was Nellie. As it was, he was almost right: the door opened, but it was Prudence, Nellie's girl, who stood there. She looked at him with malice in her child's eyes, and Shellard eyed her up like he would a cob, inspecting her young curves and considering the pleasure he could get out of her. She ignored him.

'Is your mistress in?' asked Shellard, opening his mouth to reveal his crooked teeth, smiling like a lizard.

Prudence nodded.

'I'll fetch her,' she said, hating him for coming between them, for touching Nellie.

'Fair do, lass, I know where to go,' said Shellard, stepping over the threshold of the house. He took off his cap and shoved it into his jacket pocket.

'Mister Shellard, I don't think it's right that...' gasped Prudence, stepping out of his way lest he touched her.

'Is Mister Whittle in?'

Prudence backed up against the door to the kitchen, and nodded her head.

Shellard shook his. He could tell when someone was lying - he moved in dishonest circles.

'We won't be long, you just wait on Nell, won't you, Prudence? You're a sweetheart.'

Someone coming down the stairs alerted both of them, and they turned to see Nellie come through the door from the front hallway. She shut it behind her and the three of them were alone in the brightly lit, spartan back hall. She wasn't wearing any shoes and the stone was cold beneath her stockings. Shellard noticed this and grinned lasciviously at the show of ankle between her feet and the hem of her red dress. Prudence wanted to put herself between Nellie and Shellard, throw herself like a blanket over Nellie to protect her modesty, but she was frightened of being dismissed. She didn't want to upset Nellie - she wanted to be loyal to her even if that meant being disloyal to Mister Whittle and disloyal to her own feelings about Shellard.

'Run along now, Prudence,' said Shellard, looking at her with his cold eyes. She felt his gaze touching her hip, fingering the fabric between her thighs and slipping beneath her petticoat. She glanced at Nellie. She wanted to tell her to get rid of Shellard, to pick up a poker and do away with him, anything to stop him staring. She knew what Nellie felt about her husband, so it didn't make any sense to Prudence why she was playing a game with Shellard.

'Stop that, George,' said Nellie intimately, smiling with her eyes at her lover. She nodded at Prudence. 'Don't take orders from this layabout, Prudence, he's no good. Go make that pot of tea I asked for, and bring it upstairs in half an hour.'

'Half an hour?' frowned Shellard, speaking to her as he would a cheap whore.

Nellie waited until Prudence had gone through to the kitchen, then kissed Shellard on the cheek. As she moved away from him he pulled her back and kissed her on the lips, forcing inside her with his tongue. She sighed and hugged him, then pushed him away.

'George, half an hour is all I've got. Humphrey will be back soon to get ready for the dinner John's having over at Primrose Cottage. We're both going.'

'Oh aye? I don't reckon neither of you's going to be there,' grinned Shellard, running his hand across her shoulders and across her breasts. She brushed him off then frowned at him. 'Yer see,' he continued, 'I've gorrit on good authority Councillor bloody Whittle's fer chop tonight.'

'What do you mean?' asked Nellie.

'Can we go upstairs first?' said Shellard, fondling her ear gently with his rough hands. He kissed her neck, breathing in her perfume. 'I want you now, Missis Whittle,' he whispered, touching her side, her leg. 'Fact I want you now, right 'ere,' he added, finding the loops of string on the back of her dress and beginning to unfasten them.

'George, it's too cold!' gasped Nellie, trying to push him away. He ignored her and pulled the dress down over her white shoulders, unbuttoning her petticoat and pinning her against the wall. He kissed her, touched her, and she didn't notice the feel of the plaster against her bare back. He pulled down her dress to reveal her breasts, then she grabbed at his belt, unhooking it, trying to take his trousers down as he thrust a hand up her dress to fondle her there. She could feel he was hard; she closed her eyes and smiled, imagining that it was Humphrey who had her up against the wall. She allowed him to take her weight and gripped him with her legs, pushing down on him as he entered her with a frenzy that took her by surprise. It didn't take him long to grunt with satisfaction, pleased with himself, and he let her fall back against the wall as he hitched his trousers back up to his waist.

'Come away wi me, Nell, 'fore your 'usband throws thee out on streets,' said Shellard, gasping for breath between every word.

Nellie sighed, feeling excited by their love-making but angry that it had been all too brief. Shellard had taken her like Humphrey, without a care for her feelings, and she felt her heart pounding with a mixture of unreleased energy and rage - at herself, for allowing Shellard to treat her so casually, and at Shellard, for leaving her red-faced and frustrated. She didn't look at him. She buttoned up her dress and put it back in order as best as she could, then walked away.

'Nell?' asked Shellard, following her through the door into the stairwell. She was looking at herself in a mirror on the wall, fingering her hair to pull out the knots. Pushed into the mirror's gold frame was a child's picture of a fairy queen, with a broad, inhuman smile. It reminded Shellard of her children, and he wondered whether they were upstairs, whether they'd heard him as he took their mother up against the wall. The thought made him grin all the more, and he put his arm around Nellie's shoulders.

'Don't, George,' she whispered, shrugging him off and stretching round to fasten the laces down her back. He looked at her reflection in the mirror and realised she had tears in her eyes. 'George... I can't go away with you, just like that. The children... Humphrey... and what about your family?'

'That cob, Nell, I weren't entirely up front about it all, yer see this feller

170

says as we ripped 'im off…'

Nellie looked up at him through the mirror. 'What?'

'Mister Whittle's bin taken to court, and that means it'll all come out, Nell, between me and thee, everything. Let's gerrout of Chorley, afore things get bad between us an' all an' sundry. I reckon we'll get by in Liverpool, maybe, or London.'

'George, what have you done? Have you stolen that cob? What have you done to us? To me?' cried Nellie. She turned around and pushed him away from her, using all her strength to knock him to the floor. He crawled away from her, afraid of the wild spirit that seemed to possess her, and smoothed back the few hairs on the top of his head. She towered over him, eyes blazing like the fires of hell, and Shellard feared for his life. He started to babble about how he had swapped one cob for another and conned both Whittle and a crook called Cook, and how he was sorry for not splitting the proceeds with her, but how they'd both being involved in conning Whittle. He tried to explain, but for once he couldn't find the easy words to ease his escape from an awkward position. Nellie shook her head, shaking with emotion. 'I don't want to know what you've done, George, just go.'

'Let me explain, Nell,' said Shellard, getting to his feet and smiling nervously. He had never been knocked down by a woman and it disturbed him how afraid of her he'd become.

'There's nothing to explain, George. Please, leave me alone…' said Nellie quietly.

Shellard grinned and put his cap back on, flipping it straight with a flick of his wrist. He could hear the pleading tone of her voice. He'd won back the ascendancy. He went to the door, then as he left he turned around and winked.

'Yer know where I am, lass.'

When he had gone she sat own on the stairs and cried, hating everything that had happened and despising her own wretched state. She thought of Humphrey, of the joy she'd shared with Shellard, her own glee at making Humphrey pay over the odds for the cob, the blows, the love he tried to show her in his own immature and restrained manner. She cried out loud and Prudence came to comfort her, thinking it was all over and her mistress had got rid of Shellard for good. She didn't have the strength to explain to Prudence that the worst was yet to come. She told her to go upstairs and

171

look after the children, then thought about what Shellard had said.

Humphrey would know.

It was dark before Humphrey realised his old footballing companions had left him alone in the *Rose and Crown*. The Mockett brothers had departed in merry mood in search of Garstang, who had earned a decent income playing as a professional for an association side and had retired to Chorley to run a butcher's shop. Crumblehulme had made his apologies early, missing the company of his wife, an admission that had brought cries of 'shame!' from the beery men in the public bar. Stock had stayed awhile but Humphrey had nothing except the Cup in common with him, and once that had been remembered there was little else for the two of them to do except stare at their drinks. Humphrey didn't notice him leave, and he was glad of it – apart from their time together in the scrum he realised how different their lives had been.

Humphrey sat alone, listening to the tick of the clock and the quiet conversation of widowers and lonely bachelors. The pub had changed as the economy of the nation collapsed, dragged down by doomsayers and despots determined to protect their trade. The association club didn't meet in there, or use Dole Lane, preferring its own pavilion out in the new part of town. Yet the pub's walls were familiar and comforting, and the clink of bottles and the rush of liquid poured out of the beer engine served him well.

When Cook and his lawyer Mister Berry came through the door he didn't even notice them, let alone recognise who they were. It was only when Mister Berry had placed a clerk's copy of the court summons on the table that Humphrey knew what he had waited for had finally happened.

'I've come to get the cob I paid for,' said Cook.

'Which cob?' asked Humphrey, dreading what was about to happen. He knew what cob Cook was talking about, and knew instantly that the man's grievance was true. Shellard had implicated Humphrey in some con-trick, and he had done so through Nellie, his lover.

'The one George Shellard supposedly bought on behalf of his mistress,' said Cook.

'My wife,' said Humphrey calmly. How else could he react to something he already knew? Something he'd been expecting to hear?

'Aye,' nodded Cook, 'your wife.'

Cook wanted to settle out of court. Mister Berry his solicitor explained that the matter of the cob was a delicate one, and the circumstances of the alleged fraud would prove rather embarrassing to a man of Humphrey's standing. The actual argument over possession of the cob aside - which could, after all, be blamed on George Shellard - there was the more troubling evidence that Nellie Whittle would be presented to the court as George Shellard's lover. Such a story, claimed Mister Berry, could well be the ruin of an ambitious local politician, who depended on earning the trust and respect of the town. This, he claimed, was reason enough to come to some amicable agreement that would see the cob given back to Cook and some gratuity advanced for his troubles.

Humphrey looked at Cook. He was taller than Shellard, and younger by a good few years, but they were the same. They were both cut from the same cloth, two shoddy suits with nothing of grace or style in them. Humphrey was outraged that Cook would even suggest he was man enough to make a deal with him, a deal over a cob that – as far as Humphrey was concerned – was paid for in a perfectly fair manner. He told Cook that he'd bought the cob in good faith and it was his to own; he wasn't going to make any deal. With that, he got up and told them he'd see them in court come what may, no matter what spurious rumours they wished to make public knowledge.

'Nell! Nell! Nellie Whittle!' shouted Humphrey, slamming the front door of the house and smashing his umbrella against the banisters. 'Nell, for God's sake where are you, woman! Nell, come here at once or by God you'll suffer for it! Come here now!'

The door into the kitchens opened and one of the maids appeared, a woman who had come to the house to look after the two children – Kathleen and Dorothy. She curtseyed when she saw Humphrey, then stood her ground bravely. Humphrey threw the umbrella away, its metal skeleton bent and broken. He gripped the nearest banister, as if he was about to pull the wood out of the joinery, then wiped the spittle that had stuck to the bottom hairs of his thick moustache.

'You! Where's my wife, girl?'

'Upstairs, sir, reading the wee bairns a fairy story,' answered the maid. 'I've the kettle on warming some milk for 'em, sir.'

'Where's George Shellard? Is he here?' asked Humphrey.

'No, sir.'

'Then fetch him for me. Here's a sovereign,' said Humphrey, throwing a coin on the floor like a man would toss a bone for a favoured dog. The maid picked it up, accepting this slur on her dignity for the sake of the money. 'You shall tell him that Mrs Whittle wishes to see him. Understand? If he asks you, tell him I am not here.'

The maid smiled. She'd heard the tales, and it was none of her business if a rogue like Shellard got what he deserved.

'I'll gerrim right away, Mister Whittle, and mum's the word.'

She left, and Humphrey stomped up the stairs, banging on the wall and shouting Nellie's name. He heard one of the children start to cry and he wished she would shut up. He shouted for Nellie and Prudence appeared from Nellie's room. Humphrey ignored her and stood on the balcony, shouting so loud that the glass in the nearby grandfather clock trembled and buzzed. Prudence started to say something but he stopped her speaking with a wave of his clenched fist. She cried and locked the door behind her. Both children were wailing, and with Prudence's tears the noise turned the house into a bedlam from one of the lowest circles of hell. In the centre of it all, Humphrey shivered as a cold chill ran down his spine. He looked up and saw Nellie on the stairs, with her hair hanging loose and her head hanging low.

She had betrayed him. She had slept with another man, broken her vows, broken his manhood, confirmed his failings. He realised he was out of breath. He held onto the banister rail and tried to block out the crying, scared that it would bring tears to his own eyes. He let the blackness wash over him, cleansing him of all his anger, confirming his own wretchedness in the sight of his God. She had left him, in soul if not in body, and he didn't deserve her back. It was his fault. He had failed as a man.

'Humphrey, I'm sorry…' whispered Nellie.

'You betrayed me,' said Humphrey.

Nellie wanted to hug him. She wanted to hit him. She wanted to explain why she did it, why she chose Shellard as her way of protesting about Humphrey's own betrayals. But she knew anything she said wouldn't be heard. She could see the anger in his eyes, even though he was calm. She could see how much he hated her.

Humphrey wanted to tell her how much he loved her. But there was a right way of doing things, a prescribed way for a gentleman to defend as much of his honour that could be salvaged from the humiliation.

'Nellie, the situation is clear. You have money, so I do not believe I need to look after you in such a fashion. My children will remain here, but as for you, I am afraid you have left me with no choice. You must leave. Immediately.'

'If I leave, I want the children,' said Nellie defensively.

Humphrey shook his head and hit the banister, threatening to break it asunder and send them both toppling over into the stairwell. He laughed in despair and started up the stairs towards her, measuring every step.

'You've had enough wants, Nell, now it's all over! The children are mine!'

'You've never cared about the children,' cried Nellie.

Humphrey reached her and she lifted a hand to protect herself. He grabbed it and put his other hand to her throat. He heard a voice – his father's voice – mocking him for being weak, being effeminate for caring about things too much. The voice was in his head, in his mind. He knew it wasn't real but he wondered whether strangling her would be a way to prove the voice wrong. Then he realised she was screaming and gagging, and he let go of her in shock. He felt nauseous. He pulled himself together and hit her on the side of her head, hoping that it would take some of his anger away. She staggered away from him, moaning for Prudence.

'The children are mine,' repeated Humphrey, brushing his suit down with his hands. 'Have them ready in thirty minutes, I intend to take them with me this evening to Primrose Cottage.'

He watched her go upstairs then turned to see if there were any servants at whom he could shout. But he remembered they were all given a holiday, so that they could celebrate the end of the year with their families, all save Prudence and the nursemaid. From behind the door to Nellie's rooms he could hear Prudence crying. It made him feel disgusted with everyone and everything, especially himself. He banged on the door and told her to go see to her mistress before he was minded to see to her, then he went downstairs – past paintings of primroses and portraits of dead Moreton men – to wait for George Shellard. He took a horse-whip from the stables.

Prudence remembered that dark evening with a shiver in her heart. She could hear the cries of the little children echoing through the town hall corridor, see their faces puffed up like melons by hot blood and tears. Nellie kissed them, gripped their heads so much that they yelped to be released, and told them she was having to go away for a few days. She couldn't tell them the truth – Prudence knew then that Nellie wished nothing had ever happened. She wondered whether Nellie had considered leaving with them, jumping out of the window into the middle of the cold street, or slitting their throats and Prudence's throat then her own, like an Egyptian queen. Nellie didn't say anything that night, and Prudence was the only person who left with her from Derwent Lodge.

Shellard followed the nursemaid into the house with a cocky smile. He could almost feel the touch of the clattering coins in his weskit pocket. They went in through the back door and the maid went through to the front hall, telling Shellard to wait for Mrs Whittle. He didn't mind waiting, and looked at the wall, sniffing to see whether he could smell where he'd had her. The memory brought a flush to his cheeks and he smacked his lips in anticipation of more to come.

Then the hall door opened and Humphrey Whittle strode through with his face tight beneath his top hat and his limbs stiff as a dead man. Shellard stopped grinning and in a split second realised there was nothing he could say to absolve himself from blame. He turned to escape out of the back door then Humphrey was upon him, leaping like a monkey to tackle him roughly to the stone floor.

The wind was crushed out of Shellard, and he groaned under the heavy weight of the taller man. He tried to cry out in pain but the lack of air stopped him.

'You horrible fiend, Shellard, you're nothing, I tell you, nothing, by God!' cried Humphrey, his words deafening Shellard. He dragged Shellard up by the collar then threw him against the wall. He wanted to explain to Shellard why he wasn't fit to be treated like another human being, that he was lower on the evolutionary scale than the lowest ape, but he couldn't be bothered with words. They were for the council chamber, for other gentlemen.

He took the horse-whip from his belt and thrashed at Shellard, hitting him with all the force he could muster, with every stroke removing some of his shame and anger. Shellard cried out for mercy and tried to cover his face with his hands, turning away, but this only made Humphrey concentrate harder on flaying the clothes off Shellard's back. He ripped his coat, his weskit, his shirt, then his skin. He thrashed and thrashed and thrashed as if it was the Devil before him, splattering blood on the wall until his shoulder ached and he changed hands. Then he thrashed some more, clumsily, striking Shellard low in a bloody heap on the floor. Only when Shellard had stopped crying did Humphrey stop. Then he kicked at Shellard to make sure he was alive, and dragged him through the front hall and outside onto the street. There he threw Shellard down the steps and into a pile of horse dung. Shellard moaned, realising he was free, and started to crawl away to the other side of the street.

Humphrey smiled.

'Don't ever come here or in my presence again, you snivelling wretch. Understand?' He heard Shellard say yes between sobs of relief and fear. Then he shut the door.

The affair between Nellie and Shellard became a matter of public knowledge in court. Nellie denied it but Humphrey, on hearing the evidence, agreed with the judge that his wife was indeed unfaithful, and it was this that had led her to court Shellard's favour regarding the cob. But as far as Humphrey was concerned, she had paid for the cob and the cob was his, and the fact that Nellie had been giving Shellard money was quite irrelevant to the case in hand. Mister Berry argued that Shellard's scheme was well known to Cook, who had on occasion helped Shellard out in his business affairs.

As Mister Berry argued, Shellard's scheme had been typical. He'd brought a cob from a farmer called Bond for Nellie to buy, and had stabled it with Cook. Then he brought another cob to Cook from Liverpool, and secretly removed Bond's cob and took it to Derwent Lodge. When Nellie came to Cook's to buy the cob Cook thought she was buying the Liverpool cob, but Nellie thought it was Bond's. Shellard then convinced Cook to buy Bond's cob for twenty-five pounds. Once this was done, Shellard sold the Liverpool cob that was at Derwent Lodge, and brought Bond's cob there.

This argument was refuted by Humphrey, and Shellard proved to be an unlikely witness to his defence. Shellard – in a written statement - said he'd done nothing of the sort, and hadn't had an affair. Humphrey said the cob he'd bought was his, and if Cook wanted his money back he would have to chase Shellard.

The judge agreed.

Winter slowly made way for spring. Nellie's affair and the scandal raised in court was kept out of the papers by Humphrey's friends, who all agreed it was a shame for such a promising chap and it was the least they could do to protect his feelings at a difficult time in his life. Humphrey couldn't thank them enough. Even so, they couldn't stop the news spreading from backyard to ginnel to street corner – whenever he walked the streets he could hear them talking, could sense them pointing and laughing at the cuckolded councillor. The only thing he could do was brave the taunts and keep walking.

Nellie moved to Liverpool, where she found cheap but decent accommodation for herself and Prudence. Every day she wrote a letter to Humphrey, but he never opened them - he threw them all on the fire. She also wrote to Shellard, asking him to see her, seeking some solace away from Humphrey's silence. Every night she drank enough gin to sleep, slowly drinking more and spending her inheritance. Prudence watched and worried, not wanting to see her mistress in such a state but fearing to turn to either Shellard or Humphrey for help. Whenever Shellard appeared in Liverpool he and Nellie would spend their time in gin shops and in bed, and Prudence was ashamed. She wished Shellard was dead, and wondered how much poison cost in an apothecary's shop.

Then Shellard started to shout at Nellie, and she would shout back, and it seemed to Prudence that she had gone back in time like a character in a magazine, and she was back in Derwent Lodge listening to Humphrey shout at Nellie. But Shellard wasn't Humphrey, and Nellie dominated the arguments in her clear and confident manner. She could sense Shellard cringe through the wall of their apartment, sense him knowing that he wasn't Humphrey Whittle and could never be.

Finally, after Shellard had been in Liverpool for a week in the beginning of April, Prudence watched as Nellie threw him out, followed by a small knapsack of manly things. When she closed the door on him, Nellie smiled and her face glowed like an angel's. She asked for Prudence and she went to hug and kiss her.

'Prudence,' she said, stroking her hair, 'I've got rid of him. Everything's going to be all right now.'

Prudence smiled, and let Nellie tie her hair in a plait.

14.

The Cup Final

AFTER ALL THE WAITING, the delays and the planning, the final match of the North of England Challenge Cup was played. The three months between the original date and the actual date of the final were forgotten as the teams prepared themselves for the biggest day of rugby football's short history. Yorkshire may have pioneered the idea of the cup, but the Northern Challenge Cup was something special. They believed it would become the most important cup competition in the whole of football. It would be bigger than the Calcutta Cup, the Union's pale imitation of a trophy - a cup without a competition, copied by the Union who wanted their cup to be first - played for by England and Scotland. They knew they were the pioneers for what they thought would become the pinnacle of every rugby footballer's sporting life – to play in the final of the Cup and prove one's manhood and strength against the best the north of England had to offer.

For most of those who took part in the final, the reality of the following years – when rugby football declined in Lancashire to an extent that even mighty Chorley became a 'soccer' club, when arguments over financial guarantees and allegations of impropriety forced the Cup to be scrapped – was tempered by old age and warm memories. But Humphrey wasn't the only one to regret the failed opportunities and the loss of the spirit that had made their game like no other, even if that spirit, the muscular Christian ethic, had always been susceptible to the pressures of change. The Cup was a moment of perfection they knew had passed, a moment they knew they would never have again.

Fish had no romantic ideal about the meaning and purpose of his cup competition. He didn't care that the Union's Calcutta Cup had been played for weeks earlier, beating them to it. He didn't care about those who complained about the injustice of the weather robbing their Cup of its claim to seniority. His motive was simple – to make as much money as he could before he died. He didn't believe in the idea that money was the root of all evil, and laughed at preachers who claimed no one could take their riches with them into the next world. As far as Fish was concerned, the after-life was neither here nor there, and if they didn't allow money in heaven on account of its sinful nature then he was better off in hell, where he was sure there was always a bob or two to be made among the remorseful. He'd heard some members of the Union talk about the incorruptible nature of sport and the sporting man, and it didn't make any sense to him. Whatever they said, there was always someone somewhere wanting to gamble on the fastest drop of rain on a window. If the players believed in their incorruptible nature then that was fine, as long as he could take bets on who was going to win.

On the day of the match special trains carried the Chorley team and over eight hundred supporters to Blackpool, all trimmed with the black and white colours of the town and club. The aldermen of the town and other important people honoured the team with a civic ceremony and a feast the night before of best sirloin steak. This, they said, was so that the players would be strong for the clash of the gladiators the next day. On the morning of their departure, the Whittle family treated every man on the team list to a brand new watch and a breakfast of back bacon, black pudding and spicy Cumberland sausages. Each watch was designed to fit into a weskit pocket by means of a gold catch, and was given in token of appreciation – neither the club nor the Whittles wanted the watches to be described as payments.

When his father handed over a watch to him, Humphrey found he could at last smile and thank the old man. It wasn't an expensive watch, and he had one of a far superior design, but it was something. He shook his father's hand, and they had to suffer the cheers of the crowd waiting on the steps of Primrose Cottage to escort the team to the station. The elder Whittle grimaced with embarrassment, but this turned into a laboured smile when a reporter appeared to take notes. Humphrey didn't know what to say to his father, and was relieved when it was Lever's turn to come out of the dining room to get his watch.

When each man had his watch, they climbed into a charabanc pulled by a team of six horses, and went to the station adored like honoured gladiators by the people in the streets. Harry had arranged for an engine and three coaches to take them to Blackpool, and in the night someone had stolen into the yard to paint the words 'Play Up Chorley' on the side of the gleaming black boiler. They were ushered into the first class carriage along with the club's directors, who wished they were thirty years younger.

Humphrey found a window seat and watched the town glide away with every puff and whistle of the mighty engine. He saw Primrose Cottage and the orchard where they'd let Frederick fall in the water, and the tilled earth in the fields beyond it. The train rattled over a bridge, swaying the carriage. One of the Mockett brothers started to sing a song, but Humphrey wasn't in the mood for singing. He was thinking of the Cup. He looked out at the green trees and yellow fields with the watch his father had given him cradled in his hand.

The team arrived in Blackpool, bedecked with women's fancies pinned to their shirts, and they were ushered into cars to take them to Raikes Hall like visiting royalty.

It was an unusual feeling to be a god. It was a blasphemous moment, a pagan moment, as he walked with his companions through the gardens at Raikes Hall in their brand new white shirts and black trousers. They each had a new haircut, a smooth jaw and rosettes declaring everlasting allegiance to Chorley Football Club pinned to their breasts. Humphrey led the team, a muscular Christian accepting the adulation of hundreds of men and women lining the path. He knew then what it must have been like for the gladiators of Rome to march to the circus and certain death to honour gods and emperors. It was, he realised, the most perfect moment a man could have, and after it even death was welcomed for there could be nothing close to the elation of being a god oneself. Women blew kisses, dropped dresses over their shoulders and clutched flowers in their hands. Men cheered wildly, trying to get close to the players so they could smell the hair lacquer and sweat of their betters, so they could share in the manliness of such immortals. Children followed in their wake, hoping one day to be worthy to receive the blessings of others.

The crowd in the gardens was nothing compared to the amount of people squeezed into the football ground. In the gardens the people were dispersed by trees and flower beds. In the football ground, they were shoehorned into the grandstand and squeezed into the gap between the pitch and the high wall built around it. Fish's helpers were overworked selling food and colours and taking bets, and were forced to walk on the pitch to get around the ground. In the Raikes Hall office, Fish was busy calculating how much tax he would have to pay and how small a crowd he could declare without the press becoming too suspicious. He reckoned that two thousand wouldn't seem too fallacious, and would be a respectable crowd for the enterprise, even though Raikes Hall could have almost twice that number inside its walls. It was an expedient business decision - he was sure it wouldn't become normal practice for football clubs to cheat the taxman.

The Rossendale players were already on the pitch when Humphrey arrived with the Chorley team. Rossendale, or Bacup as they sometimes called themselves (after the town in which they played), were captained by the young University man called Scheidler, who had scored the crucial try against Manchester Athletic. He had also won some acclaim as a rower and was a respectable all-rounder at cricket. He had some unusual ideas about training the body to be fit for football, and would make his men go through a series of physical jerks and small sprints to ready themselves for the actual match. It was, thought Humphrey, both undignified and counter-productive. Some of the thousand or so Chorley supporters in the crowd were laughing and mocking the Rossendale players, but most at least respected them for being finalists in the Cup.

Humphrey and his men pushed their way through the crowd and onto the pitch where there was a gap in the fence. On their arrival the Chorley supporters started to sing their praises. Others simply applauded or cheered, including the small contingent of respectable people who had come with the Rossendale team. Humphrey allowed himself to smile. Although there was a strong east wind blowing and billowing about the football ground he didn't notice it. As far as he was concerned it was a perfect day. He waved to the crowd and with that movement he had them crying out his name and that of Chorley. He was a god. He wondered whether he could try the magic again, and he waved his hand a second time. The cheers came back. He was a conductor, and the crowd his orchestra. The Rossendale players looked on enviously, knowing they were only there in a supporting role, that hardly anyone wanted them to win.

Harry came onto the pitch with the Rossendale umpire and a referee,

Mister Mounsey, whom the Union had insisted be there to make sure the match was fair and proper. He was ignored by the players, and when he offered his hand they found it to be cold and clammy. But he was the man carrying the football, and when the crowd saw him they shouted at him with impatience and anticipation. Humphrey went to the middle of the pitch and shook hands with Scheidler, noting his confident smile and rakish manner – he didn't particularly like university men, even if they had supposedly drawn up most of the rules for both codes of football. He noticed Scheidler had something going on with Harry, because they gave each other knowing looks. He ignored it and watched Mister Mounsey hold a shilling up between his fingers.

Humphrey held his breath, and offered the call to Scheidler. He opted for heads and when the coin was flipped it landed on the wet grass with the Queen staring up at them. Scheidler laughed boyishly, and Humphrey glared at him. He was sure it was going to be the only thing Scheidler won all day.

Scheidler tried to outstare Humphrey, to show how unafraid he was. But there was something frightening in Humphrey's eyes, a cold determination, that made him shiver and look to his own team to escape it.

Shellard was there when the Cup was played. There was money to be made from picking the right odds, and if that failed large crowds and plenty of beer meant people were careless about their money. They left cash in unattended coats, or put their wallets in outer pockets so big a man could put his arm inside them and the owner wouldn't even notice. And they said the women loved a footballer, and there'd be plenty of tipsy squeezes to be had if you knew the right words. He'd gone on the train that carried the team, wearing his Sunday best. The supporters were in a good mood and didn't mind that he took all their money on the turn of a card. At the match he'd found a lady's purse with five pounds in it, and feeling flush he'd found a bookie to give him the odds on who'd win. This was when the Rossendale team were out on the pitch, and the five to one offer combined with their disciplined exercises were enough to convince Shellard he was onto a good thing. He put the five pounds on Rossendale to win, and imagined what he could do with an easy woman for thirty pounds.

The ball was kicked, rising a few feet into the air before falling heavily into the waiting hands of Schiedler. The spectators, on the edges of wooden seats, gripping the shoulders of the people in front of them, roared like animals. Humphrey felt his heart punding as he ran towards Scheidler, racing ahead of his men who hung back waiting for a long kick. Schiedler smiled at Humphrey, showing no sign of fear. When Humphrey was over the centre line the Chorley fans started to wave fancy black and white flags. Scheidler stood his ground, ignoring the painful waves of urgent words. Then, still smiling at Humphrey, he passed the ball on to Aitkin, his fellow half standing a yard away, who used the tip of his boot to punt the ball into the middle of the stand.

Humphrey stopped, panting for breath, hating Scheidler. He loosened the cord at the top of his shirt, allowing the warm Spring wind to soothe his burning chest. Scheidler turned away to congratulate Aitkin for a good, clean kick. Humphrey saw the crowd moving, gesticulating. He turned to see Harry jumping up and down and shaking a fist gripping a cigar at the Rossendale umpire. Behind him, Lever was combing back his hair, whilst Leo took Humphrey's role of shepherding the forwards towards the mark where the scrum was set, on an imaginary line perpendicular to the point on the touchline where the ball had gone over. He saw Leo's lips moving but all he could hear was the loud beat of his own heart.

Scheidler jogged up to him and put out his hand. He was saying something polite, something clipped and precise with perfect vowels. A university voice.

'What?' asked Humphrey.

'No time to stand around, what?' joked Scheidler.

Humphrey smiled. 'We'll see who's standing at the end. What.'

He wiped his sweating palms on the back of his trousers, then ran to the forming scrum. Scheidler frowned.

'Is everything okay, sir?' asked Aitkin, looking at Humphrey's back.

'Let's just get on with it, shall we?'

Scheidler came out of the back of the scrum with the ball, and kicked it along the floor to Haworth, the nearest three-quarter back. But Leo had watched him drop the ball to his boots and was running up from the Chorley line as soon as the ball slapped against the hard toe-cap. He intercepted the ball and kicked it ahead of him into the middle of the pitch. The scrum to his left broke loose and all the forwards rushed after the ball like a pack of starving hounds. The Rossendale backs, confused by this sudden turn in their fortunes, hesitated enough for Leo to reach the ball a second time, and this time he managed to kick it closer to the Rossendale line just before he was shoulder-charged. As he fell to the floor Humphrey and Garstang hurdled over him, chasing the ball.

He looked around to see who had knocked him over but there wasn't a Rossendale player anywhere near him. He picked himself out of the mud, and glanced at Crumblehulme, who had moved up to join him. His fellow full-back shrugged his shoulders.

'He's keen, your brother,' he said after a moment's contemplation. Leo nodded, picking off mud from his knee, where the black cloth had ripped. In the stand, the Chorley directors were on their feet and clapping. The umpires and referee were all at the other end of the pitch, standing back from a moving scrimmage. Leo stretched his fingers, watching as a bruise blossomed up over his knuckles.

'Play up, Chorley, remember the Cup!' cried Humphrey, slapping his men on their backs as they heaved with all their might to push the Rossendale forwards off the ball and over their own goal-line. A wind whipped about them, making their eyes stream with water, gagging them when they tried to breathe. Out of the scrum, their new half-back Settle urged Humphrey to look out for a quick dribble but Humphrey ignored him. All he cared about was pushing them back, always backwards with all the energy he could muster out of his sinew-stretched pistons.

The crowd cheered as Chorley pushed Rossendale down the slope, fighting against the wind with every step. Rossendale men shouted to each other as feet slipped and shoulders were pulled to the extent of their stretch. Someone cried a warning as a socket popped and their defence crumbled. Unburdened by the opposing force, the Chorley forwards fell over their own legs and collapsed in the mud.

Humphrey ignored the crowd's applause. He didn't want their appreciation until he had won. He got to his feet and followed one of the Mockett brothers, who was dribbling with the ball at his feet. Settle and Lever followed, confusing the Rossendale backs. They argued amongst themselves until Mockett was near the line, then as he kicked the ball in front of him one of their full-backs dived for it. Mockett reacted at the same time and they both fell in heap over the ball and the goal-line.

'Howzat!' said Lever, looking at the two umpires. Harry nodded but the

Rossendale umpire shook his head and told the referee that his man had touched down first. Lever called the Rossendale umpire a cheat and Humphrey dragged him away, reminding him he was a gentleman, and a Chorley one at that. Lever agreed but went off in a sulk.

Humphrey turned to his men, who had gathered next to Harry Hibbert.

'For the Cup!' he shouted.

'For Humphrey Whittle!' cried Garstang.

'For Humphrey Whittle!' repeated Leo, in a mischievous mood.

'For Humphrey!' they all shouted, except for Lever.

Humphrey smiled, then threw himself back into the game.

The ball dropped out of the sky behind the Chorley goal-line, and the crowd gasped with amazement as it came to rest next to the posts. All thirty players on the field ran for it, shouldering each other out of the way and ignoring the noise of the crowd. Leo picked the ball up and looked to kick it clear, but he was pounced on by Scheidler and three of the Rossendale forwards. He was pinned to the ground and winded, but retained enough wits to touch the ball down before they claimed a try. Harry, who was on the spot, ruled on the matter and the referee agreed. Then the Rossendale umpire looked at his watch and suggested to the players it was half-time.

Humphrey put his hands on his knees and fought for breath. Veins were pounding in his temples. Sweat ran down his back. Blood trickled from his lip. He didn't want to stop, but he could see the rest of his men were exhausted from fighting the wind and keeping Rossendale off their line. He nodded at Harry, and the umpires stopped the game with one touchdown apiece.

'Damn it, Humphrey, they're devils!' gasped Lever, jogging up alongside him and patting his back. 'I thought the bookies favoured us!'

'We'll have the wind next half,' replied Humphrey, looking at the grandstand. People were moving about, trying to buy pies and bottles of beer. He couldn't see his father.

'With the wind in our sails, eh?' joked Lever.

Humphrey ignored him. He was looking at Scheidler, who had been called off the pitch by Fish. They seemed to be having an argument of some kind. Fish seemed nervous, worried that people could hear him. Humphrey wondered what was being said. The two of them looked back out onto the pitch and at Humphrey, then quickly looked away.

He saw them shake hands.

'Come on, Humphrey, get your chaps up the front organised!' shouted Ferguson, a reservist from Horwich who had joined them midway through the season on account of his accurate goal-kicking. The order was enough to dispel any doubts in Humphrey's mind. He only cared about the game, about winning. He slapped Lever hard on the back, then went over to his pack to put fire in their bellies.

'Come on Chorley!' shouted the crowd. Humphrey glanced up and for a moment saw that his father was on his feet and cheering with everyone else. Then, evidently embarrassed, his father sat back down awkwardly.

The wind blew away the clouds, and Rossendale's forwards wilted under the fierce gaze of the sun. Humphrey rejoiced as men fell before him, or were tackled to the ground with so much force that they refused to get back up. Marsh ran with the ball and no one could stop him except the umpires, who called offside when he threw a pass to Ferguson. But Rossendale didn't have any spirit left in them. They allowed Chorley to gain the ball and Humphrey pushed his men back up the field. In a loose scrimmage they dribbled the ball forward, keeping it at their feet, to allow Stock to cross the line for a try. The crowd was ecstatic, and men hugged each other - but then Lever missed the goal.

In the grandstand, Humphrey's father cursed the wind. Below him, in the tight space packed with younger men, Shellard held onto his ticket stub and prayed.

Rossendale charged forward, their dribbler surrounded by the rest of their forwards. The ball, slippery with mud, went out of control. The dribbler stumbled. Scheidler stepped through his own players and tried to pick up the ball but it fell out his hands. He fell on it and was jumped on by Garstang, who threw him over on his back like a Cumberland wrestler. The Rossendale forwards charged in, eneveloping Scheidler and the loose ball.

'One last push, lads!' cried Humphrey, putting his shoulder into the backs of his forwards, pushing their stumbling-feet over the ball and into the crumbling ranks of the Rossendale pack. His own feet slipped and he fell in front of the ball, looking at it with greedy eyes. He stretched out, then saw in the space between boots and legs Scheidler's knowing face. He considered punching it, then noticed that Scheidler was making no attempt to grab the ball. Humphrey hesitated, seeing in that face everything he'd feared about Fish and Raikes Hall and the evil in the world. He lunged out for the ball, or the face, not knowing which was which. Lever clambered over him and booted the ball clean away into touch near the Rossendale line.

Humphrey got to his feet, allowing Scheidler to creep away. There was only the game. He had to win the game. Nothing else mattered except the Cup. He would show his father he deserved it.

The ball was thrown out by Rossendale, and Humphrey knew he had to reach it before anyone else. He jumped through the jostling men, looking at the heavy ball rushing through the air, spinning and turning in an erratic fashion. He stretched higher, pushing Rossendale players out of his way, defying the pull of the earth to remain in the air like an angel. The ball turned, falling into his waiting arms, and he fell to the ground. The Rossendale forwards plucked and poked at him as he fell, trying to grab the ball and knock him out. Someone's elbow was jammed in his face and he felt his skull shudder and his eye socket crack. He bellowed in anger and the Rossendale forwards fell back in a mixture of fear and awe. His vision was blurred but he heard Leo calling out Ferguson's name. Behind him he heard Ferguson call him, calling for the ball. He heeled it backwards, then listened as Ferguson's boot hit the hard leather.

He wiped the blood from his eye, and saw the ball fly over the Rossendale full-backs and over the crossbar of the goals. He saw Harry running across the field with his flag in the air, and heard the crowd cheering his name. Leo was saying there was only a minute to go. Scheidler was already congratulating them.

'We've done it, Humphrey!' laughed Lever.

He had won.

15.

In Fairyland

PRUDENCE REMEMBERED THE CHANGE that came over Nellie Whittle on the day she threw out George Shellard. An alchemist's trick had transmuted her, turned her into gold. She was how Prudence imagined Ellen Moreton to have been, free and fully alive. Nellie was young again. She moved with confidence through the streets, smiling as winter turned to spring and the promise of summer was sung by birds. Bachelors and other men raised their hats to her, offered to take her hand as she stepped over puddles.

Prudence was happy because Nellie was happy. She remembered the gin bottle on the window ledge, covered in a spider's cobweb. The spider had built its nest in the crook of the window frame, throwing the web like a net between there and the green gin bottle. Prudence knew then that Nellie was rid of Shellard and Humphrey Whittle – the web was better than a telegram at telling this truth. When she'd found it she'd left it there, dusting around it but leaving it untouched.

Whittle noticed that the guests were leaving the banquet hall. They were making their excuses to Ramsbottom, the Town Clerk, since the Mayor was fast asleep with a glass of brandy in his heavy hands. Some looked at Whittle but most ignored him, knowing that there were some crosses a man had to bear by himself. They didn't want him to spoil their evening, and he understood that. In similar circumstances he knew he would have been one of the first to ostracise a man involved in a crime as perfidious as his. His friends had been too kind, too loyal to their captain. It was undeserving, and he wished they would leave him alone to suffer his sins in silent self-loathing.

He wondered how long it would be before he went insane and joined his brother in the darkness of a locked hospital room. He suspected he was madder than Frederick, madder than Jane, maybe as mad as his father had been when he'd started to see the Russian Hussar. He remembered his wedding, when he had seen that ghostly figure. He'd rationalised it away by blaming the pressures of the ceremony and his father's incessant chitter-chatter. But he knew he was fooling himself. He had seen the Hussar, of that there was no doubt. Everything that had happened since that time had only confirmed his fears, that he was about to be taken by demons in the same way as the rest of his family. They would find out and they would lock him up – then, and only then, would he be able to say what had really happened.

'Humphrey?'

One of the Mockett brothers stood over him, worrying the rim of his top hat between his hands. Whittle looked at him and for a moment hated him more than he'd ever hated George Shellard. He couldn't be left alone to forget the past. But the memory of Raikes Hall, the nostalgic recollections, were still enough to straighten his spine and remove the lines around his eyes, if only for a few brief seconds. He smiled bitterly, struggling to shape the creases of his face upwards.

'To what do I owe this pleasure?'

His words sounded cynical. Mockett, though, pretended not to hear.

'There's that young miss outside, Humphrey, askin' after thee. Seems quite insistent about it.'

Prudence. He couldn't forget her, she wouldn't go away. He knew he had to face her. He realised the room was half-empty. Someone was helping Ramsbottom to lift up the Mayor and lay him down in the cool draught of an open window. He didn't want to be left alone in the empty hall with a drunk and empty chairs. There were other ways out of the town hall, but he wouldn't take them. He had to be brave.

'I'll be out there in a minute. Tell her, won't you?'

Mockett nodded and went out. Whittle felt his heart pounding, and reached for the brandy decanter.

After Shellard had left - or rather, after she had got rid of him - Nellie decided to leave Liverpool. The Moreton family had substantial holdings in the marchlands of North Wales across the Dee estuary, and in her father's will she had been bequeathed a small house called Hollyfield in the small town of Gresford. It was ideally placed, surrounded by lush fields and copses of beech trees. It was another country, a small part of Eden left untouched by the Flood. It was a place she could call home.

When they were packing, Prudence noticed Nellie hiding a sheaf of letters away in her portmanteau. She was about to tell her to leave them, to burn them on the fire before they left for Wales, when she came across the watch under Nellie's bed. All her concerns about the letters were forgotten. The watch was a simple gold pocket watch, one Shellard had worn with pride whenever he'd come to visit Nellie. Prudence didn't know where it had come from, though she was certain Nellie had given him the watch, as she'd given him pocketfuls of gold sovereigns.

She picked it up. It had stopped ticking. On the back was inscribed, in decorative letters, the name George Moreton and the year 1823. Prudence didn't know who George Moreton was but by the date she guessed it was some ancestor of Nellie's, that the watch was a family heirloom of some sentimental value. Yet Shellard had owned it, taken it. Prudence wondered what had been going on between her mistress and Shellard. She tried to remember what she'd read about the trial, about the man who claimed Shellard had conned him and the amount of money Shellard boasted about taking from Humphrey Whittle. It was all too much for her to understand. She heard Nellie cleaning the window ledge and throwing away the gin bottle. Quickly she took the watch and put it in the front pocket of her apron.

Hollyfield was as charming as the name suggested, and on their arrival Prudence instantly fell in love with the place. It was up a small lane from Gresford, in sight of the church tower but separated from the rest of the houses by a deep-cut stream and rich green pastures. It had been a farm before it came into the possession of the Moreton family, and had its own yard and two crumbling stone out-buildings. Prudence, who had only known the crowded, filthy terraces of Chorley, had to pinch herself to make sure she hadn't travelled into some beautiful fairyland. There was a field at the back of the house rising up to a small hill where a tenant farmer grazed sheep, with a spring from where they could draw all the water they needed. Nellie said she would find some suitable servants, so that Prudence didn't have to do everything, but Prudence was happy being alone with Nellie. From her room in the attic she could look out across the flat marshes and see the serpent curves of the river, and beyond that the brown and green patchwork quilt of England. It was, thought Prudence, a perfect place for Nellie to live, a place where she could be as Prudence imagined she'd been before Humphrey Whittle and George Shellard.

Yet Nellie couldn't settle. She would stand at the window, staring at the lane down to Gresford but seeing other things. She would forget herself and pour milk instead of gravy, then watch as it drained into the grey slivers of a lamb-chop. She would listen to the Welsh postman whistling on his way up towards Wrexham, and lose her thread when knitting. Prudence would come in from a day chasing lambs in the top field to find her crying, or hiding her tears behind a widow's veil. She wanted Nellie to be happy like she was happy, surrounded by fairies, green men and kings sleeping under stones. But Nellie had taken to living her life in the hazy dream of the half-dead, wandering from room to room and never venturing out into the light of the sun. Prudence expected to be asked to fetch her a jug of ale or a bottle of something from the village, but even that pleasure seemed to be denied by Nellie.

She whispered the names of her children in the middle of the night, when she thought Prudence couldn't hear. Prudence lay awake in her own bed in the attic, staring up at the stars through the skylight and wondering what future they told. She prayed for the morning to be better than the last one.

Humphrey caught the train to see her as soon as he heard that Shellard had been in Liverpool. He found a seat in a clattering third-class carriage, travelling with pedlars and drifters to Crewe. From there he found a first-class seat where he could stretch his long bones and smoke his pipe in peace. The rattle of the wheels over uneven points soothed his anger, though in every cloud and shadow he saw Shellard's face. The train passed over the border, pushing on over the river to the slate roofs and chimney stacks of Wrexham.

Humphrey wasn't sure if there was anything he could do to punish her. The letters he'd received from her he had burned, their deceitful words turning to ashes. They had gone up the chimney to blow across the town like the slanderous gossip of backyards and gin shops. She was still his wife and the mother of his children, he still saw her face every day in their faces, and despised them for it. He didn't want to be like his own father but he had to shout at them to keep them disciplined, to make them forget their slut of a mother and learn to be proper, respectful Whittle girls. She had betrayed him again, had betrayed them. When he had thrown her out he'd expected her to behave with decorum and yet it was common knowledge amongst the scrubbers and the spinners that her house was a whore's house and Shellard her pimp. It was not the behaviour of a decent woman who deserved to be treated like the fairest flower. He hated her for the hurt she caused, the pain in his head and the demons that whispered in the middle of the street. It had to stop, or he swore on his faith that he would do whatever was necessary to retain his dignity, his manhood. He hated her for living.

He reached Hollyfield in the middle of the morning, pulled there in a hackney carriage by an illiterate, incoherent Welshman. Humphrey suffered the man's tuneless airs and Welsh gobbledegook in silence, saving his ire for Nellie. He'd hoped to find her there with Shellard. He still savoured the pleasure he'd had in thrashing the man, and had kept the blood-matted horse whip hung up in the stables as a reminder and a warning. When he was in a rage he could forget the pressures of his life and the injustices others did to him, and every stroke was a soothing hand on his brow. When he had been seventeen and a cocky young lad two knavish types had set their fox terrier to his old dog for their amusement. But they had stopped laughing when he'd kicked in the head of their terrier then punched the largest one of them flat out. The second man made his choice and saved the terrier, carrying it away as Humphrey kicked and punched the first one, cajoling him to get up and be a man until a passer-by pulled him off. Humphrey had had to go and cool down with a wash of cold water before he'd gone back to work in the Whittle office.

Prudence was in the herb garden at the front of the house, weeding the beds and turning in the blood and bones. She saw the hackney come down the road from Wrexham and recognised Humphrey's tall, straight-backed figure immediately. Only Humphrey Whittle or an undertaker would wear a top hat and black jacket on a sunny day. She picked up her basket and ran round to the back of the house and in through the kitchen. She shouted Nellie's name – Mrs Whittle - which sounded odd and formal, hoping to find her before she noticed her husband was in the lane outside the house. She heard Humphrey paying the man, offering him a tip which was greeted by a perfect English response. She heard the horses shake the livery, the driver crack the whip, and the wheels turn. She heard Humphrey's brisk step up the garden path – click, clack, click, clack on the flagstones.

She found Nellie in the sitting room, looking out at Humphrey from behind the net curtains. She was smiling, as if she expected Humphrey to bow, kiss her hand and apologise before they all went to live happily ever after at Derwent Lodge. Prudence wanted to hide and pray to God to send a lightning bolt to turn Whittle into a smouldering pile of ash, surrounded by greasy smoke. She could sense Nellie's joy, feel it in the air of the house as she rushed to the front door to greet him.

She followed Nellie, waiting in the shadows to comfort her when Humphrey had gone. Nellie opened the front door before Humphrey had time to ring the bell, and her smile disappeared. Humphrey blocked out the light, a block of granite. He didn't smile, he didn't cry. Instead he rubbed the end of his moustache and stared at Nellie as if he was looking at an applicant for charity in front of the Poor Board. He didn't enter the house, despite Nellie's desperate signals for him to do so. Prudence watched his eyes, for only there could any emotion be seen. They flashed with hatred at the house, at Wales, at Prudence, at Nellie, especially at Nellie.

'Humphrey… can I come back with you?' asked Nellie, fiddling with the front laces of her dress and avoiding his golem's stare. Prudence knew she was thinking about the children, about her own failure to be with them and the mistakes she had made. There was nothing she could do to help her.

Humphrey shook his head. Nellie started towards him to hug him and feel the firm muscles of his shoulder, to put her head there and feel his heart pounding. But he put out his hand, ready to push her off. She stopped.

'Oh, Humphrey, I'm so sorry… let's think about the children, they need their mother.'

'They need a decent mother, not a slut,' said Humphrey. The word was a cut against the grain, unbefitting his calm, patrician's manner. He chose the word deliberately, and Nellie recoiled from it. She wanted to defend herself but knew that any words she used would only make her position worse, make him believe she would never be a deserving wife. She hated the people who had made him deny his true self. He offered Nellie a brown envelope. She took it, avoiding the touch of his fingers.

'Thar's one hundred pounds. I believe that should settle things and keep you away from my children.'

'Humphrey...' she pleaded.

'I know you were with Shellard in Liverpool. A hundred pounds is enough, isn't it, for our four years of marriage?'

'Humphrey...'

'It is over. I trust now you have this money you will at least behave like an English woman. You will not see Shellard again.'

'Humphrey...' said Nellie, now crying. She threw the envelope on the floor at his feet. He shrugged and kicked it back into the house. It landed near Prudence, and for a second she glared at Humphrey with unbridled hatred. He was startled but retained his composure.

'Good bye, Nellie,' he said.

'Please stay, Humphrey,' whispered Nellie.

He shook his head.

'I can't bear to be near you any more.'

He raised his hat, the only polite gesture he'd made throughout his visit, then he walked away. Prudence stepped forward and shut the door. She wondered how one went about hiring bandits and pirates to waylay people and kill them at your bidding. She turned to comfort Nellie, but Nellie had already gone to her room, where she was shouting out his name through the window.

In the lane outside, Humphrey heard her but didn't stop.

Prudence remembered that day a year later, when she was waiting for Whittle in the town hall after he had given away the Cup. She remembered Nellie's tears.

When Mockett came back to Prudence she smiled, knowing she was about to see Whittle again. Mockett offered her a cigarette, then when she refused he lit his own and told her that Whittle would be out in a few moments. She smiled and thanked him, and he rushed away. Prudence knew he'd sensed the ghosts that were hovering about her.

As far as Shellard was concerned, he'd spent a fair bit of brass travelling to and from Liverpool and helping Nellie out with buying things. She still owed him for a cob he'd helped her buy, and he'd done that fair and square. He hadn't ripped her off like he'd ripped off her husband and his old mate Cook. It was business as far as he was concerned, he hadn't done it to prove how good or loving he was. Even so, he'd expected better treatment. She'd shown her gratitude by throwing him out without giving him what she owed - now he couldn't afford to buy a cob, not with his wife and his gambling debts. It was only fair that she had to pay him the money he'd spent on her, both for finding the cob and all his expenses. To make matters worse, when he'd decided to pawn the watch she'd given him he'd found that it had gone. At first he blamed his wife and beat her, but he soon realised he'd left it with Nellie. So he'd sent her letters, demanding what was his. He enjoyed having her but if he couldn't have her then at least he could have some money out of it.

She didn't reply to his letters, and the excuses he gave the men asking him for money didn't stop them turning him over in an alley. He didn't mind them taking what was theirs in kind. He'd done it himself, when another fellow had failed to pay what was owed and he'd attacked them at night with a club. He had to pay the debts somehow, even if that meant crawling home with a ripped suit and bruised ribs. What really made him mad was that it was her fault he'd had no money. If she hadn't thrown him out he wouldn't have had to go back to his wife and pay their bills, and he wouldn't have had to take a few risks on the roll of dice. He waited every day for a cheque but none came.

He considered attacking Humphrey, stealing his wallet and his watch, the one he'd been given for his footballing skills. But he knew he was no match for Whittle – he remembered the welts on his back. Nonetheless he watched Humphrey, spied on his movements, biding his time.

And when Humphrey went to Gresford, Shellard knew where he'd gone. He remembered the whipping, the scorn in the pub, the bet at the Cup final, Nellie's eagerness and her quick temper. He realised his life had been ruined by them, and the only way he was ever to get some peace of mind was to get what was owed to him. He knew there was something he could do that would avenge the whipping, something that would satisfy him.

He started to make plans to travel to Gresford, to finish things for good or ill. He sent her a telegram telling her he was coming over on the first of May for his watch and money, then told his wife he was leaving. She complained but he ignored her. It was too late to turn back to a life of screaming kids and indifferent bosses. When the first of May came he was up early with the sun and the children playing at Robin Hood. He walked with them as far as the ironmonger's, listening to their rhymes. Robin Hood. He was

Robin Hood all right, and he was going to show them why. He scared the children away then went inside the shop. It was time to act.

Shellard persuaded the ironmonger to give him a gun on approval. A six-chambered revolver. He couldn't resist spinning a yarn and told him he had no money to pay for it. Not yet.

Shellard arrived at Gresford train station, a tiny one-man affair on a single-track branch line. Nellie and Prudence went to meet him after dropping off the hired help at her mother's. She was suffering from a chesty cough and Nellie had agreed to give her the day off. It was, thought Prudence, a bad omen: she didn't want to be in the house alone with Shellard and Nellie. She didn't want to hear them. She didn't want to be reminded of the watch she still had in her coat pocket. She didn't know why Nellie had agreed to see Shellard, though it wasn't her place to counsel her mistress about the wisdom of her decisions.

The train puffed away, surrounding Shellard in sulphurous smoke. He grinned at Prudence like a lazy tomcat. Then he bowed at Nellie and took her hand before she could object to kiss it with all the formality of a gentleman. Nellie laughed and allowed him to linger, touching her fingers and crinkling up his eyes as if he was listening to something only he could hear. Prudence wanted to be away from him. He made her feel sick, but she couldn't leave Nellie alone with him, not after she'd read the bile-bitter words in his letters. She could see he was charming Nellie, putting her under a spell, so she bravely asked him whether he had seen anything of her own mother. Her question came as a surprise to Shellard, and he frowned and blustered, thinking only of the hatred he felt for the people in Chorley. Nellie shook her head and reprimanded Prudence for being so forward, though her warning was light-hearted. Then she remembered herself, and invited Shellard to go with them on some business at Tyncoed. They were, she said ironically, going to look at a cob.

Prudence noticed Shellard's eyes light up. She knew he thought there was more to Nellie's invitation than just a cob.

It was a long day. Prudence sat in the back of the trap, listening to Shellard making his small talk and behaving like a respectable gentleman. Nellie laughed and ignored the double meanings implicit in his weasel-twisted words. She refused to talk about money, and waved her hands to fan her face when he mentioned the watch. Prudence could feel her skin prickling as Shellard's anger built up inside him like static on an old scarf. She could tell from Nellie's gentle but restrained manner that she felt the same tension. She waited for Nellie to realise it was madness to have invited him back. It was madness behaving like a lover to help her forget some other memory. All day Prudence waited and watched but Nellie allowed Shellard to touch her shoulder, to stand close to her and brush her thighs as if by happenstance. But when he thought no one was looking, Shellard would become agitated and fidget, pacing up and down as he waited for Nellie.

They returned to Hollyfield at eight in the evening. The sun was low over the distant Welsh mountains, turning them into bottomless black holes surrounded by orange flames. Sheep complained about the heat and the damp, having forgotten the cold of winter, unaware that their lambs were soon to be slaughtered.

Shellard and Nellie went into the front room, leaving Prudence to make them some tea in the kitchen. She lit the lamps and the fire then lifted the large kettle over it. She listened to the sheep, then to Nellie and Shellard. His voice had become a whisper, a serpent's hiss. It was pleading. She heard the watch mentioned again, and felt for it in her pocket. Then she heard the voice raise in a desperate question, to which Nellie replied with a hoarse, humiliating laugh.

Outside, the sheep were excited, as if they had been disturbed by something. Prudence didn't dare look out of the window, in case there was something there, the Devil or a goblin king come to take them away to Hell.

Shellard came rushing out of the front room. Prudence jumped in her chair, startled, but he ignored her. He jerked open the back door, kicking a pebble, scaring away whatever demon had crept into the back yard. She heard Nellie sobbing. The kettle was hissing, rattling. She heard Shellard in the old brewhouse round the back, swilling himself with cold water. Nellie came into the kitchen, dabbing her eyes with a handkerchief.

'Go fetch some coal, Prudence, it's getting cold,' said Nellie.

'Is Mister Shellard staying?' asked Prudence.

Nellie shook her head.

'No, he's not staying.'

Prudence looked at Nellie's face, trying to read some secret there, but she couldn't see anything except the faint lines that had returned around Nellie's eyes. Nellie's voice was calm, relieved, as if they had all been waiting for a storm that had passed silently overhead. But Prudence could sense Shellard's presence, feel his weight crushing the wild flowers in the meadow as she went to fill a bucket with coal.

Prudence came out of the coal shed. The back door was open. The sheep had scattered up the hill, their white coats ghosts in the shadows. She thought she heard voices inside the house. She looked at the old brewhouse, afraid to go near it, afraid to be caught in the dark. The coal was heavy in the bucket, it wasn't something with which she could run.

She started walking across the yard, holding her breath. She glanced at the brewhouse and noticed the lamp there had been blown out. She noticed muddy footprints on the porch, soil stuck to the shoe-scraper. A house martin flew through the air and into the dark eaves of the brewhouse. She watched it then realised Shellard had gone.

She wondered about the voices she thought she'd heard.

Then she heard a sharp crack echo through the house, through the yard and up the hill. The sheep ran away. She dropped the bucket, spilling coal over the ground.

Someone had fired a gun.

16.

The Funeral

THE CUP WAS OLDER THAN PRUDENCE. Time had passed, so that girls like Prudence didn't understand why men like Whittle observed the rites of the football pitch. She hadn't been there when the lights failed at their floodlit match. She hadn't been there when Whittle lifted the Cup. She was there when his wife was killed.

At Nellie's funeral she had been kept away from the families by one of Whittle's companions from the Hall. She didn't know his name but she recognised him from the old picture of the Cup-winning team that hung in the drawing room. He had held her arm in a friendly but firm manner. They couldn't stop her from watching the last moments of Nellie Whittle, as her coffin was lowered into the dark earth. But they could keep her at a suitable, respectable distance. As a servant she expected no more.

Whittle stood next to the Vicar and stared into the middle distance throughout the funeral, as if he had seen something interesting amidst the green-stained stones and yew trees. The other mourners, all draped in black coats and shawls, followed every word of the Vicar. Nellie's elderly grandfather, a small man with skin like paper stuck to his bones, was the only man who cried. It was a low, pitiful sob, a cry both for the loss of his daughter's daughter and for the loss of his own dignity. The women were less restrained – Nellie's cousins wailed as the cemetery men strained on the ropes that lowered her into the ground.

Prudence couldn't cry for her friend. She had already cried enough, when she had seen her crumpled, bloody body on the bed. At the police station she had cried when they had explained to her what she had to say, and why it was necessary for her to do it. She hadn't understood until Whittle himself had said how precarious her own position was, and how easy it would be for things in Court to be misinterpreted. Prudence did what she was expected to do - but not out of duty to her master. The policeman, Deputy Chief Constable Vaughan, had been a spiteful, nasty man, who had been eager to hear all she could tell about the affair between Nellie and Shellard. His suggestions had frightened her, and in the horrible hours after the shooting she had been no match for the flint-faced Welshman. She knew what he was doing. Humphrey Whittle was a powerful man, and knew enough people even in a small town like Gresford to make sure things went his way. They all thought she was simple because she was a girl. But she had gone along with their suggestions because she was clever enough to know that poor serving girls in the employ of ladies provided an easy way to sort out complicated crimes.

She wiped a tear from her eye as the funeral finished. She looked across the grey slabs and trimmed grass at Whittle. She knew he knew she was there. His eyes flickered towards her for a brief second. Then he took out his handkerchief and blew his nose loudly. He shook his head and wiped his moustache, then turned away.

'Come on, Miss, the funeral's over, yer mistress will be in a better place by now,' said her guardian. His grip on her arm grew firmer, more insistent. 'Let's be taking you back.'

She watched the mourners shuffle away in single file, all in black, snaking between the graves. Whittle was at the front, leading them to the wake. With every step he took his stance became more relaxed, until he side-stepped onto the gravel drive and started chatting to one of his cousins about market gardens.

On the drive four black waggons were drawn up, the black coats of the horses shining with sweat and soap. The team leading the hearse, which was now the last of the four waggons, wore white roses on their reins. The drivers of each waggon had top hats and black tails, though they looked uncomfortable in such attire. The undertaker ushered the mourners in strict order of importance to the waggons, opening the side-doors for the ladies. The insides were upholstered in red velvet, and the hoods were of a dark green tarpaulin.

'Give me a moment, sir, I beg of you,' said Prudence, looking up at her guardian.

The man looked at the mourners climbing into the waggons, then at the grave where the cemetery men had started to fill in the hole.

'Very well, Prudence, but do be quick, and don't do anything silly. I promised Humphrey I would watch out for you and I don't want to betray his trust.'

He let go of her arm, and they both stepped between the gravestones and around a dying yew to reach Nellie's grave. Prudence brushed down the front of her black dress and pulled her shawl tight around her. The cemetery men, who were shovelling in the dirt which they had dug out the day before, saw her coming and nodded respectfully. The youngest man, who had not yet learnt his trade, smiled at her.

'I say, you men, can you just stop your work for a moment whilst the young lady says a prayer for Mrs Whittle?' asked the man. They nodded and moved away from the grave. Prudence smiled. He may have been a friend of Whittle's but he was a good man.

She looked in the grave. Most of the coffin was hidden under soil, but a part of the brass nameplate and the polished wood was visible. She tried to read the name but all she could see was Nellie's surname: Whittle. Nellie had never liked her husband's name. Prudence remembered a time when she heard Nellie screaming at Whittle. They were in his study, and Nellie had become angry because he was going to the Oddfellows' Hall when he had promised to go with her to a recital. Whittle had said it was not up to his wife to decide his affairs, and Nellie had told him she didn't want to be his wife. She heard Whittle hit Nellie across the face and call her a strumpet, but as long as he lived she would be nothing else but a Whittle. At that point Nellie had thrown a brick-red Roman pot at the wall, which Prudence had to clean up later, declared that she hated his name, then left the house.

The waggons moved away. She heard the rumble of the wheels and the crunch of hooves on the gravel. A few drops of rain spattered the recumbent gravestone on the other side of the hole. Prudence took a gold watch out from under her gloves. The cemetery men were not looking – they were too busy talking amongst themselves. Her guardian was looking up at the sky, watching the gathering clouds.

She threw the watch into the grave, then kicked some loose soil over it. 'I'm finished, sir,' she said.

Nellie's death was a shock to everyone who knew the Whittle family - and since Humphrey was a councillor and a member of the Poor Board, dispensing charity to the destitute and finding work for the idle, because he had been the captain of the football club in its time of glory, the town mourned. The men in the pits collected money to pay for Prudence, who had lost her employer in the cruellest of manners; the old women in the street wore black and wept whenever Whittle strode swiftly past them; the local press, warned by friends of Whittle, passed comment on the decay of society at the end of the century and the tragedy that awaited all who failed to live according to the true teachings; strangers, shocked by a few words here and there, demanded that the law on the sale of guns should be tightened to stop ruffians getting hold of them; and others, outraged by the nature of Nellie's death, attacked Shellard's family and drove them out of the town, condemning them by association for Nellie's foul murder.

Prudence was ashamed by the money that was raised. She only took it after nights spent awake in her mother's house. She had gone there after the inquiry, after Whittle decided she was to be dispensed with, free from her serving obligations. Before and during the inquiry, of course, he had made sure she was close to the family, giving her a room at Primrose Cottage where no one could persuade her to change her mind. She had been locked away in Jane's room, which was decorated with pictures of black cats and ravens, and was let out only when Whittle was away on business. The servants treated her with fear, avoiding the shadow of her black dress as if she was the embodiment of the plague, come to destroy them all. The family treated her with contempt, blaming her for what had happened to Humphrey, and what had happened to Nellie, seeing in Prudence the horror of a servant becoming a friend. Only Leo spoke to her with affection, consoling her when she cried in the middle of a large sitting room with nowhere to sit. He didn't seem to care that such action marked him out as a fluke in Primrose Cottage, a stranger in the family home, somehow less of a man than his older brother. Nor did he chastise the servants for turning his attention into what they thought was a calculated plan to seduce and bed young Prudence. Whatever his reasons, he remained honourable when he was with her, and when she was sent back to her mother's house he offered to help her in any way he could.

It was Leo Whittle who convinced her to take the money, who insisted it would help her improve her position, and that was what Nellie would have wanted. She knew he was right - she could hear Nellie telling her to take the money while it was offered and use it to start a new life far away from Chorley. She knew it was a bribe, a retainer, one which Whittle had allowed to be paid because he himself didn't have the courage to pay it. It corrupted her, made her as culpable as Shellard, as Whittle, as the men who had told her what to say and when to say it. But it offered her the chance to try and forget Whittle and Shellard, and the blood splattered over the quilt she had made for Nellie. With the money she didn't have to stay with her mother and listen to her blaming herself for failing to educate Prudence properly, as if it had somehow been Prudence's fault that Nellie had left Whittle and spurned her lover, Shellard.

Leo, of course, saw nothing wrong in helping out Prudence. He'd helped his brother out in the same way, taking care of the children throughout the traumatic week after the murder, finding them a nursemaid and reading them long and fanciful bedtime stories in which the handsome prince invariably found his princess. Humphrey said nothing about his brother's kindness. There was nothing he could say. The children could sense what had happened, Humphrey knew they could see it in his eyes whenever he stood at the door, nervously looking in. He could only watch in anguish as Leo made the children laugh and forget for a moment the black cloud that had come between their mother and father.

The newspapers in Chorley became as expensive and rare as *lapis lazuli*. They sold out so fast that the quick-thinking proprietors were forced to print more copies, changing the price to turn a profit. The brass and steel of the printing presses stamped and hammered, pistons hissed, wheels turned, guillotines cut - and still-warm papers were handed out to paperboys with boards announcing the bloody murder of Nellie Whittle and the suicide of her infamous lover. The jostling crowds surrounding the sellers recalled the day the club had won the Cup, when boys had resorted to singing the news like town criers to those who couldn't read. Those who remembered Humphrey Whittle the football captain were not slow to remind others. It was a scandal that the men who surrounded him couldn't hide, too much of a story to quietly file away after a few drinks at the Lodge.

The story they read was the story Prudence told the police in her statement, the story that was confirmed by the quick and definitive Inquests into the matter of Nellie's and Shellard's deaths by the Welsh authorities. It agreed with the eyewitness account of Police Constable Thomas Jones, a young lad not prone to poetical flourishes or leaps of imagination, who was the first man to arrive at the scene of the crime. It agreed with the scientific evidence provided by Doctor Mainsty, a man of learning and the local doctor who examined first the dying Shellard, then the body of Nellie Whittle lying on the bloodstained mattress.

The first inquest was held the day after the murder, at the Plough Inn at Gresford, close to the mine-workings. It was considered only proper that the number of reporters was kept to a minimum, as the upstairs room of the pub was crowded with witnesses, jury-men and friends of the Whittle family. Humphrey had been summoned from Chorley, appearing with his brother and the family dentist. This latter came with a bag, from which he occasionally removed a small bottle of some stiff-smelling potion to treat Humphrey's visible shock. The jury at the first inquest didn't have to leave the room to deliberate to decide that Shellard, driven by revenge, was guilty of the foul murder of Nellie Whittle. Humphrey Whittle, his face pale, his manner unsteady, remained calm as he told them of what had happened between his estranged wife and her lover. Only once did he pause, to hold his left arm as if he felt there the bullets that had killed his wife.

It was a tragic affair, one which captivated the attention of everyone in Chorley. The town's gentry, still reeling from a century of change, put preparations for the hunt to one side and warned each other of the evil that surrounded the new money of the self-publicising kings of industry. The Anglicans, Catholics, Baptists, Methodists and assorted dissenters spoke of the devil's work and pinned the blame on lust and the spiritual weakness of modern society. Other men of Humphrey's class thanked God it was him and not them caught up in such a horrible crime. And the working-classes in factories, gin shops and back yards argued amongst themselves over the virtue of Nellie Whittle and the character of her husband, forgetting for a moment their own lives.

When she'd heard the sound of the gun Prudence knew Shellard had shot her mistress. She'd run into the house, afraid he would look out of a window and shoot her, then another shot had blasted through the stone house rattling the spoons and ladles hung up on the kitchen wall. She told the jury how the smell of burnt gunpowder drifted down the stairs, how it had reminded her of walking in woods after the sportsmen had gone home. Then she'd heard Nellie scream in pain and cry out her name, and she had put all her fears to one side to do her duty, even if that meant throwing herself in front of Shellard's gun.

She cried when she spoke of the blood in pools on the floor, of Nellie slumped on the floor with one arm raised up, perhaps to plead, perhaps as a shield. She couldn't speak of the broken face, the holes where his bullets had made their mark. She could only tell of her fear when Shellard pushed her into the bedroom and shut the door, then warned her to stay away from Nellie.

She'd failed her mistress. Wanting her own life, she had watched as Nellie lost hers. She'd screamed, trying to stop the blood draining from her neck, wiping it in vain from the front of her dress. She told the police in her statement that Nellie cried out for Humphrey, apologising to her husband and muttering the names of her children as she struggled to get on the bed. And all the while, Shellard had stood there with the revolver in his shaking hand. He'd watched Prudence bring some water but before she could help Nellie he'd come to a decision and had slashed at her mistress's throat with a cut-throat razor.

'I'll see 'er die first, then shoot miself!' he'd cried, gripped with some wild insanity. Nellie's screams had died as the blood blocked her windpipe. Then, as Prudence watched, he'd put the barrel of the gun in his own mouth and fired.

Prudence had fled after that, and was being looked after by a policeman when Constable Jones discovered the suicide note. The jury had listened in silence as Jones read the note, its crumpled sheet stained brown with Shellard's blood.

Prudence Taylor is a witness that she owes me money and said she is willing to pay it. You must look that up your self. We stopped at the Royal in Lord Nelson Street, Liverpool, Number Eleven. We have made up our minds to die together. Mrs Whittle has most awfully deceived me all through the piece. She was in Liverpool with me three days last week. I kept her well. She robbed my pocket and purse on the Sunday night. She owes me thirty-four pounds and ten shillings, and her wish is for you to be paid by her guardian, Dr. Smith, of Weaverham, near Norwitch, Cheshire. She also wishes for us to be buried together at her expences. It's a sad end, but we know there is some thing worse to face. You have always been a deivel to me and drove me both from good

peace and the drink. Kiss the dear children for me as I have never had a happy home of my own, and all through you. So good by all, for ever in this world.
May the 1st, '93.

He had signed it with his name and Nellie's. The Welsh authorities agreed with the police that the letter was a foul diatribe, besmirching as it did the good name of Shellard's oppressed wife, and that of the murdered Nellie Whittle. Prudence agreed, and for the only time in the public inquiry she became animated as she said Nellie would never have stolen money, and would certainly never have condemned herself to Hell with George Shellard. She didn't mention the watch. On the matter of Nellie's character the jury agreed. The letter was a poorly argued lie, one which Shellard had hoped would give him some vengeance on the mourning Humphrey Whittle after his death. The Welshmen had no hesitation in declaring Shellard's suicide, and the murder he'd committed, the work of a mad, twisted soul. He was guilty, and his death meant there was no need for the hangman's noose.

17.

The Rites of Spring

WHITTLE REMEMBERS, SEEING THE PRESENTATION of the Cup in the bottom of a glass. It is 1879 again and he is on the field, propped up by Garstang with a cloth soaked in spirit clenched against his brow. The pain of the spirit is enough to keep him sensible of the cheering crowd encircling the players. Here there is no distinction between the heroes of Chorley and their vanquished enemies, and the Rossendale men accept the laurels of gallant footballers who have given a good game. It is, Humphrey realises with a tear in his good eye, a proper resurrection of all that was good and manly in a better age. He accepts the Cup from Fish, noticing it is already inscribed with Chorley's name. It is, says Fish, a loving cup.

The crowd cheers. Humphrey feels the cold silver under his fingers, the rough etching biting the lines of his hand. He feels the curve of the bowl, its line sensuous and tempting. It is all he has wanted, and it is his. He understands what Fish means.

It is a presentation for the fans, for the workers of Chorley saluting their bosses, all thoughts of rebellion forgotten. Humphrey lets them worship at his feet for ten minutes, then hands the Cup back to Fish so he can give it away at the proper place after their celebration meal. He knows it will be a banquet fit for Elysium, worthy of Valhalla. He raises his head to look at the diminishing crowd, and because of his wound he fails to see the red-haired man at the back staring back at him with sullen spite.

'We've won the Cup, Humphrey, m'lad!' shouts Harry excitedly. He tries to touch the Cup but it is not his. Fish takes it away to wash off the blood, so it will dazzle the eyes of the diners tonight.

Humphrey wonders where his father is. He wonders about the tomcat's smile Scheidler has, the way he glances at Fish, as if he is a cat and there is something of the fish about the eponymous General Manager of Raikes Hall Gardens.

In the bright light of the town hall Humphrey Whittle cannot forget that smile.

At the celebration tea Humphrey heard fine speeches made about the virtues of the game. His father was, for a moment, happy to be near him, sitting on an opposite table talking loudly about the ancestral strength of the Whittle family. Humphrey's eye was sore and covered in bandages and a patch, so that he resembled some Oriental pirate out of a picture story. The other players, perhaps thinking he had lost his senses, patted him gently on the back and spoke to him in whispers.

He heard Fish talk of the Chorley club nobly winning the Cup in fair and honourable competition. The words were spoken without any irony, yet he couldn't look at his father for fear of betraying his complicity. Fish spoke of the satisfactory way in which a match, so well contested, had terminated. At this the men in the room bellowed with laughter and banged their knives on the table. Humphrey's companions cheered and raised their glasses towards him. Realising he was the victim of a poor joke, Humphrey smiled weakly, knowing it wouldn't be right to be offended.

In the privacy of the Lodge where Humphrey had first met Fish, the two clubs ate their knife-and-fork tea and congratulated each other on a marvellous show of footballing prowess. When the plates had been cleared away and the air was thick with Havana tobacco, Fish presented the Cup to Harry Hibbert. It came as some surprise to the players, who had expected Humphrey to be given the honour. They looked to him to follow his lead, but he said nothing; he'd already touched it, he knew it was his and he could be generous with its siren-like allure.

'It were an 'ard tussle, it were,' grinned Harry, taking the Cup back into his possession and feigning surprise at its weight. As he spoke he looked at his audience, choosing every word to raise indignant scowls or relieved smiles.

'But, like, wi' the aid of th'elements and you'll admit, a little better play than you lads from - where is it - somewhere in Yorkshire, or near enough - my lads were enabled to pull it off. Now on behalf of Chorley Football Club, the finest in the North of England no less, I'd like to thank Mister Fish and Raikes Hall's directors. It was very noble of you to put up this

210

Cup, and it's an example to us all about industry, independence of mind, and 'onest innovation.'

The diners cheered, and looked at Humphrey. They expected him to speak. He smiled and got to his feet, holding onto the table to stop himself from falling over. The Chorley players started to stamp their feet. His father clapped politely. He put his hand in his trouser pocket and felt the watch there, its workings vibrating against his leg. His father was drunk, and was muttering to himself. Humphrey could see the old man's glazed eyes above his grumbling chops. He knew what his father was saying even though he couldn't hear above the stamping feet. Nothing had changed. He had won the Cup for his father and nothing had changed. His father hated him. He had wanted to show his father he was a man. He wanted to tell his father how he felt, what it was like to be a hero, that diligence and hard work were not the only things that made a man's character. His father hated him because he knew Humphrey was about to say those things. His father hated him for winning the Cup, for proving him wrong. He hadn't won his respect, he'd won his eternal spite.

'I'd like to propose a toast,' said Humphrey, clutching at his half-empty glass of brandy. He watched as the company followed suit. He held it in the air. 'To my dear brother Frederick, who can't be with us today, and my sister, Jane, wherever she is.'

Whittle left the banquet hall, his own words of fifteen years ago ringing in his ears. He had insulted his father and made his friends uncomfortable, mentioning unmentionables. The Rossendale men had clapped for a few seconds before they'd realised the toast - like Frederick, like Jane - was an embarrassment.

The pain in his shoulder grew as he opened the door to face Prudence. It danced like a swarm of black flies over his skin, stabbing like a sharp knife into his collar-bone, his neck and all the way down his arm to the ends of his fingers. It burrowed like a worm through his nerves, eating away at his insides and up into the space behind his eyes. It tried to seize control of his body, a pirate at the wheel of a galleon trying to turn her against the wind. It put lead weights in his feet, dragged his hand away from the handle, pushed him up against the wall like a cheap whore. He couldn't face her, but somehow the door was open and the light from the fading gas lamps betrayed his long shadow to Prudence.

Prudence didn't know how to address him. She had of course been trained by her mother and the other maids to call any gentleman of a respectable class either sir or master. Those whom she served were allowed to be called by their surnames, with the appropriate title. Mister Whittle had been his name in Derwent Lodge, but after all that had happened she only knew him as Humphrey. The name was spoken in her mind by Nellie - smiling, alive, loving, scornful of all that name represented. What Nellie had said should have been irrelevant to a young girl. It was improper of her to assume such familiarity, and she knew he would hate it as much as he hated himself for being there with her. When she hated him she thought of him as Whittle, the demon who had destroyed Nellie's life. But she knew as she saw his shadow, heard his stifled tears, that there wasn't any other way of speaking to him.

'Humphrey…' she said, a feather in her throat catching her voice and tickling her stomach. 'Humphrey Whittle? Please, I need to speak with you.'

He shut his eyes to try to squeeze out images of Nellie. Prudence even sounded like her, speaking with Nellie's gently pleading, remonstrating manner. She was a ghost sent to torment him for eternity, a barguest in the mist of a cold night. He tried to reach out and touch Nellie, to stop her from turning away from him. If only a thousand things had been different, if only this had happened instead of that, and he'd had the confidence to do all those things and more to make her happy. The images had become his litany, remembered without effort, forever on his mind like the feeble prayers of a dying monk. Again, he tried to dismiss Nellie by thinking of the working-class, the socialists and their rag-tag ideas and their hatred of all things decent. It failed. He could still hear Nellie's voice, asking him to show himself to her.

'I am here,' he said. He found his councillor's face, his businessman's back, then stepped out into the corridor. She watched him come into the light of the corridor, and stood up to meet him. In the darkness she could see Nellie's face, pleading with him, laughing in disbelief at what he was about to do. She didn't care about Shellard. She'd given the watch to Nellie to keep in the grave, in case Shellard came back from the dead to find it, to seek Prudence out in the witching hour and drag her soul down to Hell. There was little point in Prudence keeping it for Nellie's sake: it was only a watch.

Beneath her veil her skin prickled. She blamed it on the foul heat and smoke of the summer. Her red-rosy painted cheeks were marked by pale smears from the veil, which clung to her face if she moved her head too fast. She wanted to scratch her face until the skin and blood blocked up her fingernails. She wanted to rip off her clóthes and flee naked from the town hall, and run from everything until her heart burst. She had waited to confront him and now she realised she couldn't speak to him, not when his face remained as impassive as it had been throughout the Inquest when he'd listened to her lies. She remembered his urgency, the need to get the business done with in a quick manner, lest anyone guessed the truth. She remembered the only sign of emotion on his face in the Welsh court room – fear - when Jones and Mainsty had foolishly mentioned the bullets.

He frowned at her. Why was she wasting his time? He had come. What did she want of him? He wondered whether she would always follow him, stand at the back of crowds, stare through shop windows, eat from the same table. There was nothing he could do, nothing that wouldn't leave him more guilty than he already was. He shivered. He was cold. He could feel a draught in the corridor blowing out of the shadows, wrapping itself around him. He shifted on his feet, tapping the floor like a music-hall trickster.

'What is it you want, Miss Taylor? Can't you see I've given the Cup away? I have already given all I can give. I can do nothing more, my soul is doomed.'

She smiled. His pomposity, his self-importance, had ruined him, yet still he thought only of his own soul! The living surrounded by the dead! She couldn't believe in a God who passed judgement on souls, not after what had happened. It didn't make sense that a loving soul like Nellie's could be denied the chance of life by a lifeless soul like his. Yet, for all her despair and grief, all she felt for him was pity. He was scared of her, a sportsman scared of a serving girl! And they both knew why.

She heard Nellie laughing.

'You need to know something,' she said.

'If you are about to go to the police you will not get anywhere. It never happened, you know, that's the truth as far as everyone's concerned. Go now and you will be ridiculed. You will lose your means of support, and end up on the streets, or worse... you know some gossips say you had a hand in it, don't you?'

Prudence shook her head.

'But I didn't. I didn't do anything. I should have done, I should have stopped her from seeing Shellard.'

'Yes, you should,' nodded Whittle.

His quick answer shocked Prudence, who had merely been thinking aloud. She stood up and with one quick strike she slapped her former master across the cheek with the palm of her hand. He recoiled from her, the pain of it worse than any he had known. He clutched for anything, his arms flailing about in shock. He found the sill of one of the tall windows looking into the yard, and he fumbled there, knocking over a small vase of dead flowers. Prudence followed him, keeping next to his shadow, her veiled face hidden in the fading light of the gas lamps.

'I were a child, what could I have done? I saw how you treated her, I sat behind the door as you beat her.'

'I never beat her, child,' said Whittle, holding one hand up to protect himself from her. Could he have hit her as he'd hit Nellie, dealt with her to hide the truth? He had never considered it. He had sinned enough. Anything he did to Prudence he did to himself.

'Didn't you? Why lie to me? I've seen everything, I was there, remember? I saw what happened to Nellie and that bastard Shellard.'

Bastard! Whittle was shocked at the word. In the late hours of Hall and Lodge, when the bottles were empty and the candles low, men would speak to each other like navvies. But he had never heard such language from a girl as young as Prudence, a servant. It frightened him. The world was changing if a servant could swear at a gentleman. Order was collapsing, they would have everything, and it was his fault. He was Cain, marking humanity with evil, allowing the Devil to destroy everything. He was the traitor at the gates. There was, he thought, some irony in him being the precursor of the revolution, the herald of the end of the world. They had taken his dignity, his wife, his life. All he could do was watch and wait for the moment when they found out his crimes and took him away to be lynched from an electric streetlamp.

She was right. There was no point in lying to her. She had been the person Nellie had turned to in the darkest hours, the one who had shared Nellie's intimacies and received her love when her life was wrecked. She had seen everything.

'I hit her. I know. I shouldn't have done that, don't you think I know that, child? What else could I do?' said Whittle, struggling to stand up straight. His cheek blazed, burning through to the bone. A lowly clerk from Ramsbottom's office walked past and deliberately averted his gaze. He didn't greet Whittle. His steps echoed through the corridor, bouncing around in the high arches until they were smothered by the wood panels on the wall. Whittle waited for the servant's steps to disappear down the stairwell, down past the portraits of dead men who had once held power. Past his father, and the space where Harry's face would soon be, and another space that could have had his own.

'I am a failure, child, I have always been so. My father was right.'

'Oh, do stop it, sir... you don't know the meaning of it. The only person you failed was Nellie. Why didn't you see what you were doing?'

'I didn't start an affair,' argued Whittle.

'But you finished it,' said Prudence, angry at his obstinance. She had hoped to find him humble. She knew he was suffering. Everyone knew he was suffering. She had heard people in the street talking about what had happened to his father. A few even spoke of his brother and sister, mentioned only in the most oblique of terms accompanied by knowing looks. She wanted him to be humble. She wanted Nellie's ghost to rest, so she could live her own life without his dark shadow over her like the sky before a storm.

He nodded.

'I finished it. Don't you realise the sacrifice I have made in keeping silent? The compromises I've made, the worry I have that that dim-witted Welsh constable will forget himself in his cups, or some prying spy will see that the Welsh only accounted for five bullets?'

'I don't expect you to be happy. But don't worry, I won't tell, you don't have to make threats with me. It'll be on your heart every morning about what happened, as it is on mine.'

'Then what do you want? More money?' asked Whittle.

Prudence smiled. She knew he would be humbled. All she had to do was use the words like a knife slipping through his shirt.

'I don't want money, Humphrey Whittle. I owe it to Nellie. You can't avoid the truth. I want to tell you it. I want to tell you something about Nellie, about your wife. You will listen, won't you?'

'It seems you leave me with no choice,' sighed Whittle.

'It was when you argued with her, when she threw your pretty cup on the floor, when I went to find her in the snow. In the park, remember?'

He thought of the park, but remembered the day when Harry had formed the football club. It was not his memory any more. The club was as real as Robin Hood.

'She was having an affair with George Shellard! She slept in my house, child, in my house!'

'Do you know why she broke her wedding vows? Aside from you breaking yours in the streets behind the railway station.'

'Child, you shouldn't know of such places...'

'Shouldn't I? When I've friends there already old-hands at the game? Friends I've played princesses with, all running round in circles with posies in our hands?'

'Did you tell her?'

'I didn't care to know, then. But Nellie knew. All she wanted was for you to behave like a husband, like the hero you were.'

'I was never a hero, Miss Taylor. It was all a fraud,' said Whittle, struggling with his own eyes to stop them shedding tears. 'Anyway, that was years ago. The football club is dead and buried.'

'Is it?' frowned Prudence, dismissing the thought. 'You still don't understand, do you? About Nellie? About why she did what she did.'

'Madness,' said Whittle, his voice breaking. He knew. He didn't want to hear it from another's lips.

'She loved you, Humphrey, she loved you more than you deserved. And she loved you because she knew you loved her. But she wanted you to tell her that, and you never did.'

'I'm sure I did.'

'You never did. That's all she wanted, that's why she had that affair, to hurt you so much you realised you had to change. That you had to show her you loved her. It's as simple as that. She loved you. She wanted you to love her. Isn't that what every normal person wants, even a stuffed up gentleman like you?'

She looked at him, expecting an answer. He had crumpled against the window, and was looking out into the darkness. He could see her out there, her face in the glass. He wanted to see Nellie, but he found he was already forgetting what she looked like, losing that last connection he had to a moment when he was loved, when he was happy. Prudence was right. He had refused to accept it, and now he was left with his guilt and the blood that stained his hands like the hands of Shakespeare's villain.

'I could have been better. Prudence, do you see her? Are you a medium, do you believe that Spiritualists can really talk to the dead?'

'I talk to Nellie every day, sir, but only up here,' said Prudence, tapping the side of her head.

'I wish I could talk to her again. Prudence? May I call you that? What can I do? How can I find a way of apologising to her? How do I explain it was the demon inside me?'

Prudence shrugged her shoulders. She wished there was an answer. She wanted to help the shadow creature in front of her. But she had lost her faith in anything. It was up to him to find his own way of reaching Nellie. She had humbled him, but in that humbling was an empty future, a hollow past.

Midnight, three hours after the murder, Humphrey Whittle collapsed on the cold bed at Derwent Lodge. His companion, the Welsh doctor, a good Oddfellow and paid man of the Gresford mine, gave out orders to the loyal Whittle servants who had arrived minutes before to stoke the fire. Humphrey, burning with fever, looked at the familiar objects of the room melting before him. The Welsh doctor's accent was too obvious, too foolish. Where else could he have come from, arriving in the middle of the night in a clatter of turning wheels and hooves on cobbles? The Welshman had propped him up from carriage to train to carriage, covering his shoulders with a borrowed cashmere coat. He had pressed a damp towel to Humphrey's forehead, tightened the dressings on the wound. Humphrey tried to focus through the laudanum-coloured mist, seeing only phantoms of Nellie and Shellard, hearing the Welsh voices as they debated how best to make the future safe for an Oddfellow, one of us. He saw his father in the flickering polish of a Grecian urn, a naked athlete laughing like Scheidler, like Shellard. A shadow covered the walls. Nellie's blood. Couldn't the servants see it? He tried to get up but the pain in his shoulder came back, a memory he'd forgotten in the dream of the journey. He heard his own voice calling out for Nellie, for Nellie. The doctor's face appeared, holding before it a huge hypodermic needle. Humphrey saw the guilt of his own face in the drop of laudanum at the top of the needle.

'Another one when you wake up will see you through tomorrow,' the needle said. 'I'll let your friend the dentist know what to do.'

It was the first day of May, 1893. A pleasant Monday. He travelled to Hollyfield with murder on his mind. Death was the coal for his boiler, turning the wheels of his engine. He had been betrayed. He had been wronged. And now he knew that he was there with her, kissing her with his crooked lips. Humphrey would kill Shellard, and, if it came to it, he knew there was nothing left to stop him from killing his own wife too.

It was the middle of a hot day when he reached Gresford. He climbed the hill to Hollyfield and for the second time rapped at the front door. This time he was wearing thin black gloves, just right for crooked deeds. In his hands was a cut-throat razor, a common Sheffield brand anyone could buy in an ironmonger's. He imagined Shellard crouching before him, cringing in fear, pleading for mercy. He wouldn't give it. How could he hesitate? To hesitate would be to betray his own weakness. He imagined his father encouraging him from the top of some distant cloud. If he didn't see the deed through he wiould be a failure, a cuckold, less of a man than the thief who has stolen his wife. He would bring the blade down, then if she showed any pity for her dead lover, he would do to her what he had done to Shellard.

There was no answer at the door, so he walked around the back to try and find a way in. The kitchen was open, and he strode in like a shameless burglar. The house was empty. He called out her name, then the name of her girl Prudence. There was no answer save the constant purr of a black cat that had left its perch on the window to rub against his legs. He ignored it and inspected each room, in case anyone was hiding. All the fires were cold, the embers black. The lamps were unlit, the pots washed, the sheets turned back.

Humphrey returned to the kitchen and looked for something to wash the dry, burning taste out of his mouth. He found a jug of milk left near the chopping block but it had gone off. Even the cat refused to taste it when he offered it some. He wanted to smoke but could not find a flint and tinder, or any lucifers. He gripped his pipe in his mouth, lost in thought. He could see the spring bubbling up in the field, amidst the sheep. The field looked marshy but he considered it of little concern. No one was going to inspect the bottom of his trousers when the deed was done.

In the field he looked back towards England, looking across the patch-work plains and the brown smears of towns. It was a comforting sight. Time passed, and after cupping his hands to drink from the stream he sat down behind a rock to wait for her to return. The sun was warm on the back of his neck, burning his stiff collar. He folded his arms and fell asleep, waking only at the sound of movement below him. He looked down through the murk of the evening light and saw her, with him and with her girl. They were smiling at each other, confirming all he had feared. She had betrayed him. She would have to be destroyed like an unwanted letter on the fire.

He sneaked down to the farm. Hiding behind the gate to the field, he chose his moment, when Shellard was in one of the old farm buildings and Prudence in the coal shed, to slip inside on his gentle footballing feet and confront her. He would give her one last chance before he used the razor in his pocket to cut her out of his life forever.

He wiped his feet. His eyes burned as he enterd the house.

Inside the cottage all was unchanged, except for a kettle over a stoked fire in the kitchen. He passed by, seeing Prudence and maids in every shad-ow. He heard Nellie's feet moving on the floorboards upstairs. He recog-nised her heavy steps, the shuffling dance she made when she was in a good mood. It hurt him to hear it. His father's voice was in his head, asking him whether he wanted to be locked up like Frederick, forgotten like Jane. He said no, no, no! But the voice was still there. It was Shellard's cocksure sneering, Fish's crude insinuations, Leo's confident manner. He shook his head and dragged his feet up the stairs. Leaning against the rail, he listened for Shellard returning. Satisfied that he would be alone with Nellie, he jumped the last step and saw her framed by the door of her bedroom.

'Humphrey!' gasped Nellie. She was about to move towards him, to hug him and plead for her marriage, when she saw the flames in his eyes. She knew then that she was doomed. 'Humphrey,' she repeated, quieter now. 'Humphrey, what are you doing here?'

'I told you never to see him again,' said Humphrey, walking towards her, forcing her back into her sparsely furnished bedroom.

'You told me you never wanted to see me again,' answered Nellie, standing near her small dressing-table.

'I cannot allow this to go on, I cannot be shamed this way, Nell,' he said, crowding her, standing over her and arching his back like a cat on a wall. He wanted her to say something to save herself. What exactly he didn't know. His reason had deserted him. He realised he was insane. He told himself he was insane. This, he knew, was a just excuse for a violent crime. He realised it would be easier if he believed in his insanity. It was a convenient lie. 'Nell, look at me! Look at what you've done!'

'Humphrey, please stop being your father,' pleaded Nellie.

Just then he heard somebody moving on the stairs, an awkward-boned person trying to be quiet. It was Shellard. He threw Nellie on to the bed and took the razor out of his pocket. Its silver blade, snapped into position, caught the light of the bedside lamp. Nellie looked at the blade, at his eyes. He ignored her and hid in the shadow of the door. Shellard was closer now. He could hear his wheezy breathing, the swish of cloth swaying as he walked.

'Nellie, it's all over for you,' said Shellard, walking through the door. Humphrey saw his shadow cast by the light in the stairwell. He glanced at Nellie and saw terror on her face. She glanced at him for barely a second, but it was enough to warn Shellard. He grabbed the door and started to wrench it open.

Things happened quickly. Humphrey recalled every move, every emotion. It was real, like the last minutes of the Cup final. He saw Shellard turning towards him, his face torn by anger and madness. Nellie started to cough, choking on her fear. In Shellard's hands was a small revolver, which he has been pointing at her. He spun round and there was a flash of light, a crack of sound, and Humphrey felt a weight pushing against his left shoulder, trying to knock him down. He ignored it. He ignored the smell of burnt powder and warm blood, and grabbed Shellard's gun hand. Shellard was his father. Shellard smiled but there was fear on his face too. Humphrey saw it in Shellard's eyes. They had lost their arrogance, their glowing pride.

'Humphrey!' cried Nellie.

Shellard tried to pull away from Humphrey's grip and his hands come away from the gun's trigger. He shoved Humphrey in the left shoulder and his hand fell back covered in blood. Pain nibbled at Humphrey's mind now, teasing him. He wrenched the gun out of Shellard's hands and aimed it at

Shellard's head, but Shellard - free of the gun - tried to tackle him to the floor. Humphrey's arm flailed out of control as he pulled the trigger, twice in succession as he fell to the floor.

Shellard fell on top of him, and Nellie screamed,

'Dear God, Prudence, come up at once! I've been shot!'

Humphrey grabbed hold of Shellard, ignoring the pain in his shoulder. He pulled Shellard down onto him, embracing him. Shellard writhed like a snake, trying to use his knee in Humphrey's kidneys. The revolver was still in Humphrey's hands, burning hot. He pushed it between them and Shellard cried in panic as he realised what was happening. All Humphrey wanted was revenge. Shellard was his father. Shellard was everything. The barrel of the gun touched Shellard's cheek, and he shut his mouth in terror. His hair hung from his sweating forehead, tickling Humphrey.

Humphrey pinched Shellard's neck, causing him to yelp in pain. Spittle dropped from Shellard's mouth, phlegm from his nose, half-blinding Humphrey. Then Humphrey thrust the revolver inside Shellard's twisted mouth and pulled the trigger.

It was over.

Prudence watched him in the dark corridor of the town hall. She had watched him struggle with Shellard, seen him fire the gun. She'd tried to save Nellie and had listened to her cry out his name in pain. Humphrey had struggled to get Shellard off his chest, and had stood in the middle of the room in silence, blood staining his white shirt, the gun in his hand. He had shot Nellie without realising it. Prudence remembered how he'd cried, cursing Shellard and kicking the dead man in the side as if somehow it was his fault. Then he'd looked at the gun and Prudence had thought he was about to kill himself, or her. She'd got up from looking after Nellie and was ready to run away. But instead of firing, he'd thrown it to the floor.

Prudence knew there was nothing she could have done to help Nellie. She had kissed Nellie's forehead and touched her arm, looking away from the wounds in her face and neck. Then she'd heard Nellie whisper Humphrey's name. She'd wanted the pain to stop, she'd wanted him to do one last thing for her as a husband, as someone who loved her.

He found the letter in Shellard's pocket. He read it in silence, each word a barb through his heart. Shellard had wanted to kill Nellie, then kill himself. And he had done Shellard's work for him, helped him on his way with

Nellie's soul. He had killed them both with his own hands. Then he heard Nellie speak, and he knew what he had to do.

In a dream, Humphrey found the cut-throat razor and obeyed her last request, knowing he was already damned.

Prudence saw the shame in his eyes, in the way he stood stiffly in the corridor. She could hear the hum of the electricity generator as the boiler-men brought it gently to rest, stopping the fan over the reception and the other fancy gadgets. She knew what had happened, of course. Humphrey knew people in Wales, in Gresford – business associates, Oddfellows – who had spirited him away from the scene, seen to his wound, kept him con-scious for the Inquest and invented a story that Deputy Chief Constable Vaughan taught her to know by rote. She knew Humphrey wanted her to tell him he'd suffered enough. He wanted her to save him.

But she couldn't, and he knew it.

'I have to go, Miss Taylor, I have… I have to get back. Do you… do you need anything?' he asked, wiping his brow with the back of his sleeve.

'Don't forget what I've told you. I don't want her haunting me up to my death-bed,' said Prudence.

Humphrey looked at her. She had aged since they'd first taken her on. Her eyes were lined, her voice measured and mature. He thought about what she had said about the girls behind the railway station. She was older than they were.

Nellie had loved him. She had loved him and he'd been too blind to see, too deaf to hear. He had no one to blame for that. He thought of Jane. Had she loved her gardener? What show of emotion had they enjoyed, before his father had ruined her life? He had lived his life using certainties like stilts to keep him above the mire of socialism and sexual cravings, away from the anarchy of the unknown. And yet those certainties had proved to be as sub-stantial as a face in a cloud. He had nothing real. His father had been a tyrant, his wealth was a chance of birth, the club had been a passing fancy and even Raikes Hall was gone, sold to the builders of a new century.

The only thing left was charity. He couldn't bring Nellie back. He could-n't apologise. He couldn't be saved. But he could at least look after his own family, help others out, punish himself every day by doing good deeds to remind him of the love he had foolishly thrown away because of his obses-sion with pride. He knew his friends would think it unmanly, but Prudence was right. He could never forget.

He remembered Frederick, dear Freddy, locked away until Christmas. He smiled, thinking of the day he had carried him, the day he had been his horse. He would start with Frederick.

There was enough room for his brother at Derwent Lodge.